A coming of middle age story

CHAPTER 1

My fiftieth birthday started as an ordinary day.

I thought by the time I reached fifty, I'd be settled in a fulfilling career, married to my best friend, lovingly caring for our three children in our beautiful house, and we'd pack our bags and fly off to exotic locales, at least three times a year.

Sometimes fate steps in with different plans.

My name is Nicole Page but my friends call me Nikki. My parents call me Nics. My kids call me mom—if their friends aren't watching.

What really happened by the time I turned fifty?

I was still reeling from the discovery of my ex-husband's two-year affair with his much younger secretary and struggling with the aftermath of our divorce the year before. Needless to say, it's been an awful two years knowing that my life has been reduced to nothing more than a cliché. I don't know if I was angrier at him for having the affair or angrier at myself for not seeing the signs.

While my ex lived in his own version of happiness, I was stunned, stumbling through bouts of depression, unable to move forward. In those dark days, I submerged myself into the daily chores of raising three children, supporting them through their anger and pain.

When I wasn't supporting them in their endeavors, I plunged myself into my client's most vulnerable moments, working each day as a paralegal in a family law firm. When I did have those rare moments of escape, I would cry and scream into my pillow because all I could see was what was gone; all the expectations, all the dreams, the life I thought I should be living.

The farther away I roam from the divorce I see things with a little less negativity. I kept my home, still in rather decent shape, have my job, my health and most importantly, I have my three kids who I adore at least half the time, because we all know how it is with one in college, one in high school, and one in middle school.

And the job that I hoped would be fulfilling? Sometimes it's interesting, sometimes it's a bore fest and sometimes it's simply heartbreaking. Whichever way it goes, I get paid well for my work.

As a paralegal in the family law firm Able, Able, and Munch, my responsibilities vary from client to client, and situation to situation. In each case, I might draft contracts and documents, answer client calls and emails, research law, handle retainer, and client bank accounts. Like I said, sometimes it's a tedious chore; more often than not, interesting issues come up. Every once and a while, the job is painful beyond words.

I'm one of fifteen paralegals that work for the three partners and five junior partners in the firm, though I primarily work with the first Mr. Able, better known as Justin Able. I have no issues with him. He's fair, a good negotiator and his clients like him a lot.

We get along well and we chit chat when we have time, but I wouldn't call us friends. I've never gone out with him socially and the only times I've seen him outside of work was for a law firm functions, like the summer picnic at his house or the holiday party at some very nice restaurant. In those situations, I met his wife and his children: all clean, neatly dressed and well-coordinated. A picture-perfect family in a picture-perfect mansion.

Where the older brother Justin Able seemed perfect, the younger brother, Jared Able, appeared the far opposite. Justin was tall—over six feet—with permanently tanned skin, highlighted sandy blonde hair, and a dazzling white smile packaged in custom fitted suits. Jared was a head shorter, with a rounded belly and less hair. What was there was graying. His clothes were always rumpled, but his clients seemed to like him and his employees loved him more than Justin's, I would say. To be perfectly honest, Jared came across as the smarter more trustworthy of the two.

Now, about Mrs. Gertrude Munch. Everyone I know, including Justin and Jared, called her that. She was the founding partner of the law firm; a strong and sensible woman in her sixties, who did things her own way. She let her hair go silver, a perfect complement to her masculine business suits and high heels. I heard through the office grapevine that she was a great aunt of the two Able boys, which explained how she was able to hold onto them with such a tight rein.

Mrs. Munch ran the entire Illinois office as well as the satellite office in St. Louis where she lived a majority of time. I've had an opportunity to work with her on a handful of cases and was impressed by how hard she worked for her clients. And when it came to how she worked with me, I always walked away believing she had total confidence and respect for me.

I liked her very much.

I woke up on my birthday like I did every morning with an alarm clock blast. I shuffled to my closet for workout clothes and trudged to the basement for an uphill climb on my treadmill while watching the morning news. And just like every morning, I had so little time, so I jumped in a cool shower, still hot and sweaty from my workout.

After hair and makeup, I stared at my clothes in the walk-in closet. The law firm still had a conservative dress code, so I reached for my charcoal gray pantsuit with wide legs and a jacket with three quarter length sleeves. I looped the belt around my waist, grabbed my heels, and headed downstairs for a quick breakfast.

My kids began to roll out of bed. Julia was the first; I could hear the floor squeak as she walked to the bathroom. She's my thirteen-year-old middle schooler. After running a brush over her teeth and one through her hair, she bounded into the kitchen in one of her many outfits I'm too old to understand; heavy pajama bottoms, a sweatshirt and swede boots. I shook my head as she grabbed a breakfast tart and sat herself in front of the television. She'd be sugared up by the time she headed to school. I wondered if I was even a half-decent mother. I sighed and sipped my coffee.

My high schooler, Jacob, was a junior and at 5'10", he was tall and lanky and still looked very much like a little boy. But he wasn't, and I glanced at his sports bag the one he tossed by the laundry room door and left overnight, neatly packed with his basketball equipment and a clean uniform. I wondered if he had a game later today and was surprised by his new found organization.

He rolled out of bed at the last possible minute and ran the shower.

I filled my travel mug and kissed Julia on the head. "I'll be home at the regular time. I'll call if not." I said to her. She nodded absently, and took another bite of her sugared tart.

"Bye mom," she managed to say between bites.

Jacob finished his shower in record time. His heavy footsteps pounded against the carpeted floor. "Bye!" I shouted up the stairs, but it was a useless exercise. He was in his room with the door closed.

I left lunch money on the counter, grabbed my travel mug, slipped on my winter coat, and entered the garage, where I stared at my beige Toyota Camry. It might not be flashy, but it got me safely where I needed to go and took little amount of gas to do so.

While I waited for the car to heat up against the bitter wind and cold, I glanced at the clock, only seven in the morning. I took a sip of coffee, still hot in the travel mug and thought of my last big birthday, when I turned forty. I had been younger, filled with greater expectations. There had been so much in our lives at the time; we were raising younger kids, and my ex-husband Jack was growing his very successful law firm. We were happy, active and when I walked into the restaurant for my birthday dinner, and saw all of our friends and family yelling "Surprise!" I truly had been. I sighed.

As I trembled in my cold car, I put the memory away for another time, backed out of my garage and drove out of my subdivision.

Being that it was still early, didn't change the fact that around Chicagoland, rush hour was in full swing. What should take eight minutes would take me close to thirty. I punched the radio buttons, finding 94.7 FM in time for the morning celebrity quiz, fiddled around with butt warmer and heat to stave off the chill in the car.

As I crossed Rand Road, I was immediately stopped in traffic.

There were two seasons in the Chicago area: winter and construction season, and Quentin Road has been under construction for nearly three years. Originally it was new water pipes along the East side of the road, then they added a sound barrier to the west side of the road. When all that was done, they dug up the curbs to add an additional lane to both sides of the street. It's pretty much a cluster-fuck all the way around.

Ten minutes and I made it two miles, when I was finally able to turn left onto Quentin. I inched my way across the street and was stopped with my back end still in the opposite lane of traffic.

Don't turn green. Don't turn green.

I'm not sure why I mutter this, every morning, at the same spot. But every morning, sure enough, the light turned green and I'm hanging out in the wrong lane adding to the already thick snarl of traffic. When my light finally turned green again, I loosened the grip on the steering wheel and traffic lightened up. I made a full turn onto the road, drove for less than a minute and was stopped dead at the next light.

I took a deep breath as my phone buzzed and I checked the text message from Julia with a heavy sigh. She was thirteen going on forty and exactly what you'd expect from the youngest sibling of three. She was vivacious, fun, adventuresome, mouthy and sometimes simply a pain in the ass. She kept me on my toes and I never knew what to expect from her. Sometimes I was afraid to find out.

"Hi Sweetie," I said when I called her back.

"There's no bread in the drawer,"

"There's money on the counter. Buy your lunch today. I'll pick some up on the way home."

"Fine," she huffed, and the line clicked dead.

The light changed. I drove through and it was all clear until I got to the next stop light. Here, traffic cones lined the farthest right lane and traffic barriers blocked part of the opposite side of the road. I turned at the light at Route 22 and then… and that was where traffic was the worst. After jockeying for an open spot the last mile to my office, I finally made the turn into my business complex.

Four large office buildings were attached by corridors and housed small to midsize companies. The buildings were surrounded by a wide sidewalk and parking lots. Beyond the outer traffic circle were two professional golf courses with naked winter trees and almost—frozen ponds.

I was a creature of habit and always parked outside the entrance to building three, next to the cafeteria at the end of the row. I headed inside the building and though it was only 7:30, I flew up the stairs to the second floor. Juggling with one hand, I pulled out my badge and swiped it into the electronic lock.

The office was quiet, with only a handful of early employees and I was sure Justin was already in. I walked to my work area, down the wide aisle to the four cubicles that formed one large, open square. Before I reached my desk, I saw the balloons bouquet, tied to my desk chair. When I reached my cubicle, it was covered in colorful confetti, across my desktop (and even into my keyboard). It was nice to have office mates who remembered; it was even nicer that they decorated after I left last night.

I found the card on my desk, signed by the paralegals, Justin and Jared. I turned on my computer. It hummed and buzzed awake. I signed in and hung up my coat as the company system loaded.

I sat in a pile of confetti and began a scan of my emails.

There was plenty of work to do: research, document creation, phone calls, billing, invoicing. I had been working on a custody agreement for the Anders family and trust changes for the Stevens family all day yesterday, and I pulled them out to finish this morning. Until I noticed the folder for the Baker family.

I had researched and written the necessary documents and only needed Justin's signature. It was due yesterday and I had been trying to get that signature for a week. I grabbed the Baker file, and sucked in air, worried about the lateness of the file. I glanced at the clock, blew out a rather heavy sigh and headed to Justin's office.

I wish I had called first.

The offices of Able, Able and Munch were pretty much like any other place of employment. We had the know it all, the one who dates a lot of coworkers. the party planner. the gossip. In this case, the office gossip was Adrienne Mox. She sat on the other side of my office cubicle. While I'm not perfect, I try to stay away from the gossip. But I hear everything. As perfect as Justin's life appeared, there were rumors that he kept some very seedy secrets. I'm not a prude, this one irritated the hell out of me: he was sleeping with his secretary.

I didn't think about it much, it mostly popped up when I heard the gossip, but as I walked through partially open door, just wide enough for me to see too much, his administrative assistant was in a rather compromised position. My stomach roiled as I had flashbacks of my ex and his secretary. It was way too familiar. My exit from his doorway was less than graceful; I turned and tripped over the metal garbage can. The folder and papers skidded across the floor and I fell on my hands and knees in the hallway. The metal can rolled into the metal desk with a bang, and it echoed through the empty office.

"Shit," Justin said behind the semi-closed door. There was that rush and scuffle of clothes being thrown back on, zippers being zipped. I retrieved the folder and papers and scrambled back to my feet as Marcie Winkler rushed from his office holding her button down shirt closed. She blushed as she sped out of the office on her way to what I assumed was the bathroom.

People in the office would have had to be blind to not know something was going on. The amount of rumors that crossed my path led me to believe everyone in the office knew.

I wanted to leave before Justin came out but I hadn't made it. He rushed out of the office. Our eyes met and I could feel embarrassment and a bit of anger radiate from him. He momentarily caught the eye of someone behind me. I turned to see the office manager, Hector Garcia, holding back his temper; and yet he seemed helpless because of Justin's position in the law firm. I wondered just how much Human Resources could do about the situation anyway.

When I turned back to Justin, his cheeks were now rosy with the glow of embarrassment as he shuffled from foot to foot.

"I need this signed. It has to go to the client today." I held out the folder. He yanked it from my shaking hands, re-entered his office and slammed the door.

Hector was still watching, his jaw tight, his eyes wide. I was about to say something, but he held his hand up, shook his head and walked to his office, leaving me with serious questions about what was going on.

CHAPTER 2

Wilma Haynes, one of three of my office mates, was waiting for me when I returned to my desk. I smiled at her.

"Well, happy birthday?" she said with her arms spread wide.

"Thanks. And thanks for the decorations. My kids forgot." I grimaced.

"You're welcome. Lunch today?"

"Sure."

Sheila and Patti Anne, my other two office mates, made it to their cubicles as I went through my files for the day.

"Happy birthday, girl," Patti Anne said.

"Happy birthday, Nikki," Shelia added.

"Thanks, ladies. For all of this." I picked up the confetti and tossed it at Patti Anne before she took off her coat and turned on her computer.

I turned back to my work as we settled in for the day. I hadn't said anything to anyone about Justin and Marcie and I'm sure Hector said nothing either.

And yet, it spread faster than a forest fire.

As I copied and pasted, I heard the loud whispers over the wall.

"Did you hear…" Adrienne Mox asked her friend Joy Sundae. And then she mumbled.

"I heard. Linda said she came into the bathroom. Crying in front of everyone. Ruined her makeup and everything." Joy squealed.

Even retelling this, I'm embarrassed by how much I listened in. I was surprised at Adrienne. I thought she and Marcie were friends.

"Damn…" Adrienne grew quiet. "She shouldn't have done this. Not now."

"But then what would we talk about?" Joy giggled.

"We shouldn't be discussing this," Adrienne hissed.

"Sorry," Joy murmured.

I glanced over at Wilma who sat along the same wall as me, and we both looked at each other with wide eyes. Adrienne was always the instigator in the gossip, maybe she did care about Marcie.

Marcie.

If I knew Marcie better, I'd stick my nose in and tell her to sue for sexual harassment.

But there was no time for further contemplation. Wilma and the rest of the paralegals began filing into the conference room for our weekly staff meeting. I followed them inside.

It was awkward for me; I could barely make eye contact with Justin. So much so, I chose to doodle in my notebook rather than look at him. But it wasn't only me. Adrienne glanced at him with cold, angry eyes and the rest of the paralegals were silent. There were no whispers, no one asked questions, no jovial conversations before or after the meeting. If we were all shell- shocked, it wasn't so much because the rumors were true, rather, I think we were all so shocked that it happened in the office.

It was the shortest staff meeting in my tenure at the firm.

The paralegal staff dispersed and filed down our three aisles across from the conference room. I was working on a custody agreement when a client call came in.

"Yes, Mrs. Anders. That's correct and that's how it will be written into the agreement." I nodded though she couldn't see me and I answered her next question. "Yes, ma'am. I'll have that for you by the end of the week. Have a good day."

I hung up and scribbled some notes on the Anders's file. I couldn't ignore his shuffling when Justin came down my aisle. I took my time writing my notes and thoughts for the agreement. Justin stood anxiously near my desk, staring out the window at nothing in particular.

When I couldn't ignore his presence any longer, I pushed the folder to the side and cleared my throat and looked him in the eye.

He turned away, his square jaw was clenched tightly. He began to say something but stopped himself. He tossed the file on my desk and scurried away.

Wilma, Sheila, and Patti Anne watched the exchange with curiosity and watched as Justin walked away. Patti Anne stood and observed as he walked down the hallway and turned toward his office.

"That was damn gutsy," Patti Anne said with her hands on her hips. She glanced at all of us with her dark brown eyes and her lips pursed in disgust. "Why's no one stopping him or punishing him?"

Wilma and Sheila shook their heads.

"He's the boss. What are they going to do, vote him out?" I wondered what other secrets were floating around the managing partners of the firm.

"You know that's bullshit," Patti Anne said.

"Yeah. I know." I matched Patti Anne's grimace as I pulled out the document I had waited for him to sign. When I glanced at his signature, it was different, only slightly, as if he had hesitated to sign it.

"You can't force her to complain, or press charges," Wilma said.

From my personal experience with illicit relationships, sometimes both parties were equally responsible for the affair, even if one of them was the boss. It cut so close to home and I was surprised that I was taking Marcie's side in this. Maybe both of them needed to suffer consequences.

"No, I suppose we can't." Patti Anne finally sat. We stared at each other for a moment before we reluctantly returned to our work.

I pulled my pile of papers and copied all of the documents, forms and exhibits. I slipped the originals into the envelope, entered the address into the mailing system and printed the label. When the envelope was prepared for mailing, I dropped the unsealed envelope on the administrative assistant's desk for scanning and mailing.

I sat back in my chair and sighed as I debated whether or not to start my next project or give up and see what my friends had planned for lunch. My phone rang instead and my stomach roiled when I noted Hector Garcia was calling.

"Hi Hector."

"Can you come down here, please?"

To be perfectly honest, I expected to hear from him sooner and was surprised it took him so long to call me.

"On my way."

It was hard to hide from my cube mates. Patti Anne turned to me. "Justin?"

I shook my head. "I walked in on Justin and Marcie. Hector was there when I saw what happened in the office," I confided. It felt as though eyes were on me from the rest of the office. I hadn't shared that I was the one who had caught Justin and Marcie and yet; I somehow thought everyone knew it was me.

"Oh girl. That must've been a sad sight," Patti Anne said.

I started to shrug and dropped my shoulders. "It was an embarrassing surprise and a bad reminder of the end of my marriage." I bit my lip.

"And Hector wants to brush it under the rug, I suppose." Sheila wrung her hands as she spoke.

"I have no idea. I'll find out though."

The office wasn't large, but it wasn't small either. I turned the corner, walked past Justin's office to Hector's open door and knocked on the jamb. He looked up and waved me inside. "Close the door."

I sat on the other side of his desk and crossed my legs. I always had a great relationship with Hector and usually felt comfortable in his office. While my back grew wet with nervous sweat, I gripped my hands in my lap, to keep from wringing them, to hide my anxiety from Hector.

"So now you know the rumors are true."

I opened my mouth to say something about Marcie suing Justin, but kept my mouth shut instead.

"They're consenting adults," he said.

I frowned. Maybe I was projecting my feelings on my ex-husband and his affair with his secretary on Justin and Marcie. And why was I still taking her side? Was it because the other women in the paralegal department took Marcie's side? I stopped fidgeting and looked at Hector.

"It's sexual harassment. He's taking advantage of his position."

Hector took a breath. "She won't press charges. Claims it was consenting between the two of them. I've tried. And now…" He looked out the vertical window beside his closed door. It overlooked the bank of Administrative Assistant cubicles.

"They're adults and I can't do anything about it. HR knows, his brother knows. Mrs. Munch probably knows."

Do they think the affair coming to light was my fault? Is this why I was summoned here? I felt anger.

"I didn't spread the gossip this morning, if that's what you think. I think Marcie handled that on her own." I defiantly crossed my arms against my chest.

"I don't think that," Hector mumbled and glanced at his hands resting on his desk.

"I get it. They're consenting adults. If I hadn't walked in on them, I don't think I'd be this… opinionated about it."

He shook his head. "I wish it was that simple."

As people passed his office, they glanced inside, hoping to catch the latest scoop or what they might think was the latest office gossip. I suddenly felt too warm and embarrassed, wishing I hadn't been the one to catch them, forcing me to the center of their indiscretion. Frankly, I was a little afraid of my role in the office gossip.

"Is there anything else?"

Hector folded his arms on his desk and sighed. "Just be careful. Be... diligent."

I glanced at him, unable to hide my surprise and confusion. He sighed.

"I'm sorry, Nikki. We've been complicit in this, letting him get away with it. But... they're consenting adults."

"So, you call me in here and tell me to be careful because..."

He wrung his hands across his desk. "I can't be sure, but I think there's more to the affair than just sex." I opened my mouth unsure of what to say to that; he held his palms out as if to calm me. "It's... don't say anything to anyone about this. I don't have proof. I just have a ... gut feeling. Just stay alert and don't share what you know."

"Well, hell." I blurted. I observed Hector. His long face was tense, sweat broke out on his lip and along his hairline, his hands were balled tightly. He had worked for the law firm for many more years than I have.

"Just be careful. If we could have led the horse to water and made her drink..."

I fiddled with my notebook and pen trying not to laugh. "That's really cliché. And all you'd be doing is controlling her."

He held his hands out wide. "I can't discuss it any more than I already have. I just want you to be aware."

"And to tell me to be careful. What's going on, Hector? It's affecting his work." Hector raised an eyebrow.

"How so?"

I explained how it took a week to track him down to sign the documents I needed.

"You're not the first to mention something. There's a lot that makes me think something else going on." His sigh was heavy as he leaned back against his chair. "Does anyone else feel this way?" he finally asked.

I thought back to the gossip twins on the other side of the wall and shrugged. "I'm his primary paralegal so I haven't heard anything from anyone else. If I hear anything, I'll let you know."

He nodded and stood, I followed, and headed back to my cubicle with a sense that this wasn't over yet.

CHAPTER 3

The great thing about my job is that I very rarely need to take work home with me. But after catching Justin at work, I felt too awkward to ask him for information I needed. So, I packed up the case files and headed home where I could research in peace.

While my case folders and notes sat in my trunk, I fought the crowds at the grocery store, looking first for bread and then something for dinner. There were times that I wished I was a stay-at-home mom, because if I were there for my kids when they came home from school, I'd have time for home cooked meals and that would make me a better mom. But when I was home, I felt like I should be at work providing for the. I wondered if there would ever be a time when I wasn't wracked with guilt.

I tossed bread into my basket and rolled along to the deli for prepared food and stared at my options. Jacob would definitely like the pre-cooked steak, and I tossed that in the basket with the double baked potatoes and found the macaroni and cheese for Julia. I placed both in my cart as I determined if I wanted healthy or decadent and finally settled on the baked salmon for myself. I stared at the premade dinners, pushed the mom guilt deep down inside, and ran off to grab a few more items.

I'm a master shopper. I filled my cart within twenty minutes. After loading my trunk, I pulled into traffic for home.

By this time traffic was heavy. And to top that off, it started to rain. It doesn't matter how long people have lived in the Chicagoland area, driving in bad weather becomes a harrowing experience, and people forget how to drive when the street gets wet.

I sat in traffic, my attention on the car in front of me as it slowed down. I'd have driven around him but there was no room. Instead, I rubbed my temples, listened to the sound of horns honking and rolled my eyes.

Really?

It was cold and wet when I finally pulled into the garage. I dragged myself into the house, loaded with my work bag across my shoulders and bags full of bread, lunch meat, cookies, wine and dinners for the three of us. And I did it in high heels.

I skirted around Jacob's stinky workout bag and gear scattered across the laundry room floor and kicked my shoes off before depositing my bags on the island.

After I put the food away, I changed into sweats and a t-shirt and heated up the meals. It was still quiet; Jacob and Julia were in their rooms.

Before calling them down, I opened and poured myself some wine, turned on the television and channel surfed, settling on the decorating channel. Happy birthday to me, I thought, and took a sip.

"Mom!"

"Yeah?"

"Mom!"

"What do you want!" I screeched.

"Mom! Where are you?" Jacob wandered around the first floor, finally finding me on the couch.

I stared at this boy, my once tiny son, who used to crawl on to my lap and snuggle against my chest. Now, he was almost six feet tall and still gangly, with arms too long for his body. He sat beside me, damp from his shower after basketball practice.

"What's for dinner?"

"Counter." I pointed.

He looked at me with a lost expression. "I'm starving." The whining was no longer cute when they're sixteen and taller than you.

"Grab a plate and have some food. I got you the steak." I leaned back against the cushion and closed my eyes.

"You look tired," he said. His big feet hit the floor with such force when he walked. He took out the plates and they clattered against the stone counter. The silverware drawer squeaked open; the plastic food containers buckled and cracked. He loaded his plate and sauntered away with his food, I'm sure to his room to work on homework.

"Tell Julia," I called after Jacob as he lumbered upstairs. And as if on cue, my phone rang. I glanced at the caller ID, took a sip of wine and answered.

"Hi love. What's up?"

My daughter Emily was a college freshman, a great student who thrived on structure, schedules, and activities. But now that I wasn't in charge of the master schedule, she was a little unsure of herself and frequently called home. Sometimes I thought Emily was just not ready to adult yet.

"Mom!"

I could almost see her rolling her eyes.

"What's up?" I asked again. Behind me, Julia was scraping macaroni and cheese into a bowl. I didn't have to look, she'd be making a face at the green beans and loading up on macaroni and potatoes. She always did.

I turned and watched her.

"Mom. I got a C on my paper!" Emily screeched into the phone. The great student was learning that college wasn't going to be easy.

"Yeah, and?" I took another sip. It was gonna be a rough call.

"A C!" she shouted into the phone. I pulled it away from my ear.

"It happens. Did the professor tell you why?" Another sip of wine.

"Mom. It's not fair!" I rolled my eyes as Julia joined me on the sofa. She balanced the plate on her lap, her drink on the coffee table. I saw the water rings start forming. I finished my first glass of wine and poured another from the bottle on the table.

"You do realize that college IS supposed to be harder." We have had this discussion before and I wasn't sure where to go with it.

"But I ALWAYS got As in high school."

I frowned, and Julia, who could hear Emily's voice, started laughing as she ate her dinner. I held my finger up to her with my best stern look. She turned back to the tv and left me to my call.

"I've already told you. It's harder. If you're having issues, go talk to the professor about why you got the C and then go ask for help at the student center."

She was quiet on the other end while I sipped my wine. Work tomorrow was gonna suck with a hangover.

"Well," Emily's voice is soft and cautious. "Why can't you call him?"

I sighed. I had thought I raised them to take advocate for themselves, but then again, home and public school, wasn't quite like college.

"Okay. Here's the deal. You're an adult and even if I was going to talk to your professor, he won't talk to me. You either talk to him and find out what you did wrong, or get a C on the next paper. I can't help you."

"Mom. I don't think I can do this." I knew how she felt.

"Emily. I can't help you. You need to talk to the professor, keep studying and get help. It's all on you, now."

"Ugh…" she said. I waited. I had no desire to take the bait. "Fine."

I smiled when Emily hung up, proud of myself for not yelling, for not accommodating her anxiety, for gently nudging my baby bird from the nest. The world hadn't imploded, she won't hate me. Emily would survive and raise her grades. I put my legs on the table and finished my second glass of wine.

****

By the time I filled my plate with food, I was feeling the effect of the wine and found I wasn't all that hungry. It had been a weird day, not the type of day I wanted for my birthday. I picked at my dinner as I watched the designer on television paint the wall black. I was surprised by how much I liked it.

"I picked up bread and lunch meat. You can make lunch again," I said to Julia as she carried her plate to the kitchen.

It was like crickets as she and Jacob put their plates in the sink.

"Dishwasher's dirty!" I shouted and shoved potatoes into my mouth.

I thought I heard the grumbling as the dishwasher was opened and dishes clinked against dishes. The refrigerator door opened. I couldn't imagine what else my son could possibly want to eat. He came back with a small plastic container, holding a very small birthday cake.

"Happy birthday." He placed it on the coffee table, Julia followed with some plates and forks. I looked at them incredulously, very surprised, my eyes misting. I still couldn't get over the three of them forgetting my birthday initially, but at least they're trying.

I smiled widely, and wiped my damp eyes. "Thanks. Thanks for remembering."

****

I drank a lot of water and took a few pain pills to avoid the hangover headache, I was sure I'd have by morning. I was a little nauseated as I sat on my bed, covered by work folders, and turned on my computer. I opened the firm's system, pulled up the research files and began to take notes.

I scanned my go to law review websites, added what I needed for the custody agreement I was drafting. I was starting to fade from my long, emotional day. I glanced over the document for glaring mistakes and unanswered questions and saved it for the last time tonight. I logged out of the firm's system.

The phone rang and I scowled at caller ID.

"Hello?" I asked, though I knew who it was.

"Nikki?"

"Justin. What's up?" I'm a happy drunk and I was finding that the wine was masking my true feelings. While I might have sounded giddy, I was still processing what had happened early that morning. Finding Justin with Marcie at work had left me feeling anxious and maybe a little vulnerable, as if work was no longer a place for work now that such an intimate act was discovered and discussed.

But the wine. I was nearly laughing and bit my tongue to keep quiet.

It had to be awkward for Justin too because he was quiet for a moment, fidgeting with something, maybe typing, or tapping against a tablet.

"I… I wanted to talk to you about today."

I held my breath as he spoke. While I wasn't surprised he called me, I really didn't want to speak with him, especially about this. It would have been fine for me to pretend it never happened. Especially when I tried to unclench my jaw and unfurl my fingers from the tight ball I found them in. I finally let out stale air from my lungs.

"Okay."

"I'm… I'm very sorry about what happened this morning."

He was sorry he got caught.

"Apology accepted. I don't want to talk about it." There was silence between us. Neither one of us ever had a conversation about anything personal, especially this personal. But there was something in what happened today that hit so close to home. I knew it wasn't my business but I had been the wife in this situation. I knew the pain, the hurt, the distrust and the dissolution of a marriage. And while I'm usually a good employee and did the best job that I could in whatever was assigned, and never chided or spoken up to a boss or manager, I couldn't let this rest.

"No, actually. While I know you're both consenting adults, sex in your office was inappropriate." My brutal honesty truly surprised me.

Again, I held my breath as I gathered my thoughts, and let him deal with my admonishment. I'm not sure how he could justify his actions or how I could justify mine. He was, after all, my boss, and I needed this job.

"It's all a mess. It's…" he squeaked or cried.

"Justin. You don't owe me anything. No explanation and you've apologized. We're not friends, you shouldn't be talking to me."

"It's just…Nikki. I got you caught up in this. I just want us to be okay."

"It's between you and your wife. And no, we're not okay." My headache pounded against the back of my head. I pushed the folders away and leaned against the headboard. "If there's nothing else, it's late."

"I'm sorry Nikki," he said quickly. "I'm so very sorry all of this happened."

I let out an exaggerated sigh.

"I think you're sorry you got caught." It came out before I could stop it. Whatever he was doing, he stopped. There was only silence on the other end.

"I made a mistake," he whispered.

A mistake was buying the wrong type of cheese for a recipe. Cheating on your spouse but a wrong choice. I wanted to scream and yell and tell him how wrong he was. I was still stuck on my own history.

This wasn't about me.

"Justin. You're my boss. So if you want me to berate you, it's not my place. This wasn't a mistake. This was bad judgement. And I know what your wife is going through. She hurts like hell." I was still amazed at my brazenness. It wasn't like me.

"I…I know. I'm sorry."

"It's not me you have to apologize to."

"You walked in and you shouldn't have to see that or worry about my bad behavior. I'm sorry for putting you in any bad position."

That was more of an apology than I ever got from my ex. I swallowed, took a deep breath and let it out slowly.

"Thank you for saying so. If I can offer a bit of advice…"

After a beat he said, "Sure."

"End it with Marcie. Find a way to make it up to your wife and move on with your life. It's not worth destroying everything."

"It's not so simple."

"Sometimes choices are hard. I need to go. Good night Justin." I hung up the phone before he could say anything else. It wasn't my business and the conversation made me uncomfortable. He was my boss; this was his personal life.

It was late and I was feeling sick. I got myself ready for bed, took off my makeup, brushed my teeth and looked into the mirror.

"So, this is fifty," I said to my reflection.

Happy fucking birthday, I imagined my reflection saying back to me.

****

For the first time in my adult life I went to work hungover.

I was antsy through the morning drive, and that was after I had skipped my work out because I couldn't focus. Not just the hangover, but the call from Justin last night, yesterday morning in his office, my less than stellar fiftieth birthday.

After logging on to my computer, I sat with my head in my hands as my computer loaded. Even the soft humming was too much noise. I took a swig of my coffee, glanced through my emails, and printed what I needed.

The office was quiet. I enjoyed the lack of employees and the early morning. But today, I was off my game, with a brewing headache and roiling stomach. I blinked several times, unloaded my bag with the folders I worked on at home, and vowed to re-read what I had written while drunk last night. The thought made me chuckle a little.

Before I reviewed my work from last night though, I glanced at the new folders placed in my inbox after hours. There were only two.

As always, I opened each folder to glance through the notes and work needed. Usually when I received these, I had either met with Justin to discuss what work we'd be doing, or he had the meeting without me and would meet with me to discuss the case before I began on the work required for the client.

The first file wasn't a surprise. We had met with the Bakers at the beginning of the week and this was the next review of their trust agreement. I took a few notes, dropped it back in my on the pile of folders and opened the next file. It was a custody agreement for the Cabots. I had no recollection of them or their custody agreement.

I couldn't remember a time that I worked on a client file without having a meeting with the lawyer first, or a phone call with the client at the very least, or knew ahead of time that I was covering the work for another paralegal. As I read the chicken scratch notes, they weren't Justin's; the handwriting didn't ring a bell.

Confused for a moment, I logged into the client database and searched for the files for Emma and London Cabot.

I knew I had never worked with either client and had no knowledge of their ongoing divorce battle. That meant I hadn't been a part of the initial meetings or any of the other documents, calls, or meetings. If one of the paralegals was out sick or on vacation and couldn't work on this, someone would have asked me to cover for them, but that hadn't been the case and there were no notes regarding that in the file. I wasn't sure why this custody agreement had been placed on my desk.

Thinking it was just an oversight, I glanced through the Cabot file, searching the limited documentation and looked for the paralegal of record. The custody agreement was last signed out by NP.

Why are my initials attached to this document? An error?

As I scanned the files, I discovered my initials on all three of the documents in the Cabot account. My heart sped up. I could understand if someone accidently typed the wrong initials once, but three times?

Something was up.

CHAPTER 4

I prided myself on doing good work, writing concise and correct documents, entering my time correctly, taking good notes, doing more than I was asked. And even with that hangover, I couldn't help but think something was bizarre with this case file and I wanted to make sure I hadn't done something incorrectly in my work.

I opened the invoicing system where I entered my time, notes, any client bank account information, and the codes we used to describe what work had been completed. I stared at the line items for the three documents created for the Cabot family.

As a paralegal, I'm responsible for entering time and of all billable hours. I control invoicing and client accounts when a retainer is involved. But as I scrolled up through the previous entries, I noticed all of the billable hours that had already been documented. I bit my lower lip as I read the unorganized, disjointed notes. I scrolled over to see which paralegal was responsible, but noted all time was entered as JRA for Justin Robert Able.

The firm took the notation and the accuracy in the billing system very seriously. As I read Justin's notes, I couldn't make sense of the work that had been done for the Cabots and it didn't seem to jive with the thirty grand that had been billed to them in the course of their divorce case.

What is going on with this account?

Out of curiosity, I returned to the document files. The billing definitely seemed out of whack with the work that was done.

"Justin, what the hell did you do?" I muttered and glanced around to see if I was still alone. There was no one in my row and I heard no one on the other side of the wall. I was still by myself.

I pulled out my notepad, made notes on the dates, the inconsistent notations, and invoice amount.

This must have been what Hector warned me about. Problems with Justin's work.

When I finished taking notes, I exited the system, pulled the Cabot folder and my notes together, and was determined to speak to Hector. But it was only 7:00. Rather than barging in there, I took additional pain medication for my pounding headache, took a sip of my coffee, and stared at the Cabot file.

Yes, it's weird. Yes, my initials were attached to a client file that I had never worked on. Yes, I had a bad feeling in my gut that there was something going on. But this custody agreement was left on my desk to complete.

I sighed, opened the folder, pulled out the notes, and perused the first draft of the document. I reviewed point by point, marked off requested changes; there were only three and made the changes to the digital file. I did another round of spell-checking before printing off the document to show Hector. I slipped the document back in the folder and made my way to Hector's office.

He wasn't in.

Jared stood beside his administrative assistant's desk, making notes on her legal pad.

"Good morning, Nikki. You're in early." He smiled warmly. I was surprised he was in so early. He was usually in at eight and it was seven now.

"I had things I needed to get to before it got busy in here." I offered a smile and shrugged.

"What's the rush with that one?" He pointed to the folder.

"Just a custody agreement. No rush." I started to turn away.

"I didn't know Justin had a custody agreement. Who's it for?"

It was a tightrope walk when one partner wanted to know what the other was doing. I felt that if I lied or didn't answer, I was doing something wrong in the eyes of one boss. But to tell him felt like I was doing something wrong with the other. I didn't like the pull of being in the middle.

I pursed my lips. "Just the Cabot custody agreement." Jared's eyes widened for a split second. And then he smiled.

"Oh. Okay. No problem. Have a good morning." He returned to the notepad as I shoved the folder in Justin's in box.

I turned and headed back to my cubicle. As I turned the corner, I looked back. Jared was perusing the Cabot file, squinting with his tongue sticking out of his mouth. I knew it was the Cabot file; my notes were written on the cover. I stood at the corner and watched as he closed the folder and took it with him.

What the hell?

Employees began to enter the office, their voices soft and buzzed as they greeted their seat-mates and other friends. A large group chatted happily in the lunch room as they got their coffee or heated their breakfasts. Their voices wafted back into the office when the door opened. Wilma and Patti Anne were still chatting as they entered our aisle.

"Hey lady," Patti Anne said when I turned around. She glanced up and down at me and frowned. "You look like hell."

Wilma turned and assessed me. I thought I looked fine in slacks and a blouse. "She's right. What's wrong?"

It was nice to know I had friends in these ladies and that they always my back and yet, did I really look that crappy?

I told them about my night, and the alcohol, but left out my call from Justin. Patti Anne laughed. "Oh sweetie. Sorry your birthday was so shitty."

I shrugged, trying to let it go. "It is what it is. I just wish the hangover would leave." Patti Anne turned on her computer and Wilma followed. They slipped out of their coats and hung them against their cubicle walls and settled in for work. Footsteps shuffled against the carpet on the other side of the cubicle wall.

"Marcie's gone!" Joy's voice wafted over to us. "She didn't even come in with her resignation. Just emailed it to Justin. He's roaming around in a daze," Joy said happily.

"Can you keep it down," Adrienne hissed.

"I don't blame her. Sleeping with the boss, ugh," Joy added.

"Joy. Shhh…" Adrienne said. Wilma and I glanced at each other as Joy and Adrienne reverted to whispering. I edged my hip onto her desk so I could listen to them on the other side of Wilma's desk.

I wasn't proud and I was curious.

"Marcie left because she's in danger," Adrienne could barely get the words out. Again, Wilma and I glanced at each other.

41

"Why. Because they got caught? It's all his fault."

"No. She won't tell me why, but she's in danger. That's all I know. Don't tell anyone."

Their desk chairs squeaked as they stood up and the two of them left their cubicles, probably for the cafeteria downstairs and a warm breakfast.

"Marcie left. Huh?" I said, letting that sink in.

"Good for her. Justin put her in a difficult situation." Wilma turned her chair around as Justin strolled down our aisle. We all worked to not to stare at him.

"I need to talk to you Nikki," he said. He motioned for me to join him and I followed and my stomach churned as we walked to his office.

His office was a large space dominated by a half-moon shaped desk with his large ergonomic chair at the center. His shelves were stacked with law books, novels, keepsakes, and pictures of his family, kids and his wife. His law degree and college degree had been framed and hung above his desk.

He pulled a picture down of his wife and his children, all blonde, all blue eyes, and all wearing white. He held the picture as he looked at me.

"I'm so sorry." He wiped his mouth and pursed his lips. "It was the biggest mistake I have ever made. I don't think I could make it up to you. Tell me how?" He gripped the picture. I nodded toward it.

I held my hands on the chair rests, my grip so tight I was white knuckled. We weren't friends. We've never had deep discussions. "Have you apologized to them?"

He glanced down at the perfect picture. "You found me." He couldn't make eye contact.

"I'm not the one you should be apologizing to."

This was getting uncomfortable. I wasn't sure why he was trying to fix it with me. Unless this was the only relationship, he thought he could fix.

"Marcie's gone."

"I just heard."

His jaw clenched. "I just wanted to apologize again for putting you in this situation."

"You apologized last night. We're okay."

He put the picture on his desk, and I stared at the happy faces.

"I've always counted on you. Counted on your intelligence, your reliability. I just don't want to ruin that working relationship."

I stared at him. His eyes were red, circles encased them, he looked as though he hadn't slept in weeks.

"You're my boss. I'm here to do my job. Whatever you did, won't affect that." I could have said more but I said it all last night.

He looked at me expectantly. I thought he might have wanted me to admonish him some more to assuage his guilt.

"I'm…" He said slowly. "That works."

"I'm fine. I do have work to do." I stood to leave. He was wearing his suit from yesterday, only today it was rumpled. I sighed. "I put the Cabot file in your inbox. Jared removed it."

Justin glanced up at me, loss and confusion all over his face.

"The Cabot File?"

"Custody agreement after a three-year battle divorce battle."

He nodded. "I'm a little scattered right now, but I don't know the Cabot file."

I blew out stale air. He was all over that file. But then so was I and I know I hadn't worked it before. My gut churned. "I guess it could have been Jared who gave it to me then. But your initials were in the invoice system. Is there anything else?"

He shook his head and I exited and took the short walk to my desk. I stared at the folders on my desk, pulled down the first one, and read through the notes.

"What did he want?" Patti Anne asked. She was on the edge of her seat. Sheila looked on attentively as she pulled off her winter jacket.

"To apologize for putting me in an awkward position." I glanced at the three women. We had worked together for three years, supporting each other as we did our jobs. They were curious and worried.

"Mighty nice of him," Patti Anne groused.

I shrugged. "It's weird. He's so preoccupied with all of this, he forgot about a file he had given me."

"Not surprising. I bet Mrs. Justin Able isn't all that happy with what happened." Wilma said.

I debated on telling them what was really going on. But then, maybe if I shared, I could figure it out.

"There's more." I scooted my chair over by Patti Anne who was caddy-corner to me. The others followed. "Justin doesn't remember the file, but Jared saw me place it in Justin's in box; he pulled it out and took it with him."

They exchanged glances. "You sure the initials were just a mistake? It was really Jared's client?" Sheila asked.

"A mistake on three documents. He was all over that account and so was I," I said exasperated.

This time, their glances showed worry.

"Do you think this has to do with Marcie quitting and going missing?" Wilma asked.

Sheila wrung her hands with worry. Pattie Anne shook her head. "What the hell is going on with those partners?" she asked.

But we had no answer to that question, just more questions. When Wilma's phone rang, we returned to our work. My pile had grown since last night and I started again on my first folder. Last week I had a meeting with the Anders family, two moms who were setting up trust and college funds for their kids. The culmination of those agreements were in the folder, Justin's neat handwriting in various parts which needed updating.

I turned to my computer and began to work my way through the document.

****

The morning dragged on; I was grateful for lunch time and wanted to be alone. While I enjoyed my time with my work friends, I was tired and still hungover and wasn't in the mood. My office was on the third floor where it bustled with the law firm and a small accounting firm across the floor. I took the stairs to the second floor and hid myself away in one of the abandoned club chairs near the empty office and started on my sandwich. I pulled out my ear buds to listen to music when the unmistakable voice of Adrienne Mox wafted out from around the corner.

I held the buds in my hands as I listened. She was on her phone.

"Yeah. Yeah."

Silence.

"I don't know if Justin knows about it yet?"

A voice murmured from the phone.

"Justin? He's been wandering the halls. Yeah. It's hilarious." Adrienne began to laugh.

I grimaced. I didn't know what Justin was supposed to know about, but I felt in my gut that she was talking to Marcie and knew what was going on. She stopped laughing.

"Uh huh. Yeah. I'll let you know what else happens. Yeah. Be careful. It's gonna blow soon."

Adrienne never saw me as she sashayed away from her hiding spot. Her four-inch heels clicked across the marble floors. She took the elevator and I stuffed my sandwich into my bag, stood at the elevator and noticed when it hit the ground floor. I took the stairs to the first floor and found Adrienne walking toward building four. I followed, not too closely, and watched as she took the stairs to the basement.

I glanced down the wide staircase. Adrienne had stopped at the bottom and I heard the unmistakable sound of kissing.

Well, hell. Everyone's getting some but me.

Form the couches across from the staircase, I finished my sandwich and played on my phone as I waited for Adrienne to come back upstairs.

What the hell am I doing?

I had ignored that feeling in my gut that told me to leave, this was none of my business, but it was inching toward the end of lunch and I should get back to work. But before I could leave, Adrienne ran for the stairs, her short spiky hair disheveled. She saw me and frowned as she ran her fingers through her hair. If I hadn't walked in on my ex-husband and his mistress or I hadn't walked in on my boss and his, catching Adrienne walking away from something, might have made me chuckle. I glanced down at my phone as if it was the most interesting thing I owned as I waited for Adrienne to leave.

****

Every day feels busier than the last and today was no exception. I held three client meetings, mostly on my own, as Justin was preoccupied with his personal mess. He excused himself from the last two. While it irritated me, I still brought my notes from the meetings home with me. The extra weight from my messenger bag dug into my shoulders.

I reached my car and noticed Justin was outside his Lexus, parked at the edge of the lot. He was discussing something with Jared, and it was rather animated.

Though I could hear their voices I couldn't make out what they were saying. I got in, dropped my bag on the passenger side, and started my car. As it heated up, I watched Justin and Jared's argument heat up as well. I never would have said they were particularly close, and watching Jared storm off as Justin slammed his driver's side door cemented that opinion.

"What that was about?" It could have been about Marcie, or maybe the brothers always fought like that.

It was on my mind as I drove through the parking lot and out of the complex. I was still wondering when I pulled into my garage. Jacob was home, his bags scattered across the laundry room floor, and Julia's backpack was on the counter. The television was blaring and both kids were on the couch, watching a ghost chasing reality show.

"No homework?" I asked Jacob and touched his hair. It was damp after his shower.

"None," he muttered and grabbed a handful of popcorn.

Julia shrugged without looking at me. I pulled out my phone, ordered a pizza and sat on the couch between my offspring. My cell phone rang.

Pacing into the front room, I answered. "Justin."

"I didn't give you the Cabot file. I've never worked on it and I'm locked out of it," he said without greeting.

What the hell?

"Ok. That's weird considering your initials were attached to all of the Cabot's files." I leaned against the cold window and stared into the neighborhood. If Justin really didn't know about the Cabot file, did Jared take it to make sure Justin never saw it? Why? What is it about that file that I'm not seeing?

"Nikki. They're not my clients. I've never met them. What was in that file?"

I told him it had been a three-year process according to the notes. "At the same time, the custody agreement was pretty standard. Fifty-fifty, weekend and holiday rotation."

Justin was also pacing—I could hear his hard soles on a wood floor. "Anything else in the client files?"

"Yeah. A few documents, three. Not enough to justify the thirty thousand in billing though."

I heard a thump through the phone. Justin must have hit something.

"Can you get me the files? Something is off with that account."

Again, I felt like I was on a fence between one boss and the other, unsure of who I should be loyal to or even trust. "Sure. I can pull them for you. Give them to you in the morning."

"Pull the hourly billing and notes. I'd like to know what's going on."

I wanted to know that myself. The fact Justin was now concerned about the file, worried me all the more.

"No problem Justin. I can pull it tonight, give it to you tomorrow."

He stopped pacing. There was a female voice in the background. I assumed his wife but then again, after seeing him yesterday, I could be very wrong.

"Thanks Nikki. I'm sorry for all of this," he said and hung up.

A half-hour later, our pizza arrived. I shoved the worry and anxiety away for tomorrow and sat down to dinner.

CHAPTER 5

I stared at my bag, heavy with my notes on the Cabot file. I made three copies: one for me, one for Justin, and one for Hector. I put my folder back in my bag and stared at Justin's and Hector's.

Should I give Justin the files?

I felt as though I was pulled into something unseemly. Justin wasn't supposed to know, I probably wasn't supposed to know that someone was using my sign in to work the Cabot files. And yet, it was placed in my in box to work on. Did someone want me to find out what was going on? Did they not think I'd talk to my boss about a client file?

I held off on Justin's file and walked the information to Hector's office. He was always in early, before anyone else, including the partners. Both Jared's and Justin's offices were dark. I knocked on Hector's door jamb. He looked up and offered a wan smile. I wondered if what had happened with Justin was wearing on him.

"What's up, Nikki?" He motioned me in. I closed his door behind me and he cocked an eyebrow.

"Something weird is going on." I tossed the folder on his desk.

He glanced at me before opening the cover and reading my notes. He looked back at me with confusion.

"You asked me for anything that was off with Justin. His initials are all over this client file but claims he doesn't know them. I left the client folder in his in box yesterday and Jared took it." I took a deep breath and sat across from him.

"He doesn't remember a client that has his initials all over it?"

I nodded. "He missed two client meetings yesterday." Now I felt like a tattle tale. I sighed.

Hector glanced at the file for a moment and then back to me. "And you've never worked on the Cabot file?"

"Not until I got it on Tuesday. And my initials are in the invoice system as the paralegal." My voice rose an octave. I hadn't realized how much stress this was causing me.

"First Marcie and then this." Hector shook his head.

"Justin called me Tuesday night and last night. He's never called me. He's... he's..."

"Guilty. His head is elsewhere. Jared told me Justin's wife kicked him out. Apparently Justin is dealing with a lot." Hector sat back in his chair and looked at me. "I can't tell you ... certain things about what I know. Like I told you on Tuesday, just keep your head up and clear. Watch those around you."

His stare was intense; he didn't blink as he looked at me. I felt chilled by his icy glare.

"That doesn't make me feel secure."

"I'm sorry Nikki. I really am."

As I walked back to my desk, I decided I was tired of the apologies and the drama. It had only been two days since I found Justin with Marcie and that seemed to set something into motion.

The Cabot file.

Why me?

I began to wonder if it was time to look for a new job. By the time I returned to my desk, Wilma was taking off her coat.

"Hey. I wondered where you were," Wilma said as she turned on her computer.

"Hector asked me for something a few days ago. Just got him what he needed." I turned on my own computer and stared at my messenger bag. Hector's warning was stuck in my head. I decided to wait and not give Justin what he wanted.

Wilma sat and slid her desk chair to me. "There's rumors Marcie is actually missing."

I stared at Wilma and wondered if the office gossip was finally out of hand.

"What proof?" I asked. I was pretty sure Adrienne was talking to her yesterday and I was dubious that there was anything wrong. I needed proof, though. I knew I'd feel guilty if I was wrong.

Wilma pointed across the wall to Adrienne and Joy's cubicles. "I was in the bathroom just now. Adrienne seemed worried. She was calling Marcie. Leaving a message on her phone. A few, actually. She told dunderhead Joy that she went over to Marcie's house last night and Marcie was gone and the apartment was trashed. You know, like someone was looking for something."

Less dubious.

Adrienne was the great office gossip and I often thought she exaggerated. I heard her and Joy walking to their desks, saw their heads bounce with each step. I thought of Adrienne's phone conversation yesterday. It sounded like she and the unknown caller had made a plan and they was waiting for the fallout. Adrienne laughed at Justin's actions. I was sure she had been talking to Marcie.

I sucked in a breath and let it out as I stood and looked over the wall. "Did Marcie leave or is she really missing?"

Adrienne glanced at me. She wasn't angry for my intrusion and she looked concerned. Wilma watched the exchange with interest. Sheila and Patti Anne had just arrived and glanced over but stayed at their desks.

Adrienne wiped tears from her cheeks. "I went over there. She was expecting me." Her voice was high from stress.

"Did you call the police?" I asked. Adrienne looked at Joy.

"They won't do anything for twenty-four hours. I talked to her yesterday at lunch. She was fine. She was expecting me."

If she disappeared was it related to her affair with Justin? Did Justin know she was missing? Was he involved?

It seemed too coincidental.

Adrienne sat, looking dejected. I could sense her worry for her friend. How was this related to the Cabot file? To the affair? Were they related?

"Was Marcie happy that Justin's suffering the consequences of his mistake?" I was trying to put the pieces together and it slipped out before I had time to shut my mouth. I could feel my cheeks burn when Adrienne looked at me. Not quite a glare, but not friendly either.

"He used her! Yes, she was happy!"

"I'm on Marcie's side. Really, I am. I just… does this have something to do with the affair?"

Adrienne exchanged knowing glances with Joy, her look warning her off. Adrienne turned toward me. "I have no idea. If Justin did this, I could just kill him. For all of this."

I jumped when she smacked her files across her desk. Papers went flying. Adrienne stood, glared at me one last time, and ran off. Joy looked apologetic but followed after.

"Was that just too weird?" Patti Anne asked.

I debated whether to tell them everything about the Cabot account. First Justin gets caught with Marcie and she quits without warning, then I find an account he doesn't know about but has his name all over it, and now Marcie is gone. And all within three days.

Is this all connected or some cosmic coincidence?

The four of us sat back in our chairs and started our work for the day. I, however, was mostly pretending.

****

After five, the office began to clear out. There were always the stragglers, finishing up work before going home, wanting a clean slate when they returned to their families. I was the type to bring work home, at least then I was home I was there if the kids needed me. I'm not sure that actually eased my guilt, but I pretended it did.

I stared at the text Justin had left me this morning, before I came to work. He reminded me that he wanted me to bring the Cabot files to his office after Hector and Jared had left. At 5:15 my aisle was clear; Patti Anne, Shelia and Wilma had left, and Adrienne, Joy, and the rest of their aisle were long gone. It was quiet, eerily quiet as I held the files tight to my chest. I hadn't wanted to give them to him, but he was my boss, and I had no reason to withhold them from him regardless of how weird the situation seemed.

I tried not to worry that I was giving him the files. It was after all; his law firm and he should have had access to all the client files. Even so, I held my breath and walked down the hall, turned left and walked to Justin's office.

He was sitting at his desk, staring at his computer. Just staring, it seemed to me. I knocked on his door jamb.

Justin glanced up and waved me in. "Close the door," he said.

I closed the door and held out the folders. "Here's what's in the system for the Cabots. I included the invoices. And no, they don't match up to the work done and the notes in the system aren't consistent with SOP."

He cautiously took the files as if they might explode on him. He opened the cover and stared at the custody agreement I had written, and scanned the notes that had been given to me. He glanced up. "I didn't give this to you."

I let out stale air. "I thought it was weird I hadn't been part of any meetings with the Cabots. You always have me there at the beginning. So, I thought maybe the Cabot's paralegal was busy and this needed to get done. I didn't think anything of it until I looked at it in the system."

He pushed his chair from his desk and motioned for me to sit. "I'd like to see it for myself."

I logged in, pulled up the client file list and typed "Cabot." There were three entries for Cabots and none were Emma and London.

"Which one?" Justin asked.

"Emma and London. They're not here."

I returned to the search box, typed in London, nothing. Typed in Emma, got forty. There no Emmas in the system with a husband named London. "They're not here."

Justin paced behind me. It was making me anxious and I wanted to tell him to stop. I exited the client lists and pulled up the bank accounts, thinking maybe there was an account open under their names that would hold any money for retainers.

Emma and London Cabot, with a bank account. "I found them."

Justin stopped, and looked over my shoulder. "Who opened the bank account?"

I opened the Cabot file and saw the bank account form that I would normally complete for all new clients who require accounts to hold retainers or settlement funds. I scrolled to the bottom and stared at the signatures. Justin R. Able and Nicole Page. "Umm..." I pointed to the signatures.

"I didn't ask you to open that." He said calmly. Justin moved closer to the screen. Though his voice was steady, I could feel him trembling against my back. "And that's not my signature."

I stared again at our signatures. He was correct; they weren't ours. I clicked the print button and heard his printer spit out pages. I opened up the signature cards, something else I filled out and scanned into the clients' E-files each time I opened an account. Both our signature cards were in the system, but neither signature belonged to us. I printed off the cards.

When I had two copies of each, I handed Justin a set and kept one for me.

"So, what the hell is going on?" I asked him.

He shook his head. "I don't know. Marcie, she..." He leaned against his desk and looked at his hands. "I was wrong for cheating on my wife with Marcie. I never, before Tuesday, had sex with her at work. She ..." He looked up at the ceiling, at the floor, at the door. He couldn't look me in the eyes. "She suggested it. It's not her fault, I blame myself. I made a rash, awful decision, but she came to me and started it."

Finally, he looked at me. His decision and the last three days took a toll on him. He was gaunt, his jaw tight, his eyes red, his suit rumpled.

"Do you think the Cabot file had something to do with you getting caught, or her disappearance?" I asked incredulously. I was beginning to think that I received the Cabot file because I found them together. And that led to everything else since.

Justin shrugged and then his shoulders sagged. "She's missing. At least that's what I heard, though I think she left on her own. I expect the police to come around asking me where she is." He fidgeted with his hands. "I don't know. She quit, effective immediately, and that's my fault too." He sighed.

If I hadn't thought what he did was all that bad, I would have felt sorry for him. But he needed to sleep in the bed he had made. I made eye contact and held my gaze.

"So why and how are these two things related?" I still held my gaze as did he, though I think he would have liked to look away. "Did someone realize I had a file I shouldn't have had?" The thought made my stomach roil.

"But why take Marcie?" Justin rubbed his hands across his chin.

"She knew something," I suggested.

He leaned against his desk and hung his head. "You think she set me up?"

"I don't think that."

"Someone went into the system using my credentials and billed this client. She could have signed in as me. She could get into all of my accounts in the company."

He almost seemed to relax after he told that tale.

"Why take her? If someone wanted to shut her up, I would thing that person would be you?"

"I didn't hurt her. Regardless of my bad behavior, I did care for her?"

I switched tactics to see what Justin knew. Somehow, I got drawn into this. I wanted to know why. "Did she get caught doing something and just left? Or she was pissed she got caught with you. She could have just left and not gone missing," I said.

"I really screwed up."

"Yeah. You kinda did."

The whole thing seemed so far-fetched for this conservative law firm. They always thoroughly vetted employees and expected nothing less than our best work. I watched Justin for a moment. He was tired and worried.

"You go on home," he said. "I'll call you if I hear anything."

I didn't wait to be told again. I said goodbye and headed to my desk for my bag and my coat, bundled up, and headed home.

CHAPTER 6

I walked into a spaghetti fiasco. My kids, bless both of them, decided to make dinner tonight. The water in the pasta pot was boiling over. Jacob rushed to shut it off, burning. He looked at me.

"Sorry, Mom." He grimaced as he stepped away from the stove.

Julia was pouring spaghetti sauce into a bowl. It splashed against the countertop. She smiled at me.

"So, what's all this?" I asked as I used the slotted spoon to test the spaghetti. It was... a little overcooked. I pulled up the in-pot strainer, dumped the spaghetti into the waiting bowl and placed it on the counter.

Still in my suit, I grabbed the towel Jacob handed me and wiped up the spilled sauce and tossed the dirty rag in the sink.

"We wanted to make you dinner," Julia said.

"Well, that's really sweet of both of you."

Jacob pulled out the plates and silverware and helped himself a heaping pile of spaghetti, dousing it in sauce. A burnt smell filled the kitchen. I looked inside the wall oven and microwave; there was nothing inside either. I turned back to the stove, the oven was on; I opened the door. Strong smoke billowed out. I dug into the drawer beside the stove, grabbed an oven mitt and pulled out what I thought was garlic bread. I held it out for Jacob; he shrugged.

"I love you guys. And thanks for dinner." I dropped the baking sheet on the stove, filled my plate and followed my kids to the table.

"So, what's new with school?"

"Nothing," Julia said as she dug into dinner, twirling the spaghetti on her fork and shoving way more than she should in her mouth.

I grimaced and turned to Jacob. "And you?" With a full mouth, he shrugged.

"Hmmm. Eight hours and nothing." I picked at my food as I thought of the Cabot file, the invoicing, the signatures that weren't mine or Justin's.

I didn't think I was supposed to get the Cabot file. So, who gave it to me and why? And what did that have to do with Justin and Marcie and Marcie's disappearance? Was I right that it was all connected?

While I truly believed that Marcie was fine, that she simply left because they got caught. But then, if Justin wasn't lying and she did convince him to have sex in the office, did she set him up?

Why?

What she that mad at Justin for their affair. Not leaving his wife? I sighed. I was that mad at my ex.

I twirled my spaghetti and glanced up at my kids. Jacob was done with his mountain of food. He got up from the table, laid his plate in the sink and took off for his bedroom. I looked at Julia.

"Need anything else, sweetie?"

"Nope I'm good." She got up too, placed her plate in the sink, grabbed her backpack, and went to her room.

I stared at the table. It was covered in spilled sauce and parmesan cheese, the stove had boiled water and sauce hardening on it, the counter needed a good scrub, and there were dishes piled high in the sink. No longer hungry, I saved my dinner in a container, put the rest of the food away and began to scrub my kitchen.

****

I checked in on Jacob and he was reclining on his bed, reading a book, something I didn't see much of during basketball season. "Book for class?" I asked.

He glanced up and shook his head and held it out for me. *Carrie.*

"Stephen King. Very nice. Didn't know you liked horror," I said. I was pretty proud my son was taking after my reading habits.

He shrugged. "My teacher thought I'd like it." He put the book down. "Sorry about the mess. Probably should have cleaned it up."

My turn to shrug. "Probably." I sat on his bed. "I do appreciate it though. It's been a rough week."

He chuckled. "It's only Wednesday."

"Yeah. Well, some weird things are happening at work. It's a little stressful." I patted his leg. "I'll let you get back to it."

I turned to enter Julia's room when my phone rang. It was Justin—I walked to my room and closed the door before I answered.

"What's up?" I asked.

"The notes."

I sat on the bed and kicked my legs up. "Have you figured out what they meant?"

"No. There's nothing that corresponds to the work that was done. None of it makes sense."

I closed my eyes and listened to his breathing. It was shallow; he was agitated. "What might that tell you?" I asked him.

"It's a fake account."

I had the same thought. "It looks like you did this."

"It looks like you opened the account too," he said.

My stomach churned. I thought of the dinner I hadn't eaten. Glad now I hadn't. I felt anxiety grip me, my hands shook as I held the phone. I took a deep breath which didn't help to calm me. "Yeah, it does, doesn't it?"

"Listen Nikki. I'm not sure why, but I feel like I'm being set up along with you. Be careful and keep your ears and eyes open." My heart pounded. I was good at what I did. I took initiative. But when it came to dealing with people as a whole, I was the type who shied away from confrontation, always tried to be a good girl. It didn't work where my marriage was concerned and now, I felt as though I was being pushed, or used in someone else's scheme. When he said being set up and included me in that scenario, I felt as though I had had enough or at the very least needed to protect myself and my children.

I needed to be proactive, make a little noise.

"Do you think there might be other accounts out there? Similar to this?" I asked cautiously.

"I can't get into the Cabot files, but I do have access to what I assume is the rest of the client files. Though, after seeing this, there might be some I don't have access to. I don't know."

I resigned to the fact that we seemed to be in this together. I asked, "What would you like me to do?"

"Pull all of our accounts. I'd like to do an audit." Justin blew out a deep breath.

"Okay. I'll pull that tomorrow. Anything else?"

There was silence on the other end of the phone. He hung up without saying goodbye.

I beat back the urge to log in right then and readied for bed instead. I checked on the kids one last time, climbed into bed, and quickly fell asleep.

CHAPTER 7

I left for work long before the kids would wake, and tried to temper my guilt on the drive in. I pulled into the parking lot long before the rest of the staff, giving me enough time to pull the data Justin had requested, enough time to hide what I was doing. Which as I thought about it, pulling files for my boss was part of my job description. I shouldn't have felt guilt or disloyalty to the firm I had worked at for the last three years.

But here I was at my computer, long before the normal start of business hours, pulling a list of clients from the entire Able, Able and Munch client database for Justin R. Able.

While the database churned, I thought I should have pulled this list last night, but then, I was worried all those hits in the software system might attract unwanted attention.

Since last night I had pondered my role in this. Getting mixed up in whatever this was. After Hector warned me to be cautious and keep my eyes open. And yet here I was. Worried and anxious, that I might lose my job or maybe worse.

When the first list appeared my jaw dropped: there were close to a thousand clients. Many had used his services once, others in an ongoing capacity. It varied by needs. This list wouldn't tell me what he and I both wanted to know.

I added filters to the search including the invoice amount, the type of work completed, and the note fields for January through today.

While the list was considerably shorter, the report created a thick file. I sat back at my desk and began to peruse the entries. I crossed off clients' entries that were noted correctly, where the work and the invoicing matched, and the notes were accurate. Most of the accounts looked good. I circled the Cabot account and continued on.

When I finished the client entries for this year, I discovered twelve accounts that had discrepancies like the Cabot file. I glanced at the time and continued with the clients, pulling each one of the irregular entries.

I refilled the printer and let the rest of the pages spit out. I grabbed my very large stack of paper just as Adrienne and Joy walked in. They shot me a glance as they noticed all of the paper spitting from the printer. I offered a smile and returned to my desk.

Today, the voices from across the wall were barely above a whisper. I sat on Wilma's desk and put my ear to the wall. Childish yes; informative, quite possibly.

Adrienne sighed heavily. "She's gone."

"Did the police take a missing person's report?"

"Yeah. They walked the house. It was like I told them. It was a mess, like someone was looking for something. They're finally going to do something." There was genuine concern in Adrienne's voice. It had me worried.

I looked at Wilma when she got to her desk, held my finger across my lips and pointed to the wall. Wilma joined me.

"That's good. They'll find her," Joy said cheerfully.

"Shhh. Just don't tell anyone. The police were at my house last night until eleven." Her desk chair squeaked when she sat. "It wasn't supposed to happen like this," Adrienne said.

"You know, Marcie wasn't forced to sleep with Justin. She did it because she wanted to be a part of this. I would have gone to the police if it were me," Joy said.

"Well, it wasn't you!" Adrienne shouted.

Wilma and I exchanged worried glances and separated as Patti Anne and Sheila filed in. I glanced at the wall separating me from Adrienne and Joy and reluctantly sat at my desk. I stared at the huge file I pulled and tossed it in my desk drawer for later.

I didn't wait long. A few minutes later when my phone rang, it was Jared's administrative assistant, Cary Wright.

"This is Nikki."

"Hi Nikki, can you come to Justin's office?"

"On my way." I locked my computer, shared a confused glance with Patti Anne, Shelia, and Wilma and walked to Justin's office. When I turned the corner, police were entering his office. I thought about Marcie and wondered what Justin got himself into.

"What the hell's going on?" I asked.

Cary's jaw tightened; her eyes glistened with tears. She tucked her hair behind her ear in a nervous sweep.

"Don't know. But they want to talk to you."

"Me? Why?"

Cary shook her head.

A plain-clothes officer walked to us and looked at me. "You Nikki Page?"

I nodded quickly.

"I'm Detective Andy Butcher. I'd like to talk to you, if you don't mind." I followed him away from the offices into the small conference room around the corner.

"Can I ask what this is about?" My voice showed my true emotions; it was shaky and high pitched. I was familiar with the police, lawyers, and judges, and yet my heart was pounding in my chest.

He motioned me to take a seat and I did, with my hands in my lap, better to hide them when I started twisting them.

"You work for Justin Able?" he began. He looked at me with hazel eyes and his look was friendly and concerned. It sent a shiver through my belly.

"Yes." I bit my tongue and reminded myself to answer the question truthfully but only answer what they ask. At least until I knew what this was about.

"What do you do for him?"

I unclenched my hands.

"I'm a paralegal. I work on client cases with him." He wrote something on his small notepad and looked back at me.

"What does that mean?" I explained my job: meetings with clients, drafting documents, opening accounts, invoicing.

"Hmmm. I thought the lawyers did all of that stuff."

I smiled. "We're a large firm with enough paralegals to handle that work. It's cheaper for the clients if we do it." I let my hands go complete limp at my sides and shifted forward in the seat.

"And you're his paralegal only, or do you work with the other lawyers?"

"They try to assign us to certain lawyers so we build rapport, but we work with all of them at one time or another.

I primarily work with Justin and his clients." I offered a smile but Detective Butcher returned to his notebook. Each row of writing was neat and tidy, a block style lettering. I was wondering if his hand was cramping. I tried to read his notes, but he was too far away and the writing upside-down. "So, you gonna tell me what this about?" I asked, though I suspected it was about Marcie's disappearance.

"Did you work much with Marcie Winkler?"

I shook my hands in a so so motion. "I worked with her some. She's… she was Justin's admin until she quit."

He pushed his notebook to the side and crossed his hands on the desk. "I'm working Marcie Winkler's missing person's case."

I nodded in understanding.

"In the course of this investigation, I'm talking to everyone who worked with her, or knew her, trying to establish what might have happened to Marcie and where she could be. And I'm interested in speaking with Justin Able." He glanced at me.

I looked at my watch. "He should be here by now. I'm not sure why he's late."

Detective Butcher touched the table. "And that's my issue. Justin Able's car was found three blocks away from his house. He hasn't been seen since last night."

My breath stopped; my jaw tensed.

"I…"

"When was the last time you saw Justin?"

I took several shallow breaths as I tried to process the fact that Justin was now missing. "I saw him about 5:15 ish, before I left the office. He had a project he wanted me to do for him."

Andy Butcher glanced at me with curiosity on his face. He reached for his notebook again, found an empty sheet and asked, "What was the project?"

I bit my lower lip and quickly maintained a straight face. "He wanted me to pull a list of our clients for the past year. An audit of sorts."

"An audit? Is that common?"

I shrugged. "Not common, but my boss asked me to audit some clients, so I did."

"So, you left when?"

"By 5:30."

"Did he say anything about going someplace, or about Marcie when you spoke with him?"

I shook my head. "No. We established what he wanted from me and I left."

He wrote something and went back through his notes. "I've interviewed most of the administrative assistant pool. They tell me you found Justin and Marcie …" he glanced at his notes. "On Tuesday morning in a compromising position."

"Yes. I did." I sighed loudly and watched him make additional notes in his book. I wondered what the officers did with them when they concluded a case. Write up the notes, put them with evidence?

Detective Butcher looked at me and smiled. "As you can tell, our primary suspect in Marcie's disappearance is missing. That's very disconcerting. So, I'm thinking, he's either in the wind because he killed her because they were discovered at work or they are in love and decided to disappear together. Or..."

"Or?"

"Or, as his paralegal, you might know if they ran into problems with a client. Something you were all working on that might have put them and possibly you, in danger."

That thought made my stomach churn.

"That doesn't make me feel so good." I held my hand across my mouth. I didn't think I'd throw up, but I wasn't sure.

"Are you okay? Would you like a garbage can?" He turned in his seat, searching for one.

"No. No. I'm fine. The thought that I could be... no. It's fine." I placed my hands in my lap again.

"So do you know if there was a particular client problem that could have led to this?"

I glanced out the vertical window beside the door. My co-workers walked past and looked inside. I knew each and every one of them was dying to know what was going on.

"It doesn't do you any good to not answer," Detective Butcher reminded me. I knew that, and I had no reason to be dishonest, but I wasn't sure how much to share with him about the Cabot file. I had no idea if it had anything to do with this or not.

I bit my lower lip in apprehension.

"What, Mrs. Page? If you know something, now's the time to tell me." Adrienne looked inside the conference room. I met her gaze. There was something in her eyes. Worry, maybe, anxiety. Something was off. I glanced at Andy, who was looking at me expectantly.

I sat forward in my chair, the Cabot file first and foremost in my mind. Second in my mind was client attorney privilege. I glanced at him; he was looking at me still waiting.

"Is there something you want to tell me?" Andy asked.

His eyes were all cop. He saw all, recognized witness tells. I've been around police and lawyers my whole career. I know not to give more than asked. I know to answer with the truth. All I have is supposition and thoughts, and a sweaty back and underarms.

"It's client related. I'm not sure how much I'm legally able to say."

"Just tell me what you can. If it's nothing, it's nothing." He held his hands wide to encourage me to speak up. His eyes softened as he offered me a warm smile.

I felt my shoulders slump. "After I caught Justin and Marcie in his office, I received a client file." I looked at my hands. "It's probably nothing, but it had both Justin and I concerned." I looked at Detective Butcher. He remained silent and eager to hear what I said.

"I hadn't worked for the client previously, so I pulled up their account in the system, to find any notes and to see what had already been done. I discovered..." I stopped and took a breath, slipped my shaking hands under my lap. "I discovered that my initials were attached to the client entries. I thought it was a mistake so I dug around the invoicing system and found some oddities. For instance, the invoicing didn't match up to the work done."

Rather than taking notes, he looked at me with concern. I continued. "It's probably nothing."

"It had you both worried. Did you talk to Justin about the oddities?"

I shook my head. "I finished the work requested, put the file in his box. I happened to see Jared take it out of Justin's box and take it with him, after he read it."

Andy reached for his notebook and began taking notes.

"Anyway," I wrung my hands. "When I told Justin about the file, he was distracted by Marcie and called me later that day to tell me he never worked for the Cabots and couldn't get into their online files to see what it even was."

"When did he call you?"

"That night, on my cell. He asked me to pull the files and bring them to him the next day after work. That's why I stayed last night. So, we could go over the client files."

"And you think this file has something to do with Marcie's and Justin's disappearances?"

I shook my head. "I have no proof of that. You asked for something odd. That was odd."

"Okay. Tell me about this file. Who was the client and what was the issue?"

I shook my head. "You know I can't tell you that. Not without a warrant."

He sighed. "Okay. What can you tell me?"

What could I tell him? Just what the oddities were. Why they were strange.

I almost felt relieved talking to the police about what I had found. Even if it wasn't anything, I had to tell them what I might know. Hiding what I was doing from the bosses was making me anxious.

"All I can tell you was that the file was weird. The work completed didn't correspond with the amount billed and the notes were incorrectly entered. And neither Justin nor I had worked with this client before, even though our initials were all over the invoice system."

Andy Butcher wrote for a while. When he finished, he looked back at me. "And was there anything in the client files to make you think it's related to Marcie's and Justin's disappearances?"

"Nothing. You asked for weird. That was it. I have no reason to think it's related, but it's out there in case you come up with evidence for a warrant." I offered a wan smile.

"Do you believe in coincidence, Mrs. Page?"

That made me chuckle. "If I found the file at any other time, I might chalk it up to a clerical error. With Marcie and Justin… it's hard to think it's all coincidence. But then, I have no proof either way and would hate to lead you down a dead end."

He stared intently at me. "I appreciate your concern, but for now, I'm just trying to figure out where they are and if they're alive. So, Mrs. Page, as his primary paralegal, is there anything else I should know? Anything about your relationship? Would he talk to you about his personal life?"

"Justin's my boss. I saw him outside of work at company functions. I didn't see him outside of work for anything else. I wasn't sleeping with him. The only reason he came to me for help on this client file is because I received it. I don't know where he is, or where Marcie is. I know her friend Adrienne Mox is worried, and if she's worried, there's something to her disappearance."

I was hot and tired, and it was only nine in the morning. My head was pounding and making me dizzy. I wanted to leave. I crossed my legs and closed my eyes. "What?" I asked Andy Butcher, irritated. He was observing me carefully.

"What did he think of this client file?"

"Like I said earlier, he was concerned. He told me to be careful and keep my eyes and ears open."

Andy knew I was done and pulled a card out of his pocket, handed it to me, and stood. I followed suit.

"If you think of anything else that might explain where he went and why, call me. I appreciate your honesty." He held out his hand. I shook it firmly and left the room. When I stopped shaking, I grabbed my purse, ignored the inquiring glances, and took a much-needed time out.

CHAPTER 8

The police combed through Justin's office and what was left in Marcie's former desk, for any non-client information that could lead to why they were both missing. Jared oversaw the search, reviewing client files to ensure no client files were reviewed and taken.

As the police pulled files and appointments books, Andy Butcher worked his way through the paralegal staff of fifteen.

When I got back from my hasty break, Wilma, Patti Anne, and Shelia were waiting for me. They were chomping at the bit to find out what happened.

"Why didn't you wait for us, honey? We've been dying to hear. What the hell happened?" Pattie Anne asked as she scooted to the edge of her chair.

I shrugged as I put my bag in my lower drawer and sighed. "It was probably like your interviews." I glanced at all of them. They watched me intently.

"But you found Justin and Marcie," Pattie Anne reminded me.

"I told the police I don't know anything about Marcie or where Justin is." I plopped in my chair.

"So, what do you think happened?" Wilma asked. "Did Justin, do it?"

I have no idea what happened. I looked at each of them. I said nothing.

Sheila looked from Pattie Anne to Wilma, to me. She wrung her hands. "That Andy Butcher. Handsome as hell." Shelia chuckled nervously.

I met her gaze; I didn't know how to respond to that.

"I mean, we all assumed Justin killed Marcie and now he's disappeared." She continued to rub her hands together. "What's that about weird client accounts? What did you tell him 'cuz I've never seen a 'weird' account? Have you guys?" She looked from Wilma to Pattie Anne, either embarrassed by the Andy Butcher comment or just anxious about what was going on at the firm.

"It's …" I wasn't sure how much to tell them about the Cabot file. I stopped as Jared walked down the hallway past our aisle toward the other end of the office where the law library was.

I didn't want to reveal my worry. I sat back in my chair, crossed my legs. "I'm sure the police simply want to verify that it wasn't an angry client that kidnapped them. All anyone knows is, Justin and Marcie aren't where they're supposed to be." But if they had been kidnapped, any one of us could be next. The thought made me shudder.

"Don't play it down, honey. You're acting weird." Pattie Anne said.

"It's been a long week. And with all this going on, it makes me wonder, just in general. I really don't know anything. But you're probably right. It all comes down to the two of them getting caught."

"So, I asked before. Do you think he killed her and ran away or do you think they're together and all of this was a ploy for them to be together?" Wilma asked.

The odd client file made me think they weren't together and something bad happened, like one or both of them were dead. "Maybe. Maybe they're in love and wanted to run away. I don't think so, though. He called me to apologize for his bad behavior. I don't think he was planning on leaving with her. I think something else was going on."

"You know something," Sheila said excitedly as she pointed at me with a wide smile on her face.

I shook my head. "I don't. I really don't." I didn't like lying, pretending that I didn't know anything and that made me feel guilty. But all I had were guesses and suppositions. Nothing concrete and I didn't want what I knew to get all over the office. The minute I said anything, I knew everyone would know.

I glanced up. Jared was walking from the library, presumably to his office. He glanced down our aisle and looked away quickly as he continued on. Wilma, Pattie Anne, and Sheila followed my gaze and watched Jared as he turned toward his office.

"If you do know something, sweetie, you need to be careful," Pattie Anne said. They returned to their desks and their day's work, but all I could do was stare at my computer screen and think about how many people have told me to be careful in the last three days.

****

It had been a long day. Justin had texted me at 4:30 capping off the day and it led to a very strong headache. I needed to finish an adoption document before I left, but wasn't going to make it without a jolt of caffeine. I trudged my way inside the lunch room, poured a cup from the coffee machine even though it looked like it had been there all day. I added an extra teaspoon of sugar and stirred.

I glanced up, Adrienne and Joy were on the far side of the lunch room, speaking in hushed tones and looking at me. I walked over.

"How was your interview with Andy Butcher?" I blew on the coffee and took a sip. asked.

Adrienne sat straighter, narrowed her eyes. "He asked about client cases that might have caused this. What client did you tell him about?" she demanded.

"I didn't give him names. Besides, it's a reasonable question to ask," I said.

Adrienne glared. "Justin killed her. I know it! You need to stop spreading lies." It was my turn to stare at her.

"Listen, Adrienne. I know Marcie is your friend and you're worried about her. But the police can't find her until you tell them what you know."

"I… I… Bitch," Adrienne murmured. When she stood, she slammed her chair against the table and stomped out.

Joy ran after her. My hand shook as I held my coffee. Adrienne's reaction to my opinion felt so angry. Had I touched a nerve? What did Adrienne really know?

I no longer wanted my coffee and dumped the rest in the garbage can. As I walked to my desk, all I could think of was finishing the adoption agreement, so I could put this crappy day behind me.

Wilma was at the printer picking up a document. She pointed her chin in the direction of my desk where Andy Butcher was sitting. He was writing in his small notebook. After today, I thought it might be filled up.

"Hey. Find Justin yet?" I asked. He stood and let me have my desk back.

He handed me a letter, signed by Jared Able, giving me permission to speak to Andy about the client file in question. It wasn't a warrant, just a letter, and based on Jared taking the file from Justin's bin, I was surprised he agreed to it without a warrant.

"I need to print it." I opened the client file and printed the draft of the custody agreement I had prepared. Then I opened the client invoicing program, printed the invoices for Andy and motioned for him to join me. I grabbed the documents off of the printer and walked to the open conference room. I closed both doors and sat.

I slid the documents to him.

"What am I looking at?"

"I did a custody agreement for Emma and London Cabot. Apparently, the divorce had been going on for three years. I had never met the clients nor have I ever worked on any of the divorce documents for the couple. When I entered my time into the invoice system, I noticed that Justin had entered the other invoices and the notes were not SOP. I couldn't ascertain what had been done for the client and why. The work that had been done didn't correspond to the amount of the invoices. I looked in the system to find out who the paralegal was, to find out why

I got the file, and my initials are in the system for the Cabot account."

Andy cocked an eyebrow, and didn't take out his notebook to write this down. Adrienne and Joy returned to their aisle and watched me intently through the glass walls.

Andy perused the files. "This is the only work that's been done?"

"That's all that's in the system. But if you look at what's been billed, there's too much for the work completed. It shouldn't be that much." I pulled out the invoice list and showed him.

Andy took out a pen and made notes on the copies. "And Jared took the Cabot custody agreement?"

"Yes."

"But these are Justin's initials?"

"Yes."

"And Jared gave you permission to give me the file, after taking the file from Justin's inbox. Are you absolutely sure it was the Cabot file Jared took from Justin's inbox?"

"I take notes on the front cover when I need to. That's the folder he opened. Not to mention, it was the only folder in Justin's inbox that morning."

He perused the rest of the client documents. "It's rather thin for a three-year divorce dispute, wouldn't you say?"

"There's not enough work in there to justify thirty grand in billing."

Andy pulled out his notebook and started with the first page of a fresh book. There was a knock on the door. Jared Able entered and closed the door behind him. He pouted when he saw the papers on the table.

"So, you gave him the files?" Jared asked.

"Your letter gave me permission to bypass a warrant," I said rather flippantly. Jared looked shocked. He knew he should have required a warrant and began pacing along the back wall, his hand pulling his hair ZA up and out. I understood why he was stressed. I mean his brother/business partner had sex in his office and was now missing. Andy observed Jared for a moment and looked back to me.

"So, you never saw this file before you got the assignment?" he clarified.

"I've never seen this client account before. I hadn't set them up in the system, I didn't set up a bank account. I've never written anything for the client prior to this." I pulled the file closer to me and pulled out the signature cards. "I've opened hundreds of bank accounts for clients. This isn't my signature and I know Justin's. This isn't his either."

"Did Justin ever open accounts?"

"No. It's cheaper for the client if I do it." Out of the corner of my eye, I saw Jared stop and stare at us. His jaw tensed as I showed Andy the signature card.

"Is there money in that bank account?" Andy asked.

I shrugged. "I actually hadn't checked." I moved to the keyboard on the conference room table, and switched it—and the television that hung in the corner of the room—on. I pulled up the invoice system.

"You can't do that. That's confidential client information!" Jared pointed to the screen.

Andy held up the Jared's letter. "She can give me what pertains to the Cabot files. I would think you'd want to find your brother and former administrative assistant."

Jared's jaw tensed. He continued to pace along the back wall.

I pulled up the Cabot account and clicked on the bank account information. "There's nothing in the bank account right now. But that doesn't mean anything. It could have been transferred to the general law firm account as a retainer paid."

"Did Justin ever ask you to open an account and move the money to another, not the general fund?" Andy asked.

What the hell? Am I going to be investigated?

"Just from the retainer account to the general fund or the final settlement to the client's personal account."

"Through a wire?"

I nodded as Jared picked up his pace.

Andy Butcher seemed to be doing a great job of ignoring Jared's anxiety and offered me a wide smile. "Can you think of any other case where he billed the client and the money went out to other accounts not involved with the retainers or the settlements?"

I knew where Detective Andy was heading with the questioning and I didn't like it. But then, I had no proof that Justin didn't launder money into the client account and then back out. If Jared hadn't known about any suspected money laundering, he did know now. And so did the police. Jared began to sweat as he walked from one end of the room to the other.

"I don't know of any other account that had money moved in and out in this manner." I thought of the list of client accounts that had I had printed for Justin. Accounts that had odd billing that didn't match the work completed. It was still hiding in my lower desk drawer.

Jared stopped like a deer in headlights. I heard his breathing change as if he was having an asthma attack or a...

He clutched at his heart, and fell to his knees. Andy pushed away from the table and went to Jared. I ran for the phone and dialed Jared's assistant, Cary. "Something's wrong with Jared."

"I'm fine. Fine," Jared waved it away. "I'm okay. Just the shock of it."

"What's happening?" Cary shouted on the phone.

"He's okay. He's in shock maybe. Sorry to get you worked up." There was a loud click as Cary hung up, fast.

"We should call the ambulance," Andy suggested.

"No." Jared's breathing was heavy, he was red, and sweating more than normal.

Cary rushed in with a bottle of water and handed it to Jared. She looked at him, concern deep on her face. She loosened his tied, wiped sweat from his forehead with a tissue. He nodded. "Really. I'm fine." He waved her away.

Cary turned and looked at us. "It's okay. I'll call his wife. We'll get him to the hospital and home," she said as she helped him take a drink from the bottle.

Andy pulled me to the other side of the room. He glanced at Jared, sitting in a chair, speaking with Cary in low, slow tones; I assumed still convincing her, he was fine.

"Thank you for your assistance. If you think of anything else, please call me." He handed me another card. I tucked it in my pocket and nodded as I left the conference room.

Before entering my aisle, I turned and looked at the conference room wall of windows. Andy Butcher was still watching me as I walked away. I smiled weakly and returned to my desk where I closed all my programs, shut down my computer, grabbed my half-finished document and finally left for home.

CHAPTER 9

Rain poured as I pulled my car into the driveway. It was heavy yet steady and I could feel the humidity curl up my hair. I still felt shaky from my police interview, still unsettled about the Cabot client and my encounter with Adrienne. But mostly, I felt as though I shouldn't have said anything at all.

I tried to put it all away as I pulled off my jacket and slipped off my shoes. I dropped my bag on the floor. Julia was sitting on the sofa, sipping pop from a can, watching some kid's show I've never seen before.

"Whatcha doing?" I ask in my best sing-song mom voice.

Julia shrugged. "Just tv."

I joined her on the sofa and grabbed a handful of popcorn from the bowl on her lap. She gave me a look like a dog whose bone was taken away. I raised my eyebrows. "Yeah?"

"My popcorn." She crinkled her eyes and pouted. I mimicked her expression.

"I paid for it." And I stuck my tongue out and grabbed another handful. "Have a good day at school?"

Julia shrugged her usual answer.

"You don't know if you had a good day?"

She shrugged again. The door from the garage to the house opened and Jacob stepped inside, dropped his bag in the middle of the kitchen, and ran off to his room. Minutes later, the shower turned on and I glanced at the ceiling.

"Watcha want for dinner?"

Julia shrugged.

"Nice talking to you." I patted her knee and rolled my eyes at her, much like she would to me. Julia raised an eyebrow, grabbed the popcorn and returned to her television show.

The pizza place was on speed dial and I ordered a pepperoni and green pepper pizza for Jacob and myself and an Italian beef for Julia. Only my kid would hate pizza. When I finished, she offered me the bowl of popcorn, a wide smile on her face.

"You're such a dork." Still my baby, she cuddled up to me as we finished the tv show and waited for dinner to be served.

The doorbell rang immediately after my call and I jumped. I was even more shocked when I saw Andy Butcher at my front door.

"Andy." I offered my best smile that felt stilted and fake and held the door slightly closed, not inviting him in. "I have a pizza coming soon, is this going to take long?" I asked.

"I'm sorry Ms. Page, but something came up that I need to discuss with you." He glanced over my shoulder; I turned. Julia stood in the archway between the hall and the kitchen.

"Go back and watch tv, sweetie. I'll be there in a minute." She frowned and crossed her arms against her chest, watching me as I led Andy into the dining room. He sat at the end of the table and slid a legal-sized notepad over to me.

"I know you told me you never saw that Cabot file. I also know you were honest and told me about the signature card. I'd like you to write out your signature several times." He pointed to the note pad and took out a pen for me to use.

As I signed, he watched me and when I finished, he slid another sheet of paper to me. I looked at it. It was a copy of my driver's license.

My heart raced. Even though I dealt with the same banker for each client account I opened, I sent the same package to the him; the account application, a copy of my driver's license.

I sucked in the air and let it burn in my lungs as the doorbell rang. "Can I get that?"

He tilted his chin toward the door. "Sure. No problem."

I couldn't hide my fear or my anxiety. The thought of having to prove my innocence, prove that I hadn't opened that account, or wasn't responsible for this mess, weighed heavy on me. I ran for the kitchen, grabbed my money, and answered the door.

I handed a very lucky pizza delivery man way more money than dinner cost and slammed the door. "Jacob! Dinner!"

I placed the food on the kitchen island and took another breath. My hands trembled and I felt nauseated.

"Julia. Come get your dinner." She looked at me, worried, then glanced in the dining room before grabbing her sandwich and heading for the family room. Jacob walked in and looked inside the dining room. His eyebrows shot up.

"You okay, Mom?"

"Yeah. Something for work. Grab dinner and finish your homework."

He filled his plate, glared toward Andy, and stomped his way upstairs.

"Your kids are angry with me." Andy tried to smile. I sat back down.

"They see I'm stressed. I guess they blame you." I blinked away tears and stared at the copy of my identification. I thought back to the procedure I have for opening a client account: I called the banker, filled out the paperwork, and got a copy of my driver's license from my desk drawer, where I kept extras because I needed them so often. And I always kept that drawer locked. I always scanned the documents into the client computer file.

"Is that a copy of the ID or is it the actual ID that was used to open the account?"

He raised an eyebrow. "Meaning?"

"I have copies of my license in a locked drawer because I need them so often. Anyone in management could open the drawer."

"You're still telling me you didn't open this bank account?"

"Yes."

"This was what the bank had on file for the Cabot account. What do you normally do when you open the account?" he asked. I placed my shaky hands in my lap. Andy looked at me expectantly.

"I call the bank. Stuart Haines, he's the banker I always call. I tell them I'm opening the account with the name of the client. I complete the paperwork, along with my ID. That's how I was trained to do it for consistency, back when I first started at the firm."

He hunched over his little notebook and scribbled notes. When he finished, he stared at me, his gaze was warm, concerned. "Who else can open accounts like this?"

That was an easy question. "All fifteen paralegals and all the lawyers. There's three partners and five junior partners. They all have access."

I wrung my hands under the table as my chest constricted. "So, Justin could have opened the account using your ID and you wouldn't have known?"

I bit my lower lip. "I suppose it could happen. The bank knows my name. They know him. I guess he could have done it, if he didn't want anyone to know there was an account for the Cabots. But I know his signature is different on that card." I pointed to the signature card that came with the Cabot file. While it was familiar, it wasn't his.

This time, he wrote feverishly in his notebook, as if the words were pouring out of him and if he didn't catch them, they'd be lost forever. When he finished, he shook out his cramped hand.

"I'm sorry I had to disturb your evening. I just wanted to clarify the signature issue." He took a look at the signatures I scrawled across the paper and compared them to the signature card. He labeled the paper with the date and his signature, ripped it from the pad and stuck it in an evidence bag. "I'm not a handwriting expert, but even I know it's not the same signature." He stood and smiled.

"So, what's next?" I knew he couldn't tell me but I thought it wouldn't hurt to ask. He put all of the evidence in his messenger bag. About to touch my shoulders, he thought better of it and his hands fell to his side.

"I promise; I will keep you apprised. We still don't know where Justin is, so please contact me if he contacts you."

I nodded and watched as he let himself out. I locked the door behind him, grabbed slices of pizza, and ate at the counter, alone.

Nighttime noises wafted down to me; the kids were getting ready for bed.

I felt the prickling in my eyes as if I might start crying from the stress. Holding my palms to my eyes, I took several breaths. When I felt steadier, I cleaned up dinner, and headed for bed.

****

I held my driver's license and took a long, close look. I had always kept copies in my desk drawer because I sent them every time I opened or closed a client account; it was just convenient that way. My picture made me chuckle ruefully—it was neither a good hair day nor a good smile. I looked a little harried. It struck me that I had renewed my license just after I found out my husband was cheating on me. That explained the picture.

But this wasn't about that moment in time. It wasn't the smile or the eyes or the hair. Someone had gone through my locked drawer and pulled out my ID, using it for their own purposes. That scared me. Not just the invasion of privacy, which really wasn't a right I had at work, but because I was possibly being implicated in embezzlement, money laundering, fraud, or all three.

I paced back and forth past the windows in bedroom. The door squeaked open and Julia walked in, still looking worried.

"Who was that man, Mom?" I stopped my frantic pacing and sat on my bed, patting the space beside me. I took a deep breath.

"There's been some issues at work. My boss had an … improper relationship with someone who worked for him. And it seems like he might have done something illegal as well. That man was a police officer. He was asking me questions about all of it."

I glanced up; Jacob was standing at the door.

"Are you in trouble, mom?"

I wished I could tell them I wasn't in trouble, but the evidence, at least part of it, showed I had knowledge of the account and the client, and possibly knowledge of something else. I shook my head. "I think my boss did something illegal and I had access to all of his client files. And now he's missing and they're just trying to sort through the evidence."

"But you're okay, right?" Julia, usually a smart mouth, looked small and so young.

"I'm fine, love. I just want to find my boss and figure out what happened." I glanced at the clock. It was well past her bedtime. "Go on, get to bed." I smiled and touched her hair, feeling its softness. I kissed her forehead and watched as she left my room.

Jacob hardly ever came in here, but tonight he sat on my bed. "Really? What's going on?"

Across from me sat my little boy, now at sixteen, almost a man. I smiled but it didn't match my mood and I let out a sigh. "My boss slept with his secretary and the police think he might have been embezzling or laundering money. It's just a lot of seemingly separate things all at once."

"Do they suspect you?" He took my hand, something he hadn't done since he was four. I patted the back of his.

"I think they haven't figured out if I'm believable yet. It'll be fine. I promise."

Jacob looked dubious, when he raised an eyebrow. "You should get a lawyer, just in case."

For some reason, that made me laugh. "Maybe not such a bad idea. You done with homework?"

He nodded quickly.

"Try and get some sleep."

My phone buzzed. I could feel it vibrate across the bedspread. When I saw who it was, I frowned. Jacob stopped at my door, but I waved him away and he closed the door behind him.

"What do you want?"

"What the hell is going on at the office?" Justin asked. He sounded agitated, upset.

"What are you talking about?"

I wondered where or who he was getting information from. Jared, Mrs. Munch, Cary? Maybe Adrienne Mox.

"The police were there today. What were they looking for?" His voice was tired and gravely, as if he were getting a cold, or was severely stressed. I guessed the second.

"They're looking for you. Your car was found a mile from home. Where the hell are you?"

Justin was so quiet I thought he had hung up and I nearly did too. He finally said, "I can't tell you that."

"Who told you the police were there?" Again, silence. "Justin, who's telling you?"

"Adrienne Mox." I never knew Justin had any relationship with Adrienne, she never worked as a paralegal for him. Maybe it was through Marcie, which meant Adrienne really knew something.

I bit the side of my mouth, reminding me to think before I spoke. "Does that mean you're with Marcie?"

"No. I'm not. I... don't know where she is. I just know she's gone. Adrienne sent the email to Marcie and I. I don't think Marcie's in a place to pick it up."

He paced. His footsteps were heavy, angry, frantic as he moved around wherever he was.

"The police think you killed Marcie and took off. They also think you might have committed embezzlement or laundered money." I cringed when I thought of the mess, I found myself in. It was only going to get worse.

The pacing stopped for a moment and picked up again. He yelled, "What did you tell the police?"

I stared outside my bedroom window. There were no streetlights in my neighborhood and with the new moon, and clouds from the rain, I could barely see the end of my driveway.

"Nikki! What did you tell them?" Justin demanded.

"That I don't know where you are or why you left. I told them you were concerned about an account we found." My voice rose. I pursed my lips as I stared into the nothingness outside my window.

He started to pace again. "Why? Why?"

"Justin! Shut up! Just shut up! I'm not lying to the police; I'm not hiding what I may or may not know. You…" I leaned against the cool class and listened as the rain popped against it. It did little to ease the headache that was taking control.

"I'm sorry. Nikki, I'm sorry. You did what you had to do. I know they'd find out. The files would've been found." Justin was breathing hard and frantic. It sounded like he had run a long race.

"Stop. Just stop. Turn yourself in. Make this right."

He must have been thinking. Coming up with his next steps. I could almost hear the gears in his head turn.

"No. No. I can't come back, not yet. I think they're after me too. I… I need to know what other files there are. Did you find others, Nikki?"

"Where's Marcie?"

"I don't know where she is. I just know you're the only one I can trust. They have you on those accounts too. You could be next. I need your help."

If I hadn't been on the accounts with him, I would have hung up. I wasn't so much thinking about helping him as I was making sure I wouldn't get into trouble. I thought of my kids when I made my decision.

"There's fifteen accounts that were set up by you. Same notations, same billing, same lack of work." I stared at my bag, heavy with the report.

Justin stopped pacing. "I received an unmarked package at work, the day… the day after you found Marcie and… It was all the screen shots, the bank deposits, the withdrawals. Our signatures are on it. Someone set me up."

My heart raced; my stomach roiled. "You should take this to the police."

"NO! I can't. Marcie's gone. And Jared…"

"Does this have to do with the argument you had with Jared a few days ago in the parking lot."

"Damn," he murmured.

"Well?"

"Yes. I asked him if he knew the Cabot file. He turned it all around and yelled at me about my affair with Marcie. And yes, I deserved it, but that wasn't the place to do it. He reminded me that my actions affect the firm and I can lose it all."

"Did you embezzle the money or launder it?"

"No."

"So, who's framing you and me?" My voice quivered. The thought of someone framing me was jarring and I felt vulnerable. I stared at my bedroom door and thought of the kids down the hall and Emily away at school. If I was charged and convicted, if the worst happened, what would become of them? I felt nauseated all over again.

"I don't know. I have no access at all. So, I can't find the other client accounts, I can't figure out who's doing this. I need you to help me figure it out."

"Be wary of Adrienne."

"Why?"

I debated if I should tell him about her call. I broke down and did. "I think she knows something."

"She's my contact at the firm. I need you to do it. Keep me posted on the investigation." I heard Justin pound a hard surface and I jumped. "I can't believe this. I'm not perfect. I have my faults. I admit them. This, I didn't deserve!" I could hear his frustration. My own was nearing his. His pacing picked up. "I should have known something was up when Invoicing left me a message two days ago about a problem account."

He started pacing again.

"Which account?" I took out the list I had pulled at work.

"The Pouncey account. I didn't have time to look at it because Marcie went missing and I had to leave."

I found the Pouncey account. "They're on the list. Your initials are on four entries. Two invoices. Twenty grand in billing, two documents, three phone calls."

"Crap. Can you get into the accounts?"

"Give me a sec." I reached for my laptop, logged in, and pulled up the Pouncey file. "Yeah. It's here. Opened about six months ago." I pulled up the bank information. "We're both on the bank account." I zoomed in on my signature. It wasn't mine. "Same situation. We're on the accounts, and the entries in the invoicing system were initialed by you."

I opened the client work files and pulled up the two documents. "The documents are simple. One's a temporary medical permission form. The other is a medical power of attorney for the parents. These are standard forms. Not worth…"

"Not worth twenty grand. No wonder Invoicing called me."

The pounding in my chest left me nauseated and weak. I wasn't sure what to say. The problem was just getting worse. I let the tears roll down my cheeks. I sniffled.

"I'm so sorry Nikki. So, so sorry. I really fucked up. With Marcie, with the firm. This all started when I started seeing her."

"Justin. You need to talk to the police."

"Not yet. I need time to think."

"You better think fast, then."

After he hung up, I curled myself on my bed. When I stopped crying, I just stared at the clock, watching time tick away.

CHAPTER 10

I fell asleep somewhere after 4:30 in the morning. When the alarm jolted me awake, I raced through my morning routine, missed my workout, and didn't wash my hair. I had ten minutes before I was supposed to be at work when I pulled into the parking lot and found a space farther away than I normally parked. At least I'd get some exercise this morning.

I wouldn't get fired for starting after eight, but it caused me a weird anxiety as I slid my keycard into the lock and raced down the aisle to my cubicle. My seat mates were still on their way in and Hector was sitting at my desk, writing on a small note pad and sipping his coffee.

"Hector?"

He startled slightly and dropped his pen. He turned and looked tired and stressed as his jaw clenched. "Nikki. What a week, huh?"

"Yeah. It has been." Missing boss, missing administrative secretary, working while hungover. It's the most exciting week I've had here in three years. I couldn't help but worry about Justin and Marcie.

I dropped my bag beside my desk. Hector stood, grabbed my neighbor's chair and sat beside me.

"The police are asking for warrants to look at all of the accounts that Justin was working on when he disappeared. We're expecting them to be denied because it's nothing more than a fishing expedition." He looked grim and his lips tightened. I wondered if I should tell him about my call from Justin or the meeting with Andy Butcher at home.

"And how can I help you?" I sighed.

"I need you to pull any other accounts from Justin that look like he's embezzled or laundered money through the client account."

I glanced around the office. Employees were quickly arriving and settling in. I pulled the report out of my bag and handed it to Hector. "Before Justin went missing, he asked me for this report," I whispered. Hector raised a questioning eyebrow. "He thinks he's being set up, so he wanted to know the extent. So far, I found about fifteen files that have the same issues as the Cabot file. Lots of billing, little work, all attributed to Justin."

Hector glanced at the list of accounts, and quickly reviewed my notes. "Nikki, did you know about these accounts?"

I shook my head. Patti Anne walked to her desk, glanced at us, but turned away to her morning routine. I moved closer to Hector. "Not until I entered the Cabot file and told Justin about it. I don't know what's going on here, but someone got into my desk and took my copies of my ID to open the accounts. Detective Butcher came to my house last night and questioned me about it," I whispered.

Hector's mouth opened in surprise. "What did you know?" he asked, a little harshly. Pattie Anne glanced up; her expression filled with concern.

"I didn't know anything. This is all new to me and it feels like someone is setting me up as well." Wilma and Sheila arrived, stared at Hector and I and then to Pattie Anne who shook her head. Hector tensed.

He motioned me to join him. I grabbed my bag and glanced at Patti Anne as I followed Hector to his office. He closed the door behind us.

"What do you know?" Hector asked. He was pacing behind his desk. The space was all of six feet across.

"How do I know you didn't do this?" My voice was harsher than expected.

He turned and looked at me. "I have the police and Jared pressuring me. Mrs. Munch is coming here to find out what's going on with her nephews. I need to have something to tell her." He met my gaze. "And I didn't do this."

I reached into my bag and pulled out the rest of my notes. "This is all I know. The Cabot file was in my inbox. Never met the client, and when I worked on the custody agreement—the first thing I did for them—I entered it into the system. The notes were off; the billing amounts didn't match the work. Marcie quit the next day and when I told Justin about the file, he didn't know what I was talking about. Since that day, he's contacted me multiple times. His signature and my signature are on the bank accounts; his initials are all over the Cabot file." I pushed the folder to Hector. He looked at the bank information and then to me.

"They think he embezzled money and then killed Marcie because she knew about it," Hector said.

"Those signatures are fake. I see his all the time. It's not his."

Hector looked back down, held the signature out for a better view. He looked back at me. "Okay. I agree, it doesn't look like his." He shoved it back inside the folder and pushed the folder to me. "Do you know where he is? He needs to get his ass back here and fix this."

I leaned back in the chair and crossed my arms against my chest. "I told him that. He knows we're being set up but he won't come back. He wants me to help him because guess what, he's been kicked out of the system. He can't get in."

Hector tapped his fingers against his desk top as he thought. In an instant, he turned toward his computer and entered the system. He pulled up whatever it was he was looking for and stared at his screen. "He's been locked out. I didn't do it and that's my responsibility. I set up everyone into the system, I remove them when they quit." He chewed on his lip.

"Can you tell who did it?"

He looked at me. "According to this, it was Justin."

Laughter bubbled up and out. I shouldn't be laughing. It was just too much. "Awesome. He's either a really good actor, or he is being set up. If I wasn't involved, I'd think he did it."

"And I think I'd agree with you." Hector got out of the system and turned back to me.

"He needs to come back and sort this out. If not, he will lose his license. If he didn't do this, he needs to come back and help figure it out." He motioned me to take the file I had started and handed me back Justin's client report. He leaned against his chair. "How much more bizarre can this get? Just to let you know, Mrs. Munch wants to speak with you tomorrow."

"How much trouble am I in?"

He looked at me. I wasn't sure if I saw pity or fear in his eyes. "Can you prove the signature isn't yours?"

"Andy Butcher stopped by my house last night. He watched me sign a sheet of paper multiple times and he took it with him as evidence."

"I'm sorry, Nikki. It appears this might have been in the works for a while. I just don't get why it's surfacing now."

"Is this what you couldn't tell me earlier this week?"

He nodded. "I'm sorry. Really. I've gotten a few messages from the billing department about one of the off accounts. I've been doing some research but the account files aren't in my wheelhouse. I just don't know what I'm looking at."

I was an aficionado of mystery novels. I always had a theory. I knew it might be way out there, but this was the best I could offer.

"If I had to make a guess, I think finding Justin with Marcie set the ball rolling. I find them and all of a sudden, a secret client file is left in my inbox, like it was left there on purpose. And now they're both gone. The police need to find Marcie because she either knows something or is being used. And Justin is either another victim or the mastermind. Either way, Justin's in trouble."

Hector nodded. "You're assessing that right, I think. We'll have the computer forensic specialist look for any other client files that have a large amount of billing without the work to show for it."

"That'll take a while." All data files were stored in St. Louis; there were thousands of electronic and paper files stored there.

"Yeah. This was a cluster fuck waiting to happen." Hector stood. "I need you to continue with your regular case load. But I think since you've already started, keep looking for other client files like the Cabots. Not just Justin's clients but all of them."

I nodded, though I wasn't sure how long I could be any help. "I'll get you what you need as soon as I can." I looked at the Cabot file. "Is Jared, okay? He seemed very distressed when the police were here."

"He's been completely caught off guard by all of this." Hector shook his head.

"When I dropped the Cabot file in Justin's inbox, Jared was there. I saw him grab the file and look at it. He left with it."

Hector cocked an eyebrow.

"I saw them fighting in the parking lot after I told Justin I finished the custody agreement for the Cabots. Jared knows something."

Hector rubbed his temple. "I am so sorry, Nikki."

"So am I."

****

Long after my conversation with Hector, long after I forced myself to concentrate on my daily work load, and not long after the longest staff meeting, that warned of possible legal trouble for Justin, I found myself flipping a grilled cheese sandwich on the grill on my stove.

When I have time, I do know how to cook from scratch, but tonight, grilled cheese and tomato soup seemed like the logical option. I stirred the soup to keep it from burning and returned the sandwich. I pulled it up to check its doneness. The cheese was getting stretchy; almost there.

Have I ever told you I'm a multitasker? I was also on the phone with my mother.

"So, what do you think happened to your boss?" my mother asked as I put the first sandwich on the plate and turned off the soup.

"All I can say is that he's gone and the police are looking for him. From what I understand, he claims innocence." I laid another sandwich on the grill.

"Did you help him?"

I rubbed a hand across my chin, glanced up at the ceiling and took a cleansing breath. "I don't know anything about where he is or who's involved with what client files. I just don't know anything." I hoped Justin would turn himself in and this nightmare would end.

"He was such a nice boy," Mom said, which was funny. She really wouldn't know. She never met Justin. "So, are you going to jail?"

"No. I didn't do anything wrong."

"Will he?"

I sucked in air and blew it out slowly. "If he did something illegal, yes."

"Will you lose your job?"

I thought about that for a moment. If it came to it, how much business did Justin bring in? If he goes to jail, would there be enough to sustain the law firm? The thought left me queasy as I checked the sandwich.

Even after all of this, I would probably still lose my job; a good job with good pay and that scared me. Even with my savings, alimony, and child support, losing my salary would be tough. "If the law firm goes under and I lose my job, I'll be fine. I'll get a new one." I shook my head. I couldn't tell her now, not how worried I was becoming over this situation. Losing my job was only part of the problem. What if the police believed I was involved?

"But you worked for a crook. Who'll hire you?"

Oh God.

"I'll be fine." My mom finally changed the subject and told me all about Aunt Linnie's knee replacement. I looked around my kitchen. Warm grilled cheese and tomato soup were ready. "Okay. As interesting as Aunt Linnie is, I need to go."

"Okay, Nics. Call me as you as you know something."

My computer sat on the island and I signed into the firm's site. I pulled up the client files and did a preliminary search on all accounts with over $20,000 in invoices for a five-year period with under ten documents in the client file, removing Justin as a filter. I had a sinking feeling that I'd find more than I could imagine—and I could imagine a lot.

As the computer ran, I pulled out bowls, plates and spoons. My phone rang. I flinched and answered.

"Hey Susie," I said as enthusiastically as I could. Susie and I have been friends since fourth grade, when we lived four houses apart. We did everything together growing up, remained friends after attending and graduating from different colleges, stood up in each other's weddings, and generally stayed in touch our entire adult lives. But that was where the similarities ended. I was divorced with three kids; she was a happily married mother of six.

"Hi sweetie. How's things?"

How are things? I asked myself as I held my hand over the speaker and yelled for the kids to come down. "Well, my boss is missing, I was interviewed by the police twice this week, and there are some questions about my involvement in a shady legal deal."

"No shit! Wow! Justin Able the missing guy that's all over the news is your boss!"

I explained the best I could about the last few days without saying much at all.

"Wow. That's pretty sucky. Especially since I missed your birthday."

I chuckled. Ever since I'd known Susie, she always remembered my birthday several days after. It's like getting a birthday, part two.

"Yeah. You always remember, just not on the day."

Jacob and Julia grabbed sandwiches and poured soup in their bowls. Julia sat in front of the television and Jacob headed back upstairs. I should have checked to make sure it was to do homework, but I didn't follow. While I watched my kids settle in, Susie told me about all six kids; Audrey, Henry, Sandy, Lisa, Jordy, the baby, Bobby, and didn't leave out her husband, Gary. I was exhausted by her life, let alone mine.

"So how are the kids?" she finally asked.

"Emily's learning how to advocate for herself. Jacob's playing basketball and Julia is Julia. They're doing well. Good students and staying out of trouble."

"That's good to hear. There was something else I wanted to tell you but maybe I shouldn't."

I rolled my eyes. Once I knew there was something to know, I wanted to know it. You know?

"Just tell me so I don't lie awake wondering." I took a bite of my sandwich and waited with anticipation.

"Okay. I saw Jack and his bitch last night." Susie referred to my ex and the woman he cheated on me with. I really didn't want to know. I asked anyway.

"And?"

"She's pregnant and wearing a ring the size of a potato. It looked gaudy and so did that belly, that homewrecker, tramp."

I held my breath. I really hadn't wanted to know that. We had only been divorced a year and she was big and pregnant, which meant it hadn't taken much time. I sighed.

"I'm sorry. I shouldn't have said anything."

I knew the fiancé. Her name was Amber Levy and had been his secretary for two years. She had just turned twenty-eight and hated my children. Thankfully for me, I'd only seen her a handful of times, because when my ex had the kids, she'd be conveniently out of town. But lately I soon realized, when she was out of town, so was he.

"Don't worry about it. It's a part of life. She hates my kids and they hate her. I don't have to worry about her or him for that matter."

I should have found it sad that my kids no longer had their dad around, but they're fairly well adjusted and it was one less thing for me to worry about. And yet…

"I'm sorry. I know it sucks. You really need to find a man." So said my friend with six kids.

"Bad timing. My life, as of yesterday, is now one complicated, big, old mess."

"You need to date. Take your mind off of your big old mess. I know someone you'd really like." Susie had been trying to fix me up for most of the year since the divorce was final. I'd been too tired and too disinterested to go down that road again.

She continued to tell me about her kids' new school. I heard all about Mrs. Monticello at the bakery. I had already heard the story of the woman and how she slipped and broke her hip in the store.

Thirty minutes later, I managed to hang up. The kid's dirty dishes were in the dishwasher and my dinner was cold. I put it in the microwave and when it came out, it was too hot to eat.

CHAPTER 11

It was ten o'clock when I finally opened the query, I had run earlier that evening. I wasn't sure if I had sufficient filters, but as I stared at the list of seven client accounts, all with the same criteria, I cringed.

I stared at the list: not a single name I recognized.

There were so many. All with my initials attached. I printed the list and opened the first client name. All of the signature cards had my signature, but not mine, scrawled across them. The criteria on all the accounts were the same, high billing, with low end generic custody agreements, or trust fund documents, or power of attorney, or temporary guardian documents. Nothing that justified the $20,000 in billing.

My heart skipped a beat.

I plowed through the list of clients, pulled all the pertinent information, changed the filters, and ran a new report. I logged out of the system and pulled up my spreadsheet and began tracking all of the invoices with the date and the amounts. Each invoice had been paid, but not every invoice had a corresponding document, phone call, or other work function attached to it.

At the end of an intense hour of sorting through documents and numbers, I printed my spreadsheet, put my computer away, and placed any printed documents into my work bag to take to Hector in the morning.

I was wired, exhausted, and upset. If I couldn't prove I had nothing to do with these accounts, I could be in serious trouble. Like Jacob suggested, I thought it was time to call my lawyer.

Tomorrow.

I glanced at the clock; it was after 11pm. I blinked away the dryness in my eyes, and looked at my phone when it rang. I grimaced. I didn't think the police could tap my phone or bug my room but I took a quick glance around my room before answering.

"Justin," I said.

"I need to talk to you."

My hand shook with anger. "Now why?"

He let out a heavy sigh. "I'm still completely locked out of the system." I glanced at my computer and the work I had done.

"What do you need from it?" I leaned against my headboard and closed my eyes.

"I need to build a case. I need to prove I didn't do anything. I need the bank account numbers for the Cabot file and the rest of the files that are similar."

All the account numbers, fraudulently opened, sat in my bag. The weight of it hurt my chest.

"Where are you?" I strained to hear any background noise. It was quiet, empty.

"Stop asking me that! I can't tell you!"

I was tired and becoming increasingly irritated by him. "So, you expect me to get you the data? Is that because you need me to prove you're innocent or are you going to dispose of the evidence that proves you committed bank fraud and laundered money through the law firm?"

"Jesus, Nikki! What the hell happened there? Really? Adrienne didn't tell me about that!"

While he stopped talking, he began to pace. His footsteps were loud against a hard floor. He muttered something, but I couldn't hear what he said. Then he said, "Why can't you just help me out?"

I still had a good job and my life was stable. I couldn't imagine what it would take to get me to risk it all to help Justin now.

"No more! I can't and won't help you. The police are waiting on warrants to pull all clients you were working on.

Whatever you had in those files will be with the police by the end of this week. If you want to help yourself, turn yourself in. Tell them where Marcie is. Don't call me again." I wished I had an old fashioned wall phone that I could slam down, loudly enough to express my true feelings without saying a word.

"Nikki. You're the only one who can help me. Please?"

"No! I have kids and I need this job. Go to the police. You're an ass and I hope you get disbarred!" I clicked off the phone but it wasn't the same as slamming it in its receiver. I tried to maintain a steady breath but I couldn't. And even though it was after eleven, I decided not to wait until morning and called my old friend Will Mann, a family lawyer that I went to undergraduate school with.

"Well, Nikki Page. It's been a long time. How's it going?" I smiled at his familiar voice, felt my anxiety lessen. I thought it might not be so bad.

"You're awfully cheerful for so late. And I'm sorry to be calling at eleven."

He was quiet for a moment. "It's okay. I'm guessing this might have something to do with Justin Able's disappearance."

Justin's disappearance did make the news, but more than that, there was a large legal community in and around Lake County, Illinois. I'm sure the news had filtered through every law firm in this, and several other counties.

"Actually, it is. I think I might need a lawyer." For now, I gave him the basics. Client accounts I knew nothing about, my name on the signature cards for the bank accounts, the stolen ID. Will typed on his keyboard, as I explained my dilemma.

"Okay. Did the cops ask for your signature?" he asked cautiously.

"Yesterday I had a home visit from Detective Andy Butcher with the Lake Zurich police department. His opinion is, my signature and the one on the bank account don't match." My breathing was ragged. I felt the same anxiety I felt every time I had spoken to Andy Butcher. Tears welled in my eyes.

"First of all, yes, I'll represent you. Second, if they want to speak with you again, at work or at home, call me. And if a subpoena comes in for you to appear anywhere, let me know right away. I wouldn't worry about this. You're the most honest person I know."

I tried to laugh but my gut churned. What I needed was a toilet.

"Thanks. The other thing. Justin called me several times. I implored him to call the police. Now he wants the account numbers from the client accounts and other pertinent information. I told him no."

Will was quiet for a moment. "Call the police detective and tell him about Justin's calls. But don't allow them to conduct another full interview with you, unless I'm there."

"Okay." I sighed heavily. I felt dizzy, as if I might pass out, and was thankful I was on my bed. "I feel so helpless."

Will seldom had a temper. But tonight, he sounded wired, like he was vibrating. His voice sounded a little higher than normal. Maybe he felt some stress too. He was a good man, abided by the law and sometimes bumped against the legal line without going over. He was a good lawyer and did well for his clients.

"You're anything but helpless. Call the police, tell them about Justin's calls. I can come out by your house tomorrow after work. Maybe around seven and we can talk about it. Okay?"

"Yeah, thanks."

"You know the drill. Answer with the truth." Even with the pledge to help, the tears thickened and ran down my cheeks.

"Thanks. Again. Really. I'm starting to freak. And before I forget my manners…" I wiped tears from my cheek. "How's Janelle?" Janelle was Will's wife. I remembered their wedding; the food was excellent, the dancing lasted well into the night, and Janelle drank so much she threw up in the punch bowl. The memory made me chuckle.

"Wow. It has been a while since we talked. Janelle and I are divorced. Well, in the process. Divorce is never easy, with or without kids. And how are you otherwise? You, okay?"

"If I keep my job, I'll be fine. Otherwise, life is pretty much settled and good." I think I was really trying to convince myself.

"I'll see you tomorrow. Don't worry and try to sleep."

We said goodbye and I packed up my work, hiding everything in my closet for now. Exhausted, I dragged myself to bed and hoped to get a few hours of sleep.

****

I called Andy Butcher after my first cup of coffee. "Hi Mrs. Page. How can I help you?" It was early and he was formal. I took a sip of coffee before I answered.

"My lawyer advised me to contact you and let you know that Justin's been calling me about the case." If he was formal, I could be formal and I needed to let him know I've involved a lawyer. Andy remained silent on the other end of the line. I waited patiently and enjoyed a second sip of coffee.

"What did Justin want?" Andy finally asked.

I explained that he wanted to get information on the Cabot file and the account numbers to help prove himself innocent. While I explained my various conversations with Justin, Andy typed on his keyboard. There were voices in the background. "You didn't give them to him, did you?"

"If I did, do you think I'd be calling you?"

Andy chuckled softly, lightening the mood. "No, I suppose you wouldn't. It's interesting that he doesn't have them with him." Andy was thoughtful for a moment. "Did he by any chance say where he was?"

"No. He just wants to prove his innocence and asked for the numbers."

I could almost hear the gears in Andy Butcher's head turn. I waited for the obvious. "We may have to tap your cell phone so we can figure out where he is."

"For that I'll give you my lawyer's name and phone number and you can work it through with him." I couldn't make my voice any less chilled.

"Is it necessary to bring in a lawyer?" he asked, rather surprised.

"Yes, I do."

It wasn't very pleasant after that, but we did say goodbye and I finished getting ready for work. Traffic was just as awful as it was every morning and I ran so fast up the two flights of stairs, I nearly twisted my ankle on one of the slippery steps.

With my ankle still hurting, I hobbled to the doorway, my key card in my hand, just about to swipe through. Pangs of anxiety whipped through me, my hands began to shake, and my vision blurred.

"Hey Nikki." Hector caught me at the door, opened it and ushered me inside. "You look a little pale. You, okay?"

I licked my dried lips and nodded. "Sorry. I'm all churned up about Justin." I glanced at him, embarrassed by my reaction and rushed down the aisle to my desk. I sat, turned on my computer and held my face in my hands.

"Nikki." The voice was gravelly, the sound that smokers make after thirty years of smoking, and it was very familiar. I turned quickly; Mrs. Munch was standing behind me.

"Mrs. Munch," I said. I slipped off my jacket and hung it on the back of my chair before straightening my button-down shirt.

"Can we talk?" she asked softly. I glanced at my computer and back to her and nodded. She walked with a quick pace and I nearly ran to keep up. When we were inside her office, she motioned for me to sit before closing the door.

I've only worked directly with Mrs. Munch on a few client cases. She was an easy lawyer to work for as long as you did your work in a timely manner and without error. While I had done good work for her, she primarily used paralegals in St. Louis. Other employees may have felt she was overbearing or overwhelming; I wasn't one of them. I observed her as she watched me. This was the first time I had ever felt anxious in her presence.

"I know this is rather stressful for you." It was a statement rather than a question. I wasn't surprised by her perception. Her violet eyes softened as she looked at me. "We have no intention of pursuing you as complicit in this matter and have told the police so." She leaned in and rested her hands on her very clean and clear desk. "I just want to hear what you know."

I returned her gaze and placed my hands on the desk mimicking her confidence, though I felt little of that right now. "All I can tell you is this: the file for the Cabot custody agreement was left in my inbox. I assumed it was from Justin, though as his primary paralegal, I had never seen the client account before. When I opened the invoicing system to track my time, I noticed how little work there was and for such a high bill. Maybe I shouldn't have explained that to Detective Butcher when he asked me if there were any strange client files that could account for Justin's disappearance, but I'm not up for lying to the police."

Mrs. Munch listened intently without taking notes or taking her eyes off of me. That added to my anxiety and I began to wring my hands, now sweaty in my lap. She waited for me to continue.

"I never saw the Cabot file before, I never opened the bank accounts, though I do keep copies of my ID in my locked drawer. One had been used but the signature on the bank cards are not mine." My voice rose as anger boiled to the top. I cleared my throat and leaned back in the chair.

"That idiot!" I jumped at her tone. She looked embarrassed after shouting out. "He's going to ruin this firm if he's not found."

I thought, for just a moment, about telling her he had called me and decided against it and then re-decided. "He's been calling me." No need to have her find out from the police that he had made contact several times. When she looked at me, her face was hard, her eyes catching everything.

"Where is he?" she said through gritted teeth.

I shook my head. "I wish I knew. I've been telling him to come to the police. He's not having it."

"What does he want?" she asked. She was no longer expressing anger. Her voice sounded defeated.

Do I tell her what he wanted?

I bit my lower lip as I looked at my hands.

"To prove himself innocent."

"Is he with Marcie Winkler?" She let out an irritated sigh.

"He says he's not. He says he has a contact here that's keeping him informed. He wants information from me so I can help him prove his innocence. I haven't given him anything."

Mrs. Munch made several notes on a legal pad of paper she kept on her desk. Her handwriting was mostly scribbles and would have been difficult to read right side up let alone upside down. She ripped off the sheet from the pad, folded it, and stuck it in her shirt pocket. "Hector asked you to follow the money, yes?"

I thought of the folders in my bag, along with the spreadsheet. "Yes."

"You do that away from here. We'll get the data on the client accounts and hopefully by next week we'll know how many clients he used to embezzle money."

"I did a search last night. I found seven more," I blurted out. Her eyes widened.

"Seven?" She rubbed her hands against her leathery skin.

"It was my first pass at it. I re-filtered and will look again when I get home."

When she motioned me away, she looked crushed, as if everything she had worked for her entire life might be slowly slipping away.

****

There are turning points in our lives that change the very path we walk on. The day I caught my husband with his secretary and the day I found Justin with his. Forever after this, I would see and feel the stares directed at me, the office gossips pointing and murmuring, the warm friendliness that I once felt here, now chilled. It pained me as I walked to my cubicle and wondered if I would ever feel normal here again.

"Nikki?" Patti Anne asked. At least my seat mates were still friends, I thought. She came and gave me a hug. "What's going on, sweetie? No one's telling us anything."

I shook my head. "I can't. It's just bad." I wiped a tear from my cheek. I was soon surrounded by Wilma and Shelia as well.

"We figured it was bad. Hector and Mrs. Munch. You sure you can't tell us?" Wilma asked.

Again, I shook my head. "It's just... I worked a lot with Justin. Now he's missing and there are some issues with some of his accounts."

Wilma, Patti Anne and Shelia shared glances. "Can we do anything?" Shelia asked.

I sighed. "I wish you could. I just have to get through this and handle what's expected of me. At least until Justin is found."

"Is he alive? Is Marcie alive?" Wilma asked.

I couldn't tell them what I knew. Not because I was asked not to, but I knew witnesses shouldn't talk in an investigation like this. I shouldn't tell them my thoughts. Hearsay wouldn't help Justin in the end.

"Right now, all it's about, is finding anything that could help find Justin. That includes files I've worked."

There was movement along the main passageway and we separated. They each gave me the look of pity and touched my shoulder. I'm sure even though they were my friends, they were glad it wasn't them.

CHAPTER 12

I signed back into my computer, grabbed the first folder in my inbox and began the tedious art of researching the law. After quality time with the database, I finished up my other work. As I put the files for the custody agreement in the folder for lawyer review, I realized that it would need to go to Jared now.

I stopped outside Jared's closed door and glanced at Cary, his administrative assistant.

"Hi Nikki." She motioned for me to come to her desk.

"Hi Cary. Have you heard from Marcie?"

Cary looked tired, sad almost. She shook her head. "No. I was wondering what you knew about all of this?"

"Not much. I just know it has to do with some client files. But I don't know beyond that." At that moment, a thought popped in my overly stuffed brain. Adrienne. I had heard on the phone with someone who knew what was going on. When I was done with Jared, I might have a talk with her.

Cary stared at me. "If you hear anything, let me know." I nodded and knocked on Jared's door.

"Come in."

Jared was sitting at his desk. It was just a desk, not too small or too large, just big enough to be covered in piles of folders and papers and stacks of handwritten notes, completely opposite of his brothers clean desk.

"I have a few files that should go to Justin, but…"

He waved me closer and took the files.

"There's the Johannsen custody agreement, some letters, some other simple documents," I told him.

He perused the files quickly.

"The notes are in the digital file?"

I nodded.

"Mrs. Munch and I would like to clear off as much open work as we can from Justin's current case load," he said. It was only mid-morning but his beige slacks and white shirt were already rumpled and his hair was mussed from running a hand through it several times already.

"How are you holding up?" I asked. I wasn't sure if small talk was necessarily required, but he seemed so bedraggled, I wanted to offer what support I could.

"I'm holding up as well as could be expected. My sister-in-law and the kids have been troopers. No one seems to know where Justin is or if he's even alive."

"He's alive," I said quickly. He glanced at me, wide eyes, surprised at my announcement.

"How do you know? Have you seen him?" He began to wring his hands. I can't imagine this has been easy for him or the family. Not with all of this coming out.

"No. Justin called me. He claims he's innocent." I explained the last call I received. Jared looked anxious and bit his lower lip.

"You haven't helped him, have you?"

I shook my head. "No. I told him to go to the police. He's adamant he's innocent. His actions say otherwise."

Jared nodded so quickly; I thought his head would fly off his neck. "That's right. You're absolutely correct. He needs to come in. Clear this up. It could be nothing." Jared's eyes seemed wild... or I was projecting my own anxiety.

"Is there anything I can do?" I asked him.

He looked at me almost as if he forgot I was there. "No. I just want you to keep at the open client files as you can. Come to me or Mrs. Munch for anything. We'll be splitting the active clients that haven't left yet."

He hadn't dismissed me, so I smiled and nodded. "Is there anything else?"

"I … I. The files have been restricted and I wasn't able to get in. Is there anything I should know about the Cabot files?"

I shook my head, thinking that was odd since I saw him take the Cabot file from Justin's inbox. "Nothing that I haven't already shared."

He shook his head absently; he was thinking of something else. "If you have the bank account numbers, please email them to me. I need to determine what Justin did. It's bad enough he embezzled money, but now he's left us holding the bag." He glanced at the vertical window beside his door. As people went about their day, they glanced inside the office or did all they could to ignore us. It felt like we were in a glass bowl where everyone could see and know what we were doing.

"Okay. I'll see what I can pull."

"Thanks Nikki." He looked up at me. "We need to put this to rest. Make sure the clients are reimbursed or not involved." He smiled, but it felt cold and empty. When he dismissed me, I left the office and closed his door behind me. Justin and Marcie were missing, there was possible illegal activities running through client accounts, and Jared seemed… out of it. Maybe it was how he dealt with stress, but something about his demeanor seemed wrong. With my trembling hands, and nauseated gut, I felt as though I was feeling more stress than he was. But then again, Hector acted unsurprised by this. Maybe Jared knew more than he was letting on.

I felt the stares and heard the whispers for the second time today; they followed me through the law offices to my cubicle. I took a seat, pulled up the Cabot file and saw firsthand that it was blocked from viewing.

****

It was a cool day and staying inside at lunch, didn't feel like an option for me. I bundled up and took my walk around the four buildings that made up the business complex. They were stacked from one end to another and if I walked the sidewalk around the buildings twice, I would have a good two-mile walk completed.

When I finished the first walk around, I spotted a Sheriff's car parked beside mine. He wasn't touching my car but he was looking inside. My heart sped up at what felt like a violation of my privacy and rather than engaging with him, I continued my second lap around the buildings.

A light breeze brushed up against me, my phone rang and I looked to the screen and saw the school calling me. My heart couldn't have sunk any further. "Hello?"

"I'm in the principal's office." Julia sound embarrassed with her small voice. I wasn't sure if she was afraid of the principal's office or my reaction to her being there.

"Oh Julia. Will I be getting a call? A note?"

"Yeah," she said rather sheepishly. She was usually blunter than this.

"What did you do to earn a trip to the principal's office?"

"Well. We were playing at lunch, like we do outside when the weather's nice and, well, I was teaching everyone how to play poker."

I had made it to building three where I worked, and stopped at the edge of the parking lot. The sheriff's officer was leaning against his car, working on his phone waiting. It seemed odd he was out here, rather than inside, but I had a feeling he was there to see me. Between that and Julia's adventure, I felt my shoulders slump, there was no fighting the inevitable. When I returned to my car, I leaned against the trunk, noticed he was holding an envelope. He noticed me there, slipped his phone in his pants pocket and began to walk toward me.

"Daughter, in the principal's office." I said and turned my attention back to Julia. In that moment, it all seemed funny and I tried to stifle a laugh.

"Did you at least win some lunch money from those hapless kids?" I couldn't stop the smile or the laugh.

"Mom? You, okay?"

"Yeah. How much did you win?" I said when I was composed.

"Twenty bucks."

"Okay. You're a knucklehead. Seriously, on school property. What the hell are you thinking? Are you getting a detention, suspension, expulsion?"

"Not sure, Mommy."

I blew out air. "I have to go. I better have a note from the school waiting for me when I get home. I'm so glad I taught you how to play." I hung up and stared at the Sheriff's officer. When I tucked my phone away, he sauntered over.

"Hi, Ma'am. Sorry to have to do this." He handed me an envelope with my name scrawled across the front. I figured by his demeanor; it was a subpoena. Having no choice, I took the envelope, he saluted me once and headed back toward his car. I watched him climb inside and pull his car out.

When he was gone, I opened the envelope, and glanced over the notice to appear at the FBI building on Monday. I sighed, made a quick call to Will.

"Hey Will, it's Nikki. I need to be at the FBI office in Chicago on Monday morning. Sorry to leave a message. Call me."

When I hung up, my head was spinning. I tucked the paperwork in my car and headed back up to work.

CHAPTER 13

This had been an excruciatingly long day. I glanced up as I shut off my computer and Adrienne Mox was staring down at me. "Can I help you?" I asked cautiously. Though I had wanted to speak with Adrienne to find out what she knew, her presence standing over me, made me feel vulnerable.

"You know something," she said and leaned a hip on my desk.

"Not really. What do you know?" I stood up and put on my jacket. She watched me intently. I glanced at my clock. Will was, after all, coming over tonight and it was the weekend. I thought this could wait until Monday and I wanted nothing to do with work tonight.

"Nothing," she said quickly. I couldn't help but think of her phone call days ago.

"You sure about that? I get the feeling Marcie and Justin know exactly what's going on. I just can't seem to decide who's updating them."

Adrienne pursed her lips, clenched her hands in fists. "He is calling you, isn't he?" she hissed.

Why does that bother her?

"I'm not sure what you know or your role in whatever's going on, but I don't want to know any more of it. I know more than I want. So, tell your friend Marcie, to come forward with whatever she knows and tell her boyfriend to turn himself in."

Adrienne unclenched her fists. "She can't. Not yet," she nearly whispered.

Before I could speak again, Adrienne turned and walked away.

I grabbed my bag, waved to my seatmates who had been watching the exchange with curiosity and left the office.

I had plenty of time before Will would be at my house so I sat in the seating area off to the side of the stairs, out of direct view from anyone coming down the stairs. My anxiety was high as I pulled out a book, pretending to read, while I waited for Adrienne to come down stairs. I've never done anything like this as I watched, from over the top of my book, for my co-workers to leave for the weekend.

Adrienne and Joy left together.

When they exited the building, I got up and followed them out of the door. My car was parked farther away than normal, which worked out well for me. They stood at Joy's car, which was parked on the far side of the pretty shed that housed the garbage cans. I stood on the other side which just happened to be beside my car.

"That bitch!" Adrienne pounded on Joy's car.

"She probably doesn't know anything. If Justin's calling her, he's trying to find out what's going on. He doesn't know, so she doesn't."

"I told Marcie this was a bad idea."

"Adrienne. You should tell the police where Marcie is. She didn't do this and you know she'll put the nail in Justin's coffin. If you do this now, you won't get in trouble. Just a bystander. Right?"

"It's not that simple. I know stuff. Not all of it, but enough. And Nikki knows too. I know she does."

"Maybe you can implicate Nikki. Act like she knows more. If you report Justin to the police, you can say she was his favorite paralegal and he trusted her the most. Make it seem like they were in love and did this together." Joy sounded gleeful at the suggestion. My stomach roiled and I wish I could have seen Adrienne's face.

"You idiot!" Adrienne said. "It's too many lies." Her shoes clicked on the pavement. "Though, maybe I can convince Marcie to implicate her further."

My heart raced. Adrienne and Joy knew about the plan or parts of it. And I was going to be their fall guy.

"But it was Nikki's signature on those bank accounts. Her ID was used."

People streamed from the office buildings. Some were coming out as far as our parking spots. I opened my door.

"She'll know it wasn't her signature. If she could prove it was faked... Just don't say anything. I'll let you know what happens after I see Marcie tonight. Maybe I can get to Nikki. Maybe..."

Joy's car door slammed. I climbed inside my car and started the engine.

How do I prove what Adrienne knows?

I pulled out of the parking spot and drove home, my leg shaking, my hands trembling. I was being set up, by my co-workers, possibly my boss, his secretary.

Why me?

The tears fell faster, the closer I was to home.

****

I rushed inside the house, saw Julia's note from school, and breathed a sigh of relief; she was only getting a week of detention. I don't know why I thought of Julia's friend Macy, the poor girl who got a two-week grounding for coming home ten minutes late one night. Why I wondered what her very strict mother would have thought about this was just another form of guilt on my part and made no sense. I thought maybe I should punish Julia at home, but then, the twenty bucks she won sat on the counter and I couldn't stop giggling.

Pushing aside my guilt and putting aside thoughts of strict parents, I pocketed the money, placed the note on the refrigerator. I turned when the garage door opened. Jacob was followed by a girl, Penny or Peri—I could never remember.

"What's for dinner, mom?"

"Leftovers. Help yourself to whatever. I have a meeting tonight at seven."

"A date-like meeting," Jacob teased. I glanced at Peri or Penny, she blushed.

"No. Not a date-like meeting. My friend Will the lawyer, is coming over. I have some things going on at work and he's going to help me."

Jacob raised his eyebrows. I shook my head. He shrugged and the two of them headed to the basement. I did the mom thing and propped the basement door open with a chair, just in case they were planning on more than studying. It was Friday afternoon, after all.

Julia poked her face out from around the hallway wall.

"I'm not grounding you. That seems like too much work for too little reward. I'm just gonna ask: what the hell were you thinking?"

Julia shrugged. "They were easy marks." Great, my kid, the con woman.

"The school frowns on gambling on school grounds. If you're gonna do it, do it here or don't do it at all. That would be better. Not at all."

She came over to me, placed her thin arms around me and squeezed. "Thanks, Mom."

"Don't "thanks, Mom" me. I'm a little pissed at you right now. You're lucky you're smart and do well in school. Go finish your homework."

****

I ate my heated leftovers in the dining room and re-read the subpoena. My case notes were spread across the table and I wrote my thoughts out on my legal pad.

Julia quietly completed her homework in the den while Jacob and Penny or Peri were downstairs with the door still open and the television on.

I was nervous as I put dinner dishes in the dishwasher. I began to clean the kitchen, the stove top, the sink, the counters. When the doorbell rang, I felt my stomach churn and wished I had time to change my clothes.

Will hadn't changed in all the years I've known him, except maybe a little wider and broader. Otherwise, he aged well, with salt and pepper—mostly peppered— hair, cut short. His blue eyes sparkled as he leaned in and kissed my cheek.

"Well, look at you. It's been a long time." He smiled broadly.

"Way too long." I smiled back. "And thanks so much for coming." He followed me into the dining room and sat at the side chair. "Coffee?" I asked.

He nodded and I passed him the subpoena. He looked it over as I made him a cup.

"It looks like the LZPD called the FBI when there were hints of illegal activities at the firm. It's a standard subpoena. They just want to talk to you in person." I handed him the cup, placed a packet of creamer and sugar beside him. "I'll pick you up here and drive you in."

I had tea for myself. When I sat down, he was making copious notes on a legal pad.

"How much are you going to charge?"

He glanced up and smiled.

"Dinner should cover it. So has anything else happened since yesterday?"

"The office manager has me pulling any other accounts with the same high invoicing that doesn't coincide with the amount of work done. I've found seven accounts so far. I'll pull more tonight. I talked to Mrs. Munch. She believes I'm not involved, for what that's worth. And Jared is taking over some of the cases and he asked if I had the bank account numbers for the Cabot file. Oh, and the office gossip, her name is Adrienne Mox. She's in contact with the missing Marcie Winkler and alluded to knowing what's going on."

He cocked an eyebrow. Pretty sexy and yet I mentally gave myself a palm plant to the forehead. I needed to focus on this not on my once college crush.

"You have evidence to that?"

I shook my head. "Not physical proof. She questioned me about what I knew. So, I did the adult thing and listened in on her conversation."

"Okay," he said cautiously. "What did she say in this conversation?"

I held my breath as I remembered what Adrienne had said about my role in all of this. "I'm being set up. There's a from me to Justin. My name is all over bank accounts, my ID was used. Andy Butcher, the LZPD officer had me sign a blank sheet of paper to prove it wasn't me who opened the accounts."

Will rubbed his hand against his chin.

"From this point forward, only speak with the police if I'm there. Between the office gossip admitting to framing you, to Jared worried about the accounts, I'm thinking there's someone else in charge of the operation and you could be in serious trouble." He wrote something else in his notes and looked up to me. "Do you know if Jared knows anything else?"

I shook my head. "I have a gut feeling he knows. He acts like he's just been found out. He nearly passed out when I was being interviewed by the police. But then he seems out of it, and doesn't have access to client bank account information?" "I asked incredulously, the octave in my voice rising with my anxiety. "And Mrs. Munch, she's calm and cool and then she blows up, pissed as hell at what Justin's done. And Justin claims he knows nothing. I thought I understood people but nothing makes sense. I mean, it looks like a criminal enterprise and they could all be in on it and really good liars." I felt my face flush. I took a sip of warm tea.

He took my hand and offered a squeeze. "You have me to help you sort this. It sounds like a cluster fuck in the making."

I nodded. I had nothing to add to that. I watched Will make more notes. He looked up at me and smiled.

"You look stressed. And that makes me feel guilty. How did we lose touch?"

"Life has a funny way about that," I said. Had he really been my crush once or did Jack wipe all those memories of my life before him?

"After this, we need to change that."

I nodded. He went right back to his notes.

"So, there's Justin, Jared and Mrs. Munch. Any of them could be lying and it's a good assumption that they probably all are. You found out about this when you got the Cabot file to work on. So, the question is, who gave you the file? I can't believe it would be Justin, Jared or Mrs. Munch. Why risk this getting out. Who do you think wanted this to come out?"

I sat back in my chair, still nursing my tea. "I found Justin and Marcie in a compromising position. The day after, I got the file. It seems like too much of a coincidence. She was Justin's administrative assistant. She could know what's going on."

I closed my eyes as Will's pen scratched across the paper.

"How is Adrienne Mox, the office gossip involved."

"Marcie's friend."

Did Marcie tell Adrienne what was going on? Was Marcie that angry with Justin, that she put the file out there so someone would find out? If they're setting me up, why give it to me?

I shuddered.

"You, okay?" Will asked.

I could feel my eyes sting with tears. I told him what I thought.

"You think Marcie gave you the file so the truth would come out because of her failed affair with her boss. That's motive. But why frame you? Have you ever had bad blood with Marcie, Adrienne or the partners?"

"Nothing that I knew of."

Could I have read everyone that incorrectly that I didn't know they'd use me as a fall guy for their scheme? I felt vulnerable and frightened by that.

"Anyone else in management who might know about this?"

I thought about everyone who knew something. I could only think of Hector.

"Hector Garcia is the Human Resources manager. He knew about the affair but couldn't convince Marcie to file a sexual harassment charge. He seemed to know something was amiss when I showed him what Justin asked me to find and he wants me to go further with it. He's got access to the files, so, I'm not giving him anything he can't get for himself."

I held my tea but didn't sip it. I looked at Will.

"Does Jared know you're looking into this?

I shook my head. "No, but Mrs. Munch does. I never told any of them that Justin's called me more than once. And before you could tell me again, I told Detective Butcher he called me." I was rambling with nerves.

"Do you think Hector could be in on this and asking you to look into this is just his way of diverting attention from himself?"

I shrugged. "I wouldn't have thought Marcie would do something like this, so I have no idea what Hector would do. I don't know."

"From here on out, only talk to me and the police. Keep working on what Hector requests and do your job as normal. Watch out for the partners. I wouldn't be surprised if Jared, especially, knew what was going on."

"I am very sorry we lost touch." I sighed.

Will smiled and touched my forearm. "I'm sorry we hadn't stayed in touch, too. But you're right, life does have a way of getting in the way." His hand was warm against my skin and my stomach fluttered. Crush. I don't know where that was coming from. Maybe it was because at this moment, he was my knight in shining armor. I was glad he had my back.

"We always had fun. Music, food, beer and movies." I stifled a yawn. I hadn't realized how tired I was until that moment.

"It was fun. And then you met Jack and I met Janelle and you know the story." He put his notepad in his briefcase and sipped his coffee.

"I appreciate you helping me with this. It's been upsetting. And I'm... scared."

"Don't be. From what you've told me, you have proof you didn't open the account. You'll tell the FBI that."

"We haven't talked in so long and then I call you out of the blue. I feel like I'm using you."

"Don't worry about calling me out of the blue to represent you on this. I'm glad you called me." I offered a smile. He chuckled.

"You'll buy me dinner. No using involved." He opened his arms as if to prove his point.

I sighed.

"Don't worry about it. You know depositions. They've been notified of the possibility of embezzlement and money laundering and they're collecting data."

I shook my head; it didn't ease the anxiety.

"Nikki. You get stressed if you can't get work done on time, or if you forget to leave a tip. You're so honest. I don't think I've ever known you to tell a lie." He shook his head. "I can't see you lying or committing a crime for anyone, especially a boss."

"I know. You're right. I feel guilty over lots of stuff." I touched his hand. "I'll buy you dinner when this is over. Whether it's finding Justin or figuring out what's going on."

"Try and get sleep. And try to enjoy your weekend."

Will and I chatted for another half hour, and at the door, he reached in and kissed my cheek. "Don't worry."

I watched him walk to his car and pull out of my crooked driveway in his Jaguar convertible. When I could no longer see his taillights, I dragged myself upstairs to continue to search for the "weird" accounts.

****

My cell phone rang at 3:11 am. The lights in my room were still on, my computer screen was blank, and across my bed were the lists of other client accounts that I had found that evening.

I grumbled at my ring tone, didn't look at the caller ID as I answered the phone. "Hello..." I mumbled.

"Nikki, I need to meet you." Justin's voice was raspy, as if he were sick or just tired. My eyes popped open as the cobwebs cleared from my mind.

"Justin. It's three in the morning. I told you to call the police. I can't and won't help you."

"I didn't embezzle or launder that money," he pleaded.

Now fully awake, I pushed the papers into a pile and leaned against the headboard. "You ran. You implicated yourself. What did you know and when did you know it?"

It was quiet on his end. I could imagine crickets. He had either hung up or he was thinking of his answer or excuse. "Hello?" I asked.

"I'm here. I'm just not sure how to answer."

I rolled my eyes.

"It's a simple question. When did you find out and what do you know?"

I pulled the blankets across my lap because my room was chilly and my house was quiet and felt lonely.

"When you told me about the Cabot file, it rang a bell for me. I tried to pull it up on the system and couldn't. And there was an invoicing question on that one. There have been odd things over the years, but this was really odd."

"So, you've had gut feelings but nothing concrete. Or you need my help to cover up what you've done. Do you think I'm stupid?"

"No, I don't." He was quiet, contemplative. "I don't think you're stupid. But I do need your help. I need to prove I didn't do this and figure out who did it."

He was so insistent that he hadn't done what everyone thought he did. I understood that feeling because I knew I hadn't opened those client accounts. I knew for certain I was being set up. I thought of Adrienne Mox and Marcie Walker. If they were setting me up, why couldn't they be setting him up as well

"Is Marcie keeping you updated on what's going on at the firm?" I asked.

"Yes."

"Everyone thinks you killed her or she's alive and hiding with you."

"She's not. I'm alone." He sounded defeated, remorseful even.

Thoughts and ideas were jumbled in my head. If Marcie was leading Justin around, was it Adrienne who was telling her what was going on? Who was telling Adrienne? Was it the same person who had access to Justin's invoicing?

When I signed in to the system, I could click on the initials field and my initials would populate it because I was logged in. With Justin's initials in the fields, it meant that someone signed in with Justin's credentials. That couldn't be overridden. Was it Marcie? Adrienne? Jared? Hector?

"Who has access to your login for the invoicing system?"

He was quiet, but not still. I could hear his footsteps on the floor wherever he was hiding. "Marcie and Cary."

The administrative assistants. That would make sense. Were they involved or did they pass the information on to someone else, which would make them involved? I sighed loudly.

"Yeah. Exactly. I can see why Marcie would set me up, but not Cary. Why would they do this?"

"Someone else got to them and is paying them, or in Marcie's case, she hates you and wants to see you suffer behind bars."

He stopped, stilled his active body. "It could be anyone in the law firm."

Or Jared and Mrs. Munch, I thought to myself. Not that I had a reason to believe they would do this. But as I had read through the notes that were written beside each invoice entry, they were so chaotic, so nonsensical, I had to believe they were put there to lead an investigator away from someone who knew what should be used in the notes. Or it was someone who didn't know at all how we coded invoices. I thought of Adrienne Mox again. She knew enough to do a bad job, set him up. But why?

"What does Adrienne Mox have to do with this?" I asked Justin.

"She's friends with Marcie. She must be the one keeping Marcie up to date," he said quickly.

"Could she have helped Marcie set you up? I mean, Marcie wouldn't know all of the codes for the legal work. Adrienne could have told her what to do or not to do or how to get around the system."

"If I could have those account numbers and access, then I could prove I didn't do this and find out who did and why. Nikki. You gotta believe me, I didn't do this! I need your help!"

I knew that wasn't the answer to Justin's problems. What he needed to do was turn himself in, face hard questioning. Then the truth could come out. I knew if I gave him those account numbers, I truly believed the accounts would be emptied and Justin would be gone for good.

But if he was framed like me…

"I'm not giving you that information. Just tell me what you're looking for."

He let out a heavy sigh as if that wasn't what he wanted to hear. "Signatures for starters. The signature cards were forged. I'm sure of it." He was adamant about that. "You could be in trouble. I need you to help me and you need to help yourself."

Each time I discovered how little I trusted my boss. While I knew it was possible to be framed, the fact that he wouldn't come in and deal with it, that he had run from it, made me think he was guilty, that I was still the scape goat. If I was going to do anything, it would be to protect myself.

"The police watched me sign my signature and they're comparing it to the signature cards. I'm sure there are copies of your signature in the system so they can compare the two and confirm the signature cards were forged."

"Marcie signed my name to several documents. She was pretty spot-on."

"That sucks for you."

"Why are you being such a bitch about this?" First Adrienne, now Justin. I rolled my eyes, if only for myself.

"I'm not a bitch, I'm not your secretary. If you didn't do this, come forward and defend yourself, but don't ask me to do this."

"I'm sorry, Nikki."

"Yeah. So am I. Turn yourself in. I did nothing, and now Adrienne knows I figured out what's been going on. I'm not going to let whoever is doing this set me up. For all I know, it was Marcie, or it could be you." My breath was ragged, my heart pounded in my chest. I heard footsteps coming down the hallway. I think I woke my kids.

"Help me and it'll help you."

There was a knock on my door. I stomped to the door, opened it, and both of my kids were staring at me with fear in their eyes. I held my hand over the speaker. "Go to bed." I gave them my sternest look. They reluctantly went back to their rooms. I slammed my door closed.

"Where are you?" I listened carefully to his silence, but wherever he was, it was quiet and he seemed well hidden.

"I can't tell you that."

"Fine. They're thinking of bugging my phone. You can't contact me again without being found."

"Damn." He pounded on something hard. My eye twitched.

"Besides the signature cards, what else are you looking for? I'm not giving you the account numbers, but I can search if you give me the direction. I can give the police what I find."

"I don't know what to look for specifically. But you'll know when the accounts are off. You saw it with the Cabot file. You'll see the irregularities. You'll know."

I felt his frustration. It was the same that rose inside of me and it was making my head pound.

"I'm already looking. But having said that, you need to call the police." I clicked off the phone. I slid the folders, filled with the documents I've been collecting, under the chair in my room and shut off my bedroom light. I didn't fall asleep again for the rest of the night as my thoughts stumbled between my children scared in their room and all of the things that I should be looking for in the files I had just found. It was as if everything hinged on that, and hoped the answers would be in there.

CHAPTER 14

I loved Saturday mornings. This one was dark and colder, and Julia had no activities on the weekends unless you counted getting sugared up and watching cartoons. After the week I had, I could live with that.

Jacob, a driver and fully responsible for his schedule, woke early and worked out before eating breakfast: usually cereal, sausage, an egg.

I sauntered downstairs and did my own workout, though this morning it felt rather lackadaisical. I showered after, and stood under the hot jets, letting the water pound against my skin, hopefully reducing the stiffness I felt. Ready for the day, I grabbed a toasted peanut butter sandwich, checked in on my offspring and locked myself in my room to perform more queries.

I pulled up my last search from Friday night and noticed that I was now up to twenty client accounts that followed the Cabot model. All clients had been invoiced twenty to thirty thousand with little to no work for that amount.

I printed the list and began to pull up all the accounts, looking at the documents, the notes in the invoice system, the banking records. It took me all morning to print hundreds of documents and I had loaded my printer twice. I was feeling surly when I finished, and decided it was time for a break. I headed to the kitchen to make Julia's favorite, macaroni and cheese.

The only noise in the house came from the television. Julia was sprawled across the sofa watching a sponge and a starfish. Jacob had left for a few pickup basketball games at the Y. Standing at the refrigerator, I found the ingredients: butter, milk, cheese, noodles. I found my large casserole dish. I don't always cook because of the work required, but today seemed like the kind of day to nest a little.

After preparing the food, I sat beside Julia on the couch. She was quiet and still as we waited for our casserole to bake.

"You, okay?" I finally asked. It was just too much to pretend to watch the cartoon. She turned and looked at me.

"Yeah. Fine. You, okay?"

"I am. Sorry about last night. It's getting really hard at work."

"Are you going to jail?"

I grimaced and let out a sigh. "No, Sweetie. I didn't do anything. I'm stuck between my boss and the law firm and the police. They all want something." I thought of the hundreds of pages upstairs.

"You were so mad last night."

"I was. My boss keeps calling. I think he did something. Or someone did something to make it look like Justin did it. I don't know." I rubbed at my temple; the headache was growing deeper as my stress level went up. Julia scooted over and sat beside me and laid her head on my shoulder.

We sat in silence until the casserole finished. I served it up and we ate in silence. Julia was occupied with the screen and my mind wandered back to the client files in my bedroom.

Telling Julia, realizing how this is affecting my children, left me feeling rather paralyzed; all I could do was leave the dirty dishes soaking in the sink. But after only a few minutes on the couch, I had the need to grab my computer and start additional queries. Because I had found twenty client accounts in the last five years, I suspected if I searched before that time period, I'd find even more problematic client accounts. I returned to my searches, changed the criteria, and let the computer run. The television held no interest for me, and yet, I couldn't take my mind off of the cartoon.

"I'm sorry, Mom," Julia said. I shifted and turned my attention to her.

"About?"

"I shouldn't gamble on school grounds."

I chuckled. "Well, duh. I probably shouldn't have taught you to play poker yet. You're too young." I kissed her forehead.

"It was kinda funny though, right?" she beamed at me with a wide smile. I shook my head but laughed.

"Only you, kid."

"I am sorry."

"I know, baby." I pulled the winnings from my jeans pocket. "Could I trust you to get this back to the kids you took it from?"

"Yeah."

I held the money for her but yanked it away before she could grab it. "Really?"

She nodded and took the money. When the computer finished pulling the reports, I picked it up to go print them off.

I used the printing time to start reading the actual files, noting anything odd, or as Justin reminded me, looking for something off. The first folder I read was for the Posey family. While the billing amount had only hit $10,000, I noted the amount of work completed didn't equal that amount.

I read through the ownership documents that had been created for a company called Asset Investments.

Asset Investments?

It sounded familiar. Maybe I had worked with them before. I pulled them up on my computer.

It was a one-page website that described the company as an investment firm with a P.O. box for an address. What I found strangest was the lack of a phone number or email address. There was no mention of employees or who owned the company. I scrolled down and noted that the page copyright was ten years old. I printed the page.

I pulled Asset Investments up on the Better Business Bureau website; there was no listing for the company. I did another search on the Illinois business database to see when and if the company had ever been incorporated.

Nothing.

I printed both pages, showing that Asset Management was virtually unknown. I added the documents to my growing collection. I stared at the printout of the website.

Where have I heard this name before?

I dropped all of my new documents on my desk and pulled up the Cabot file. I found a list of assets for the Cabots. Asset Investments was one of them.

I bit my lip and searched for the Cabots and the Poseys online. I expected nothing, and that's what I got. Nothing on Emma and London Cabot or Francine and Frank Posey on the Better Business Association website or on the

Asset Investment website, nothing on Facebook, Twitter, Instagram.

With all of the odd client accounts, I took one at a time, looking for anything about Asset Investments.

****

After two hours, I finally learned that Asset Investments wasn't registered as a company in Illinois, it was registered in the Cayman Islands. That alone raised my eyebrows, but only slightly. It had a board of directors: Emma and London Cabot, J. Able, Francine and Frank Posey, Donald Silvio Family Trust, and Michael Maximillian. I printed what I could from the website I had finally found and stared at the owners of Asset Investments.

J. Able.

While it was most likely Justin, it could have been Jared. Much like the website I found, the company itself appeared to have few to no employees and no physical structure. It had no physical assets and only claimed to be worth about $10 million.

I supposed a business management expert could tell me what I was missing, but for now, I had spent the entire bulk of my Saturday researching these odd accounts looking for the answers. I arranged all of my documents, saved what I had found on my computer, and made three sets of copies: one for Hector, one for the FBI, and one for me.

I wondered if Justin had figured it out and that's why he ran or maybe someone was setting up both Able brothers.

I hid my files on the floor of my closet behind my laundry basket. I wound my way to the kitchen to feed my children.

****

This wasn't how I wanted to spend my Sunday, but here I was parked outside of Marcie Walker's house. The building contained four condos, two on the top floor and two on the bottom. She was on the top floor; the curtains were closed and the lights were off. I had backed into the parking spot that faced the back window.

From my location, I could see if she left her cul-de-sac and there was only one way out of the apartment complex. After an hour, I figured she was either hiding inside or really had left for other locales. I turned on my car, and watched a gray Lexus pull into her cul-de-sac. It looked like Justin was coming to Marcie's house.

I exited the car without any thoughts of repercussions and ran around to the front door. When I saw him using the key to get in, my only thought was to convince him to go to the police and end this ridiculousness.

"This is what you do instead of turning yourself in?" I said.

He dropped the keys and looked at me. "What are you doing here?" He bent over to pick them up.

"I was thinking Marcie knew something and I was thinking she might come back here. I wasted an hour waiting for something to happen and then you showed up."

"You shouldn't be here." He opened the door and stepped inside. I grabbed it before he could lock me out and followed him in.

"Yeah. You're right. I shouldn't be. I should be at home with my kids, relaxing and enjoying my day. But I'm not. I'm here trying to figure out who might be framing me. I'm going to make sure I don't lose everything because of you." We walked the open staircase to Marcie's apartment and he unlocked the door. We stepped inside.

It had been trashed. The television was cracked and lying in the middle of the room, books were scattered across the carpet, glass figurines had been shattered. I walked down the hallway glanced into the kitchen to see overturned cereal boxes, their contents across the floor. I continued toward the bedrooms. Clothes and other items from the closet and drawers were scattered across unmade beds. Pictures hung askew. The bathrooms weren't any better. The house had been ransacked,

"Who and what?" I asked Justin as he joined me in Marcie's bedroom.

"I don't know. If I knew, we wouldn't be in this trouble."

I only stared at the mess around me, afraid to touch anything, afraid to make my presence here known. But Justin didn't seem to care as he picked up Marcie's fancy negligee from the floor and tossed it on the bed. He took a good look at the room. "The headboard's been slashed." It was a French caned headboard, possibly antique. I held my breath for a moment and let it out slowly.

"Marcie set you up. You do realize that, don't you?"

He looked at me and plopped on the bed, as if he were too exhausted to stand any longer.

"You're right. You're right." He tossed up his hands. "I think Marcie gave you the file and quit." He put his head in his hands, his body trembled. I touched his shoulder. "You need to go to the police. You need to tell your side of this."

I backed away from him and glanced inside her closet. Everything had been yanked off the hangers, purses were scattered across the floor, shoes had been tossed into the bedroom. I walked inside and looked around. I knelt in the corner of the closet where the carpet wasn't flat. I pulled out a tissue from my purse and pulled up the edge of the carpet. "I think I know what they were looking for."

He joined me in the closet. Under the carpet was a floor safe. It had been untouched, or undiscovered. "I didn't know she had that," Justin said.

"Unless she took what she hid in here, I'm guessing some answers are here."

He leaned against the door jamb. "Maybe it's her birthday. March 23, 1977."

Still using the tissue, I typed the date, 032377, 03231977, 32377 and 3231977. "Nope."

"Mine is July 1, 1966."

I typed all iterations of his birthday. "Nada." I looked at him, his skin was nearly transparent. "What does Adrienne have to do with this?"

Justin shook his head. "I'm not sure. If Marcie really did set me up, I'm guessing Adrienne helped her. Told her how to set up the accounts, or fill them in. But they were all wrong." He sighed. "She's emailing me, keeping me apprised."

Seeing all of this, hearing Justin's realization that he had been set up but Marcie, made me additionally fearful of what I had been dragged in. And I realized that because I was being set up, I shouldn't have come here. I shouldn't have put myself in danger.

I no longer wanted to be here. I was no longer going to be stupid and further implicate myself in this. I touched Justin's shoulder and headed out, careful to not touch anything on my way out and I drove home.

CHAPTER 15

On Monday morning, I sent Hector an email, advising him briefly of what I found and reminding him I was subpoenaed to appear at the FBI offices, and sat on my front porch step as I waited for Will. My dark purple suit hid dirt well so no one would know I had been sitting on the stoop.

I had my hand on my purse as it hung around my shoulders. I breathed a sigh of relief when Will pulled into my driveway in his silver Jaguar. I climbed inside and he kissed my cheek.

"You, okay?" he asked as he pulled into traffic.

"Yeah." I fiddled with the purse strap and stared out the window, intently.

"How's the research coming?"

I glanced at him, freshly shaven, hair combed neatly, his suit without creases. He was definitely a nice-looking man, but that wasn't why I was relieved to have him with me. It was that brain, all his knowledge, and simply his friendly face. "It's going. I pulled additional queries. I have twenty possible accounts all with ties to a company called Asset Investments." I pursed my lips.

"And is this company real?"

"Caymans." Alone, that didn't make it a false company but it made me suspicious, and what I had found—or hadn't found— made me believe it's only there for the purpose of embezzlement or money laundering.

"The FBI will know these things. Just answer the questions they ask." He patted my hand that was carelessly laying on my lap. I tried to smile back, but I hadn't eaten breakfast and my stomach was tied in knots.

I followed Will through the lobby of the FBI building on West Roosevelt Road in Chicago. We ran for the elevators; I wish we had taken our time, because standing inside was my ex-husband, Jack. My stomach roiled.

"Nikki? What are you doing here?" He reached to give me a kiss, I moved away before he could, slightly leaving him hanging. I bit my lip to keep from laughing.

"Nothing you need to worry about."

Will glanced at Jack. They were the same height, roughly five-eleven. Jack returned Will's gaze. "Will?" he asked.

Will and Jack shook hands.

"So, what's this all about?" Jack demanded.

All my past guilt, all of my past anger was nothing at this moment. I no longer owed him an explanation or a single word.

"It's not your concern," I told him. Thankfully, the door to our floor opened and Will whisked me out of there. When I turned back, Jack had a confused, sad expression as the doors closed.

"When was the last time you saw him?" Will still had a hand at the small of my back as he led me toward the FBI office.

"About three months ago. The last time he saw the kids." I stopped at the FBI office door. It was thick and wide glass, with a full view of the lobby. The floor was covered in beige tile, the walls were white, and windows lined the back wall looking out over Chicago.

"It'll be okay." Will pushed open the door and led me inside. He spoke to the receptionist who had us wait in basic brown chairs.

I looked around. Basic government building. "The FBI takes up this whole floor?"

"Yes. Jack knows you're at the FBI."

I sighed audibly as we waited for my meeting.

****

The FBI Agents were Sylvia Rutger and Myles Stanton. Both wore dark blue suits; he wore black oxfords, she wore pumps. She was dark-complected, he was light.

I sat with my hands in my lap and watched as they reorganized their pile of folders, moved their coffee cups to the side and took a seat across from me. Will squeezed my hand and offered a smile, I bit my lip and looked nervous.

"So, Mrs. Page." Sylvia began the interview and I turned my gaze to her. "As you know, in the course of the investigation into the disappearance of Marcie Winkler and now Justin Able, you gave us information about an Emma and Landon Cabot." She pushed the Cabot file toward me, I opened the cover and recognized the several documents, the invoices, the signature cards, the signatures I wrote out for Andy Butcher. I nodded.

"So, you recognize all of these documents?" Silvia asked.

"Yes. I do." I was wringing my hands in my lap. Thankfully they were covered by the table top.

"How long have you worked for Justin Able?"

It should have been an easy question and yet I had to think. Julia was thirteen, I started when she was ten. "Three years." My mouth was dry, I nearly choked on my words.

Myles left his seat and headed to the bank of cabinets behind me. I turned as he handed me a glass of water. "Thanks," I murmured.

"Three years?" She took notes and looked back at me. "As his paralegal, what do you do for him?" Again, it was an easy question. This time I rambled out my duties.

"I answer client phone calls, research law, write the contracts, file subpoenas, write out the deposition questions, take notes during meetings, review case files, open and maintain client bank accounts for retainers, and hourly billing or if there's a jury award." I glanced at Will. He nodded with a smile.

Special agent Silvia Rutger pulled out the signature card from the bank account for the Cabots and slid it to me. "Did you sign that?" I picked up the signature card. I knew it wasn't my signature.

I shook my head. "No. This isn't my signature." I watched Silvia pull out another sheet of paper. It was the paper Andy Butcher had me sign my name on, multiple times. She slid it to me.

"You signed this for Detective Andy Butcher of the Lake Zurich Police Department?"

"Yes." I slid it back to her.

"So, this is the issue we have." Silvia rested her hands on the table. "We only have the one account. We are unable to enter the client system at Able, Able and Munch without a warrant. But as you stated to Detective Butcher, there was something odd in the Cabot file. We've gone through the file."

I nodded and glanced at the file under Silvia's hands.

"What do you know about Asset Investments?"

I glanced at Will. He leaned over so I could whisper in his ear. "Should I give them everything?"

He nodded.

I pulled out the folder I had, pulled out the information I was able to find on the company. "All I know is the company has a one-page website, isn't listed anywhere in the US. I finally found them incorporated in the Caymans." I pushed the information from Asset Investments to them. They both looked at me.

"You were able to find a lot," Myles said. He pushed the documents back to me.

"Yes."

They both looked at me with serious expressions. "How had you come across the company?"

I glanced at Will and he nodded. "After finding the Cabot file, my superiors, Mrs. Gertrude Munch and Mr. Hector Garcia, both asked me to find similar files to the Cabots. I did that and found all of the files had ties to Asset Investments."

This time, Silvia and Myles turned to glance at each other.

"How many files have you found?" Silvia asked.

"Twenty."

"Criteria?" Myles asked.

"Client accounts with twenty to thirty grand in billing with very little work in the files. I pulled for the last five years and found twenty clients."

Silvia slid a sheet of paper toward Will. He opened it and read the document. "It's a warrant, Nikki. They are unable to get a warrant to walk through the client files of Able, Able and Munch. But they can in the course of the investigation ask you for similar files."

I gulped, opened the file I had in front of me and pulled out the client list. I slid it to Silvia.

Both of them reviewed the list. "Each of the codes in the note field is wrong. That was something else I noted in the files," I offered and Will didn't shake his head this time.

"Anything else about this?" Myles asked.

"All of the information was entered using Justin's initials, that meant someone signed into the system as him. We click on that field and it automatically populates to the initials of the person's sign on. Also, I was listed as the paralegal on all the bank accounts and my ID was used."

Both Silvia and Myles were taking extensive notes in their notebooks. Silvia looked at me. "Did you do any work for these twenty clients?" Sylvia asked me as she ripped the page from the notepad and stuck it in their folder, one that was already very thick. I wondered what they already had.

She sat across from me with a lot of patience as I formulated my answer. "I have never met, spoken to, or conducted any business for the Cabot family until I received the custody agreement last week. And the rest of the list, the clients are unfamiliar to me as well." It always paid to be honest, even though it roiled in my belly.

"You didn't set up this bank account for the Cabot family?" Sylvia slid another document to me. It was the bank account application. I had seen hundreds of these and I held my breath as I looked at the attached copy of my ID.

I shook my head. "No. I didn't open this account."

"Is that your ID?" Myles asked this time. His voice was stern and authoritative, his face was doughy, his hair curly, and long enough to fall over his ears. He looked like a six-foot-tall hobbit.

"That's my ID."

"How does the bank have that ID?" he asked. He put his pen down and folded his hands on the table. His face softened and he smiled. I don't think he liked playing bad cop.

"I keep copies of my ID in my locked desk drawer. I open accounts all the time and rather than running to the copier when I need to send it to the bank, I have them ready."

Myles and Silvia glanced at each other.

"What is your procedure for opening an account?" Sylvia asked this time. I could feel nervous sweat bead on my lower back and under my arms.

"I call the bank. I always speak to Stuart Haines. I give him the client information. Name, address, phone number. I give him my information like always. He faxes me the account forms, I fill them in, get approval from Justin, Jared, or Mrs. Munch, depending on whose client it is. I fax the bank back with the information, including my ID and then mail them the originals. The law firm keeps all of the E-documents."

Myles took additional notes. They filled the entire page of the legal note pad. He turned over the next page and wrote additional information. His handwriting was scribbles; I couldn't read it even if it was right side up.

"And you have the only key to your desk?" Sylvia asked.

"I couldn't tell you that for certain. I have a key that I keep on my key chain. If someone wanted it and I wasn't at my desk, I suppose they could have lifted it from my purse and unlocked the drawer. I actually don't lock the drawer where I keep my purse." I frowned. I'd have to start doing that, it seemed.

"Is it common for Justin to open accounts without your knowledge or work on clients that you never, see?" Myles asked.

"It would be very rare for Justin to handle administrative functions for the client. As a paralegal, that's my responsibility. I almost always handle the bulk of the work. I write almost all the documents, always for his approval. I take customer calls because my time is billed at a lower rate than his. It's not common to have that many files opened by him and only worked by him. However, while I primarily work for him, he had—on occasion—used other paralegals for client cases. Again, I'm on all of these accounts." I pointed to the list.

I felt the weight of the folders in my bag against my leg. Silvia and Myles looked at me, surprise and shock on their faces.

"Do you have the documents for these clients?" Myles asked.

I waited for Will to say yes.

"Go ahead Nikki. The warrant covers that."

I felt bad. I hadn't given the rest of the files to Hector yet, but I pulled out the bundle I marked for the FBI; Hector's was in my car at home, and I passed the twenty client files to the agents. "All of these client files consist of high billing and low work. All of the clients in the billing system are coded incorrectly. And they are all related to Asset Investments."

"Who else knows about this?"

I no longer felt nervous, maybe now a little apprehensive as I watch Myles and Silvia scan the files.

"Hector and Mrs. Munch know that I'm looking into this and are waiting for the same files. Jared isn't fully apprised but I don't know why. And Justin wants this information, but he doesn't have access to it."

They both glanced at me. "Have you been in contact with Justin?" Silvia asked.

I shook my head. "It's more like he's been in contact with me." I gave them a brief synopsis of our phone calls. I debated with myself for a moment, whether or not to tell them about my being at Marcie's condo and seeing Justin there. How much trouble could I be in if I didn't tell them.

"There's something else," I blurted out. I told them about seeing Justin at Marcie's home and what he said.

Will looked at me with a deep frown. Silvia and Myles stared at me with a look I could only think was skepticism.

"When was this and what were you trying to accomplish?" Silvia asked.

"Saturday. And I'm trying to protect myself. It's occurred to me this week that someone is setting me up. I didn't do this." My hands trembled under the table. Will held my hand and squeezed.

"Right now, based on the signature cards, and what Mrs. Munch has told us, we're not looking at you for this. But we do think Justin implicated himself by running. What I'd like to know from you, regardless of his claiming he didn't do this. Do you think he could have? Or would you have expected Justin to do this?" Silvia asked. Her voice was calm and steady and yet it hadn't calmed me.

"He claims he didn't. I wouldn't have thought he'd do this, but I've read through all of these files. Someone did something."

When they both finished with their notes or circles or doodles, they both looked back at me. I felt my face flush.

"And he never asked you to help him open the accounts or transfer money out?" Myles asked.

I shook my head. "No. I've never seen any of those accounts. He's never asked me to move money in or out of them." I felt defeated as I leaned back in my chair.

"So why did Justin Able give the Cabot file to you? Surely he'd know you'd find something odd about it." Silvia asked incredulously.

I shook my head. "I can't say for certain that he gave me the client file. I found it in my inbox. It never felt right, from the beginning."

"Justin Able never asked you to research law, or write documents, or handle the money on any of these accounts you found?" Silvia was trying to trip me up, get me to change my answers or wear me down. Her mouth was turned down, her eyes slits as she glared at me. Will still had a firm hold of my hand.

"No. I have a spreadsheet I use when I'm handed a new client with work to complete. I mark it there so I know what's still outstanding and what's been finished. I've never dealt with those twenty clients."

"You could've erased them from the list," Ms. Smarty pants groused.

"I'm sure your computer forensic tech will be able to prove whether or not I've deleted the names from my spreadsheet or worked on any of those accounts. All he has to do is spot check the backup files. From what I understand, they're good for a year before they're dumped." I offered Silvia a smile and her partner bit his tongue to hold back his laugh.

"So, Justin wants your help? Exactly what is he asking of you?" Myles asked.

I exhaled and wrung my hands in my lap. "At first, he wanted me to get at the files. He needed the account numbers. He still says he needs the account numbers to help prove his innocence. He still claims he didn't do this."

"Have you agreed to help him?" Silvia asked.

I shook my head. "No. I'm looking into the client files per Hector's request, but I have no intention of helping Justin." I glanced at the copies of their file, still wanting to know what was in there.

"Do you think Justin did this?"

"Someone forged my signature; someone could have forged his. But realistically, he ran, he's asking for the account numbers, and he cheated on his wife with his secretary, in his office."

Silvia cocked an eyebrow. "You were the one who discovered that?"

"Yep. Marcie went missing the next day and now Justin." I scowled.

"Is Justin with Marcie?" Myles asked.

"I don't know. Maybe. He tells me he isn't. I have a hard time believing that Marcie's disappearance had nothing to do with the Cabot file. Everything happened after that."

"Is there anything else you can tell us about this?" Myles asked.

I looked at Will and he moved in closer. "I only have suppositions. No proof. They have the files now."

He nodded. "I think Mrs. Page has no other evidence to give. Everything else is merely supposition and can't be proven."

"Have you told Justin what's going on in the office?" Silvia asked.

"Someone else is doing that. I don't have proof of anything," I said.

"We're going to officially ask to trace your phone so that we can track Justin. If he calls again, tell him it will be in his best interest to turn himself in. It's not looking good for him," Myles said.

I nodded. "If he calls, I'll let him know, again. But I would like a warrant before you mess with my phone."

"I guess for now, that's it. We'll contact you with a warrant for your phone. And if we have additional questions, we'll let you know. Don't leave town."

****

We left the FBI offices and I could almost breathe until we came to the building lobby. Jack was sitting on one of the benches, peering over a newspaper. When he saw us coming out of the elevator, he bolted to us.

"Why were you visiting the FBI?" he asked as he steered me away from Will. Will followed closely with even, easy steps.

"I'm not in trouble, so you don't need to worry about getting the kids dropped in your lap." Though I didn't think that was his major concern.

"You're too honest to get into trouble. This has to do with Justin Able, doesn't it?" Jack demanded. I was sick of his demands, and his cheating and his lying. I pulled my arm away.

"The kids won't be plopped into your perfect home. I'm fine." I turned and began to walk away.

Jack reached for me and spun me around. "I'm worried. I'm allowed to be worried about you." He pushed loose hair around my ear, I jerked my head away.

"You lost that right when you slept with your secretary." I could see something in his face: embarrassment, guilt, remorse? I held my breath.

"Nikki. Not that, not now. I just want to make sure you're okay." He was about to put his hand on my shoulder and stopped, letting his arm fall to his side.

"It's about Justin Able but that's all I can tell you."

This time I let him touch my upper arm. He smiled at me, looked at Will and nodded. "If you need anything…" he didn't finish, but I nodded. I began to step away from him but turned back.

"Congrats on the baby." He seemed genuinely surprised that I knew; he should have been sorry he hadn't told me himself. I bet he even wondered who told me.

Will put a strong arm around my shoulder. He led me away from Jack and to the door to the parking garage at the end of the lobby.

When we made it to the car, he made sure I was safely tucked inside and pulled out.

"For what it's worth, he seemed genuinely upset that you could be in trouble." Will looked both ways and headed toward the expressway. I glanced at the clock. It was noon; I expected traffic on I90 would be ok.

"He's just worried I'll go to jail and he'll get stuck with the kids. His baby mama doesn't like them." I watched the city pass before me, a blurry gray. Even after meeting, after getting Myles Stanton's card and promising to call if Justin called me again, the sourness in my belly was just as strong as it was this morning when I arrived at the FBI offices.

I remained quiet throughout the drive to the Northwest suburbs, my thoughts racing. I didn't realize we had arrived at my house until I saw the yellowish stucco and blue French shutters. "Thanks. You were really helpful today." I squeezed his hand.

He followed me to the side door. I opened it and stood there with my hand on the curved burnished copper handle.

Will kissed me lightly on my cheek and lingered so close I could smell his spicy scent. He smiled and pulled away, placing his hands on my shoulders. "Call me any time about this. Call me any time not about this. We used to hang out a lot in our younger days. I miss that."

He kissed my forehead and headed to his Jaguar. I watched him back down the oddly curved driveway and head out. I called the office and let them know I was working from home the rest of the day.

CHAPTER 16

I liked the quiet of the house in the afternoon when the sun was still out. It felt warm and soothing, though I knew in minutes the kids would come home with their welcome chaos and that would change. Until I realized Julia had detention all week.

I took out my computer, pulled up my work, and began to sort through the next assigned document. This time it was for Jared, a simple custodian agreement for parents who were attending a wedding out of town. I was surprised he handed this to me; this was a standard document we had on file and should have been given to the parents a long time ago.

Regardless, I pulled it up as my phone rang. I didn't read the screen, just swiped and answered.

"Hello?" I saved the document and printed it off.

"Nikki?" I had dated Jack for two years in college before we became engaged and we were married for twenty years. I hadn't ever forgotten his voice, the sound of it when it was just the two of us, or when he was concerned, really concerned—not the fake he managed as our marriage crumbled. My heart skipped a beat.

"Jack." I couldn't retract the coolness of my voice, even a year after the divorce. I couldn't remove the icy feelings, even when his voice was warm with concern.

"What's going on?"

I finally let out the stale air I was holding in while I waited for him to speak. "It's complicated and I'm not sure if I should reveal what's going on."

"You're still…" I knew how he had planned to finish that. I was still the mother of his kids. But with the pregnant girlfriend, he hadn't acted much like a father to them.

"I'm sorry, Jack, but it's complicated. It has to do with Justin. It's a police investigation."

"It looked like an FBI investigation to me. If you're in trouble, I can help you. I'm a defense attorney for fuck's sake!" His emotion about my situation surprised me. It was bad enough my kids were concerned, but his worry was something I didn't want hanging over me. I gave him just the basics.

"Listen, I appreciate your concern, but it appears that Justin was illegally handling the money. And it seems like

I was brought into it without my knowledge. I have a lawyer and it will sort itself out." My voice had risen higher than typical when I was upset or angry and that left me embarrassed. I never wanted to show Jack my vulnerability. Not ever again.

"Nikki." He seemed to be formulating his question or debating whether he should ask. He had been great at patience and then springing his attack; it made him a great lawyer and a shitty husband. "Has he been found, at least?" he finally asked, though I didn't think that was what he wanted to know.

"No. He's alive and he's trying to get me to help him. He claims he's innocent. I'm not sure what I think."

"Do you need any help? Any extra representation."

For whatever reason, I laughed. For the first time since I found that file and entered my time into the invoicing system, I really laughed. I don't think his offer was meant to be funny, but the irony of him asking, now of all times, was too much.

"Glad I could help," he groused.

"I'm sorry, Jack. It's..."

"If I gave you that kind of caring and emotion we'd still be married," he said quietly.

I raised an eyebrow, surprised by his insight. I didn't want to tackle the breakdown of our marriage. Not here, and not again in the future. He moved on and I was working toward the same thing.

Rather than antagonize him further, I said, "If I did need help, I'm pretty sure I wouldn't come to you, though I really do appreciate the offer and the concern." As I pulled up the next document in my work cue, another standard document the firm has on file for small clients that didn't need customization, I began to feel like I've received a demotion at work. I was trained to write legal documents; this was reviewing documents that didn't need reviewing.

"I want you to tell me if something happens. I can help."

I pulled away from the disappointing work load, returning to Jack. He wants to help. I appreciate the effort but realistically, he was good with the money for the kids, but not so much for the time with them.

"I know. Thanks again for your concern. But this, all I can really say is, it's about money."

Now he laughed. "It's always about money."

****

It took the rest of the afternoon to review and prepare the documents I brought home. I printed, sorted, and stowed them inside the client file folders and slipped them in my bag for the morning. Julia would have been home an hour ago, but there was that pesky detention.

While I waited, I started on my big project.

I opened the spreadsheet of odd client accounts. I had marked each payment with the date, account numbers, whether it was a wire transfer or check, and what work was completed. The newest field I added was a simple yes or no to any association to Asset Investments. Eighteen of the twenty client accounts had a "yes".

Why not the other two?

I re-read those two client files; they clients were linked to Investments Unlimited.

Both!

After pulling all of these client accounts, there was a gut feeling that was growing stronger. I had no reason up until now to perform a background check on these clients. But the more I dug, the more unusual data I was finding made me wonder if the clients and their accounts were fake.

I started with London and Emma Cabot. While I had done a simple search of them already, I decided to go off procedure and complete a full background check on them. I opened the background review software and started with their credit history.

There was something odd right off the bat as I pulled down the first five clients on my list. While I had names, ages, and genders, I didn't find credit history filled with mortgages, credit cards, bank accounts, or car loans.

I searched those first five clients on social media. And while the clients were almost all over forty, which could explain some of it, I came up dry for all of them. I pulled the background checks for rest of the twenty clients, printed what I found, and noted what I couldn't find. I updated the spreadsheet with additional notes, glanced at the clock, and realized Julia would be home within minutes.

As I had done previously, I placed all of my work in my bag and hid it in my closet along with my computer. I heard the garage door open and went down to meet Julia in the kitchen.

She looked at me. "You're home?" She squinted her eyes and planted her hands on her hips as she waited for an answer.

"I had an early meeting downtown. Came home to finish my other work. Got homework?" I asked nonchalantly. Julia knew she was still in trouble for gambling on school grounds and she watched me with caution, not knowing when or if I'd spring a punishment on her.

I pulled out a donut from the box on the kitchen island and handed it to her. She took it gratefully and dropped her backpack on the floor. "I have homework," she said and she took a big bite.

"I expect the dishwasher empty when you're done." I smiled and she groaned around a mouthful of donut.

My phone rang. I hesitated, worried it was Jack again. This time it was Will; I smiled. It must have looked weird on my face—Julia gave me a questioning look before heading to her homework.

I chuckled and answered.

"Hey. How's it going? You feeling okay after this morning?" Will was stirring something in a cup. The sound was crystal clear as if he were here with me.

"I'm okay. Worked from home this afternoon."

He was silent for a minute, I assumed taking a sip of whatever he was drinking.

"How's the research going?"

"It's odd." I hesitated, as I hadn't given anything to Hector or Mrs. Munch yet. But then, he was my lawyer and the only one I completely trusted. "Well, I have dates, times, and work completed. I decided to pull a credit report and background check on the first five client accounts."

"Huh? Do you normally run background checks on clients?"

"No. But I was thinking, what if the clients are fake as well as the files."

"OK. And did the credit checks illuminate that for you?"

"I think so. I personally have more than one bank account and more than one credit card. I have social media. There's hardly anything online for these clients."

"Are you going to tackle the other... fifteen?"

I let out a deep breath. "I probably should, but I thought five would be enough to take to Hector, at least for now."

He was silent again. A soft female voice spoke to him. He pulled the phone away from his mouth and answered before returning to me. "Sorry. Still the work day. Have you told the office yet?"

"No. I'm going tomorrow as I normally would. I'll give Hector and Mrs. Munch what I've discovered and they can do what they want with it. If they're in on it, who knows what's gonna happen. But at least I did my job." I sighed. My stomach churned; I hadn't eaten much in the last few days. I wasn't sure when I'd feel hungry again.

"I'm not sure a pattern will help Justin."

"No, it won't. But it will prove money laundering or embezzlement. I'm not exactly sure what was going on. Not until I find out where the money came from. For all I know, they could be real clients and Justin was bilking them and stealing the money."

"Any other similarities?"

"Eighteen clients had some contact with a company called Asset Investments. And two of the clients were associated with Investments Unlimited."

"And have you found them?"

"Asset Investments is in the Caymans, nothing substantial online. I just found the other company, haven't looked into it yet. If I was a betting individual, I'd say they were Caymans as well."

He was thoughtful for a moment or maybe was sipping his drink. "Promise me you'll be careful. If Justin's behind it, he had help. If he's not, someone else in the firm is doing this. They won't want to be caught. Call me if something happens."

"I will. I promise."

We talked easily together for a few minutes longer and after I said goodbye, I wondered how our once close relationship became so lost.

****

Once I placed the casserole in front of Jacob, he hunkered over his plate to better shovel in his food. Julia and I looked at him and glanced at each other before shrugging simultaneously.

Jacob was halfway through his dinner before I sat down and he finished before I had my second bite.

"Homework," he said when he stood up. He rinsed his plate, put it in the dishwasher, and ran upstairs. It took all of five minutes.

"Damn," I said as I watched after him.

"Damn," Julia said and took her first bite.

I shook my head and chuckled before eating my dinner. But I didn't do more than play with my food. I still wasn't hungry and still knew I should run a few more clients.

I left Julia to her homework, or her television show. Either way, I needed her busy as I pulled up the next name on my list. It was the Hillary family: mother, father, two boys. I had worked out the kinks on my first go-around with the Cabots and pulled their credit history as well as their background information. I filled in the gaps of my spreadsheet. adding columns and noting that I would need to pull the account numbers and see where they originated.

I had smoothly pulled background information for another ten clients and was starting the eleventh when the doorbell rang. It was after 9 p.m. I cautiously walked downstairs and answered the door.

Justin was staring at me. He was in his casual wear, sweats and a sweatshirt, with stains across his chest. His hair was unkempt, the shoelace on his left gym shoe was undone. His disappearance was clearly taking a toll on him.

He didn't wait for me to invite him in, rather he pushed past me and began pacing my kitchen.

"Where are the account numbers?" he growled.

Calmly, and I can't believe that I stayed that way, I pulled out the remaining casserole and put it in the microwave. I grabbed my phone, texted Will and let him know that Justin was here. I didn't yet send it and held my phone to Justin.

"I'll hit send if you piss me off. You can have some dinner. Take a shower if you want. And then you leave. I have no account numbers. But I do think I know what you did."

He looked at me. His eyes were wild, his mouth in a snarl. "I didn't do this. Someone else did." He blinked rapidly when the food was done. I placed it in front of him with a fork. He shoveled the food in as if he hadn't eaten in days. I'm guessing that was probably true.

"What did they do?" he asked.

"Who's they?"

He pushed the empty container away from him and slouched in the chair. "I don't know." He ran his fingers through his hair. "Jared, maybe. Marcie. I don't know who did this. I've been listening to Marcie but she seems to be making it harder for me to find out what's going on."

He wiped his hand across his mouth and then down his sweatshirt. I grimaced. "The only way to prove your innocence is to turn yourself in. Defend yourself. If you didn't do this, defend yourself."

"Nikki. I can't get in to get the files. I know if I could see them carefully, review them, I could find the proof. They can compare signatures, look at my schedule and compare it to what's in the system. I didn't do this."

"You keep saying that, but you offer no proof." I may have sounded calm, but I felt hysterical. My breathing was heavy, I was tired and desperately wanted to get under the covers and hide from all of this.

Justin stood and paced the length of my kitchen and into my den. To make a circuit, he walked around the table and around the sofa and back again, turning at the island at the center of the kitchen. I was getting dizzy watching him.

"I've gotta think. Gotta think." He tapped his fist against his temple.

"Justin, who wants you out? Why this way?"

"Money. It was always about the money. Bet whoever did it thought Justin would be good and caught by now." He pounded his fist on the stone island and laughed. I'm not an expert but he seemed to becoming unhinged. I glanced at the ceiling as if I could see through the floors to my kids, safe in their rooms. But I didn't feel safe with Justin here and now. I held out my phone.

"I'm pushing the send. It'll alert my lawyer who'll alert the police. You need to leave."

"No! Nikki, please, just tell me what's in the files!" Justin grabbed my arms and shook me, my phone slipped to the floor. Again, I glanced at the ceiling where the kids' rooms were. I hoped they'd stay put out of harm as I braced myself for an escape.

Justin wasn't himself, at least not the self I knew from work. When he stopped shaking me, his hands were still tight on my upper arms and my hands continued to tremble. He looked at me pleadingly.

I choked back the tears, took a deep breath.

"There's... there's invoicing that doesn't match the work completed. Notes that make no sense. Clients with light backgrounds. Companies that don't exist."

He looked at me. Confused, or in the throes of a deep though. "Embezzlement?"

"Money laundering?" I asked.

His jaw tightened and he gripped my upper arms tighter. "My name is attached to all of the files?"

"We both are."

"You claim you didn't do it. So why don't you believe me?"

He let go of my arms. I gulped in air; I must have been holding my breath. I watched him pace liked a caged animal, as he ran his hands through his hair, that in a week had grown below the tops of his ears.

It took all I had to remain standing, my legs were now shaky and weak.

"I don't believe you because you have access to my desk. To my records. I work mostly for you." I couldn't control my voice. I took a deep breath and watched Justin take another spin around my downstairs. "You need to stop and go to the police!" I gripped his arms and pulled him toward me. I held him firmly as I looked into his eyes. He could barely make eye contact with me. "Call the police."

"I need to go."

He yanked his arms from my grasp and ran from the house, leaving the door open. I watched him run into the moonlit night. I couldn't even tell which way he went once he left my yard.

Footsteps padded behind me. I slammed the door shut and locked it tight.

"Mom?" Julia stood there in her unicorn footie pajamas. Even though she was thirteen she sometimes still looked like my baby. "Was that your boss?" She had tears in her eyes, she was shaking.

I put my arms around her. "Yeah. I can't help him if he won't help himself. And now he seems to have nothing left to lose."

"What did he do?" She lay her head on my shoulder, sweet and innocent like she used to do when she was a baby, before she learned how to con her eighth-grade class.

"He stole money from the company and hid it somewhere. He was caught and he ran away."

"Why did he come here?" She buried her head on my chin.

"He wants me to help prove he didn't do what everyone says he did. But there's overwhelming proof."

"So you're not going to help him?" She looked up at me confused by my reluctance.

"It's illegal for me to give him what he wants me to give him. But I'm wondering if someone might have set him up."

"So, you'll help him?"

"No. Not really. I can't give him what I have. I tell him as little as possible. I could get in trouble if I give him more." I kissed her cheek. She hugged me tight.

"Dad's girlfriend is pregnant."

I sighed and wondered how she heard as I brushed her hair with my hands. "I know. I heard that too."

"He doesn't love us anymore, does he?"

I didn't know what to tell her. I wish I could tell her he did, that he wanted his children in his life, but he hadn't made them a priority. I had to believe that in the end, he'd realize what he was doing. Maybe not.

"I know he loves the three of you. He's just not doing a good job of showing it." I wished I believed what I was saying, but I really didn't know if he cared.

"This week sucks."

"Yeah. This week sucks."

CHAPTER 17

When the alarm blasted through my dark room, my heart pounded, and my hands shook. I almost hit snooze and skipped my workout. But I needed to get it in, to feel the treadmill under my feet, the sweat run down my back and feel my legs go rubbery. I slammed my palm against the clock and tossed off the blankets. I still had to drag myself out of bed.

The run, even on the treadmill, was jarring and woke me quickly. I ate breakfast while I cooled down, and when I was mostly done sweating, I showered and dressed.

There were only three other cars in the parking lot. One belonged to Jared, one to Hector, and the other I assumed was Mrs. Munch's. The lot was covered in puddles, and I hopped over several or skirted around them as I made my way inside.

When I got to my desk, I pulled off my jacket and tossed it on my chair. While my computer loaded, I prepared the client files I collected, and spreadsheet I created. I dropped the information into two separate envelopes and sealed them both.

Hector was already on the phone when I knocked on the door jamb. It sounded like he was talking to his wife, Maria, and I found the way they were with each other endearing. When he hung up, he smiled. "Sorry. Forgot my lunch today. You're in early."

I held up the envelope. "I found twenty odd accounts. These are the first five that I picked apart."

Hector took the folder, unsealed it, and slid the items out. He stared at the spreadsheet first. After getting his bearings, he pulled out the Cabot file and read the background check. He looked up at me.

"Are they all like this?"

"Yes. The first five had light histories. The account numbers are on the spreadsheet. I think the money needs to be traced back to whoever actually paid the invoices. My first thought is a company called Asset Investments. Ever hear of it?"

He stayed still as he read the spreadsheet and then turned his attention to the client file. "You think the invoice payment is generated from there?" Hector caught on to what I was thinking, Asset Investments might be funneling the money to Able, Able, and Munch, but he was keeping his feelings close to the vest by not making eye contact with me. Either he already knew this because he was involved or he knew something I didn't and my information confirmed what he already knew.

I nodded. "The first five clients had mentions of the company. Nothing specific."

"I wonder why this came out now," Hector murmured.

I didn't have an answer for him, and he really wasn't asking. "I have no proof, but I think someone wanted us to know and gave me the Cabot file."

"Sure," Hector said as he turned the page and read additional information in the files.

"It's always about the money. Maybe someone wasn't getting their fair share and decided to come forward."

"It's always money." His voice was quiet as he immersed himself in my notes.

His finger traced one of the rows in the spreadsheet, then he stopped and flipped through a client folder in his pile until he found what he was looking for.

"Asset Investments, yes," Hector murmured to himself.

"Did you find something?"

I had seen all of the information that he now possessed, but I wasn't sure what it was that he saw. While the client files were odd, nothing gave me an "ah ha" moment that would make my jaw tense and get lost in my thoughts like it did for him.

"I don't think he did this," I said, unsure of what Hector was surmising that I had missed.

He glanced at me. "Mrs. Munch and I, we don't think you did anything wrong."

"I think Justin was framed."

Hector shook his head. "I don't know Nikki. I just don't know." He looked back at the pile of papers and then back at me. "Thanks again for all of this work. Finish the rest of the twenty when you get a chance. The more we have, the better." I stood to leave.

"If you want me to keep going I will. I would like to trace the payments, but I don't have access to that."

"I'll see that you get it. I … how was the FBI yesterday?" I didn't think he was all that interested; I guessed his mind was still on the client files on his desk.

"I told them what I knew. Gave them the files per their warrant."

"Yeah, okay. Thanks again Nikki." But Hector was already pouring over the spreadsheet again.

****

My fingers flew across the keyboard as I worked through a to-do list that had grown quite large overnight, full of tasks for Jared and Mrs. Munch. . After I perused each file and took preliminary notes, I began drafting my first document.

After my first hours, I felt as though my workload was almost insurmountable; I wasn't through half of my first document.

As I finally sunk into the work, checking off each point Mrs. Munch wanted done, the phone rang for the fourth time that morning. It was another client, this one asking about work in progress. I was grateful to not have to answer another call about Justin. I was tired of skirting the line between professional courtesy and outright lying. After I hung up, I leaned back against my chair and closed my eyes.

"Busy day," Wilma said. I sat up and looked at her. She wasn't the only one watching me. Sheila and Patti Anne looked concerned. It was nice to have some friends in the firm who weren't trying to implicate me in a crime. But would I know it if Wilma, Shelia, and Patti Anne were part of this. My gut told me no.

"Yeah. Busy day."

"What happened at the FBI, hon?" Patti Anne asked me.

I shrugged. "There's not much to tell them. They have everything we have. I think they just want to sort through what's there and determine what's been done or hasn't been done." I sighed.

"What did Justin do? We've heard embezzlement, laundering, possible murder." I glanced at Sheila. She was often the most gullible of the four of us.

"We… I don't know. I just don't know what he did. There's…" I looked past Patti Anne, across the aisle where Hector was rushing down the hallway. I glanced at my friends and shook my head. "There's odd accounts with billing that doesn't correspond to completed work. There's several accounts, but we just don't know what they mean."

Patti Anne scooted herself to me, still in her desk chair. "Oh honey." She placed her arms around me. If I could have, I would have stayed there in her protective embrace. Any thoughts my friends were involved drifted off. Reluctantly, I pulled away a short moment after.

"I'm fine. Really. It's stressful and weird, but I'm dealing." I offered a smile but it felt forced. I knew I wasn't really fine and all I wanted to do was escape to my house and sleep.

My seat mates separated as Adrienne Mox strolled down the aisle. "We need to talk," she said. I rolled my eyes and followed her into the empty cafeteria.

Adrienne turned to face me and slapped my cheek. I was so shocked; I placed my hand on my cheek and gaped at her with an open mouth. "What the hell was that?"

"What are you doing?" Adrienne's voice was barely an angry whisper.

"You hit me, so I could ask the same question. What the hell is the matter with you?"

Adrienne paced in a three-foot section of the cafeteria. If I stuck my leg out, I could have tripped her. I bit my tongue instead.

"You were at her house with Justin!"

I leaned against the table and crossed my arms against my chest. "Who's watching her apartment and why?"

It took all I had to not shake, to not squeak my voice, to convince her I was in charge. Adrienne looked at me.

"This is all your fault." She gritted her teeth. She was seething and I couldn't help but laugh.

"Please don't deflect this on me. I know you and Joy are planning on framing me for the client accounts. And if that's the case, that means you put the Cabot file in my inbox." I pointed to her. Adrienne flinched.

The cafeteria door opened; Wilma peaked inside. I turned, shook my head and she backed out and closed the door.

"What the hell did you think would happen when you gave me that file? I'd just do the work and it would be okay? Someone wanted that file out. Who told you to put it in my inbox?"

Adrienne's face burned brightly and she shook her head. I knew I was right when she wrapped her arms around herself. Her lip trembled and she bowed her head, defeated.

"Who?" I demanded.

"Marcie asked me to drop it in your box," she said above a whisper.

"And you didn't question why she was bringing me into this? Why she had to implicate me?" I stepped away from her, turned and faced the opposite of the room. I didn't think the deep breaths I was taking would reduce the anger I was feeling.

"You never should have told the police about the Cabot file. Marcie would here and fine if you kept your mouth shut."

"If you didn't put the file in my inbox, Marcie would also be fine."

Adrienne didn't respond, and hadn't made a movement to leave. When I turned, she wiped a tear from her cheek, smudging her makeup. "What's going on?" she asked with a small, childlike voice.

I dropped my arms, they hung loosely at my sides. Seeing Adrienne so lost made me lose my own fight. I had the sudden feeling we were both being used.

"I was going to ask you the same thing. Where is Marcie? Why did she ask you to put the file in my inbox? What are you telling her about what's going on around here? And who told you I was with Justin at her apartment?"

Adrienne shook her head again. "I can't tell you." Her voice was so soft and quiet I moved closer to her.

"What was that?"

"I can't tell you, because I don't know. Marcie won't tell me. She's in danger and she won't tell me how to help her," Adrienne cried out. For the first time, I saw her worry for her friend and maybe a little remorse.

I touched Adrienne's shoulder and squeezed. "You know more than you're telling me. You could help Marcie by telling the police, or tell Hector or Mrs. Munch what you know."

At Mrs. Munch's name, Adrienne shook her head. "No."

"Then talk to the police. Tell Justin to do the same. Call the FBI, tell Hector. I don't care. Just tell them what you know. And whoever told you I was at Marcie's tell them I wanted to talk to her and I wanted to find Justin. But guess what? He showed up. He let me in and we took a look around. Her place was destroyed. But her safe seemed intact."

I pulled away from the table. Adrienne gave me a questioning look. "Safe?"

"Yeah. The safe I found. You both know what's going on and you need to tell the police."

"Nikki!"

I turned.

"I can't tell you where she is. But she's fine, for now."

"Tell her to go to the police. They can help her. You can help her."

Adrienne stared at her feet. "I just need you to…"

"You need me to what?"

She glanced back up and scowled. "Stop talking to the police, to the FBI. You're getting in the way!"

My jaw clenched shut with tension. When I could pry it open, I marched up to Adrienne, cornering her.

"*I'm* getting in the way?" I took a deep breath. "Ask her why she wanted me to have the file. Ask her who told her to get it to me. And then ask yourself why *you* agreed to do this. You're just as responsible for the embezzlement and money laundering." At that suggestion, Adrienne's eyes widened, her jaw dropped.

"That's not it. That's Justin. That's what he did and now she's in danger. She asked to help because she had to leave. She's hiding but if she comes out, she put herself in danger."

I had worried that might be the case, but I didn't think Marcie left because she thought she was in danger. The one thing I was sure of was that someone would come after her.

"I heard you and Joy, at her car the other day."

Adrienne began to tremble. "Marcie doesn't deserve this," she whispered.

"And your solution is to frame me?"

She stared at me but still admitted nothing.

"I know what you're planning for me. I suggest you find another option and leave me alone. If you hit me again, or yell and me again, I'll report you to HR. If the FBI comes to me again, I'll be sure to mention this discussion with them."

I turned and walked away, Adrienne was softly crying, slumped against the wall of the cafeteria. I didn't look back.

I didn't return to my desk and took a few minutes to walk the perimeter of the four buildings as I cleared my head. When I returned to my desk, I shook my head at my seat mates as I logged into my computer and pulled up the tedious document, I had been working on for Mrs. Munch. But my focus wasn't there and had to re-read the first paragraph of the document for a third time when my work phone rang.

I grabbed it and answered, not paying attention to the caller ID or the time. "Nicole Page. How can I help you?"

"Nicole Page. This is Emma Cabot. I need to talk to you." I had begun to believe that Emma Cabot and the others were fictional characters. Maybe they were. Maybe it was someone pretending. Either way, my stomach churned when the woman on the phone told me who she was. After what I had found (or not found) online, it couldn't really be Emma Cabot.

Could it?

"Yes. Mrs. Cabot. What can I assist you with today?" I said when I finally found my voice. I was embarrassed by how it quivered when I spoke. I pulled up the Cabot client file and stared at the screen; numbers and letters jumped in front of me and I felt nauseated.

"I know you've been looking into me. I think it's time you stopped."

My throat felt dry, my mouth parched. I could barely speak. "I'm sorry, but I'm not sure what you're talking about."

"You've been wading in some serious shit, Nicole Page. Quit your job, go on vacation. Forget you ever heard about me."

"What is Asset Investments?" That seemed to be the glue that held most of the clients together. I could hear her audibly gasp when I asked. She began to laugh but it sounded angry.

"You need to leave it be. It would be a shame if Emily had to care for Jacob and Julia."

The woman who claimed to be Emma Cabot slammed down the receiver, it seemed to reverberate through my body.

Mrs. Cabot is real. She just threatened me. Why?

I ran from my desk with my cell phone, leaving anxious looks behind and dialed Will.

"I thought the clients might not have been real people. But she called me. Emma Cabot threatened me," I said.

"What did she say?" Will asked with alarm in his voice.

"She knows I'm looking into her. Thought it would be a shame if Emily had to care for Jacob and Julia."

I sat in my car watching other employees exit the building or re-enter from lunch. They were light, happy, seemingly stress free. I felt the tears burn my eyes.

"It's more than Justin and Marcie. And it's someone who knows you well. I suggest you be careful, with everyone there and not tell anyone what you know."

I told him about my encounter with Adrienne Mox.

"The gossip?"

I nodded, felt foolish and then answered. "Yes. She blames me."

"She's feeling guilty. I'm going to call Andy Butcher and get a restraining order against Emma Cabot. You call the FBI and let them know what's going on. They need to know about Adrienne Mox."

"Okay. I just feel so…"

"I'm sorry you're going through this. I hate to say it but I think it's time to look for a new job."

I chuckled, cracked under the stress.

"It will be okay. I promise you that."

"I know. I don't think the police think I did this. It's just… the threat."

"I'll take care of the legal documents; you inform the FBI. If you need me to come over tonight, I can."

"Thanks, Will."

"You're on the right track and someone is scared."

"Yeah." I sighed.

"Be careful."

****

After hanging up with Will I called Myles Stanton. He answered quickly. "Mrs. Page. I'm glad you called. I was just about to contact you. How can I help you?"

"Justin's still calling me, he came to my house last night. He wants the files I've been collecting to try and prove his innocence. I told him no. And this morning, I was threatened by the client whose file started this all. Emma Cabot."

It came out in a string of consciousness. I took a deep breath to catch up. Myles typed on his keyboard. "I'm glad you called. While I can't tell you the specifics, I do want you to know that what you gave us has sped up our process."

"Okay?"

"Mrs. Page. I have a warrant to trace your phone. I would like to come out and do that, especially since you heard from Emma Cabot. I assume you, as we did, thought all of the accounts were fake. It's disconcerting that these might be real clients. Do you concur?"

I took a deep breath and let it out fast. "I still think they're fake accounts. It could be anyone pretending to be Emma Cabot." My voice was still shaky and my hands trembled as I watched several co-workers pull into the parking lot and enter the building.

"May I come by tonight and put in the bug? I really want to make sure you're safe."

"Yeah, whatever." I sighed.

He typed something on his keyboard.

"Mrs. Page. You receiving this file has put you in danger. Is there someplace you could go that would be safe? Maybe take a vacation, away from work?"

"I can't. I have kids!"

"I suppose that would be difficult." He was quiet for a moment. "I suggest maybe have the local police complete safety drive bys around your neighborhood. I could set that up for you."

"That I can get behind." The thought my kids were in danger sat in the pit of my gut. I ran through all the times they were in public and vulnerable. I might ask a friend to pick Julia up from school every day.

"What you discovered seemed to upset someone. I implore you to be vigilant and careful. Watch your back. Would it help if we assign a body guard to you?"

"That might make it worse. I think I'll get someone to pick up my daughter from school. My lawyer is putting together documentation for a restraining order against Emma Cabot, whoever she may be."

"I strongly suggest we take you to a safe house. With your children."

I thought of Emily away at school. Julia who walked home every day, Jacob, his own car."

"I'll think about it. I'm pretty sure it's someone in the office. Someone knows I'm working on this. I suspect you have enough to get a warrant and pull the files. I want this over. I have children." I so badly wanted to scream, so badly wished I had an old-fashioned phone so I could hang up on him.

"Have you told Justin Able to turn himself in?" Myles asked.

"Repeatedly. There was something else."

"Yes?"

I told him about Adrienne Mox and my confrontation with her less than an hour ago.

"She gave you the folder? She's helping Marcie?"

"Yes."

"Thank you for that information. I can't speak directly about her interview, but that does help us. I wish there was more I could do for you. We're limited in what we're able to pull. But this, could help us make additional connections.

So glad to help.

"And you'll send an agent to track my phone?"

"We will. If the local police can't help with additional drivebys, I'll try to get someone from our end. It's not our jurisdiction. In the meantime, please, please watch yourself."

My stomach rumbled; I had missed lunch. I left my car and walked to the pond on the edge of the parking lot still connected to Myles Stanton. I watched a goose fly above me.

"Thank you. I appreciate your help."

"I do wish I could tell you more or help you more securely. And as always, please tell Justin to come in. He could clear this all up."

"I'm starting to think he isn't the problem. That he's just as much of a victim as I am." My hand shook as I held the phone.

"You have evidence it's not Justin?"

"Gut feeling. He seems genuinely upset and confused by the whole thing. I think it would be in everyone's best interest to consider he might not be the one laundering and embezzling money."

There was more typing. "We are looking at everyone. I never commit to one suspect right away. He could have been framed. Not likely. If he calls again, implore him to come back to answer our questions." He sighed and typed and then said, "Call me anytime."

"Thanks again."

It was past my lunch hour. I was unsettled, almost afraid to go back to work. I called Will.

"How did it go?"

"Pretty much call the LZPD, get additional drivebys. They'll track my phone and if LZPD can't help, they'll try."

"And Adrienne?"

"I think it clarified something for Myles. The FBI thinks I should leave."

"It's not feasible with the kids. I have the request for a restraining order at the police department and Andy will send out cruisers. Maybe talk to Emily, make her aware. And Julia…" He didn't finish.

"I'm thinking of having someone pick her up after school."

"If you need help with securing the house let me know. I can help. But in the meantime, I think you should limit who and what you talk about at work."

"It's time to find a new job."

"Probably."

I didn't feel any better after hanging up with him. I walked through the back hallway that led directly to my cubicle. It was quiet as I moved through the office, and I thought I could feel all of their eyes on me, as if I were the center of what was happening.

Mrs. Munch was near my section of cubicles, it appeared without purpose. I'd never known her to go wandering aimlessly through the department while visiting. Today, she watched me intently as I made my way down the aisle to my desk. I had expected her to follow me there, but she didn't. I logged back in to the computer but felt no desire to work. Instead, I grabbed m lunch and ran to the lunchroom to see if I could force myself to eat.

CHAPTER 18

I played with my salad and took a drink of my pop. The cafeteria, usually packed between noon and one, was nearly empty. I spied Jared at the far end beside the patio doors. It was November, and the wind was chilly. No one would brave the outside patio until the first warm day in March.

Jared ate his sandwich, slowly, methodically. I wondered if he counted how many times he chewed. Each bite seemed specifically planned. When he was done with his sandwich, he opened the bag of chips. One at a time; another long bout of chewing before swallowing.

He finished the bag, balled it up and laid it on the plate where his sandwich had been. Jared pressed down the edges of the lid on his fountain pop and sipped. When he finished, he pulled his dessert closer and began to nibble away at what appeared to be a slice of chocolate cake. I looked away, unable to watch his methodical eating any longer. It was making anxious and impatient.

I looked down at my half-eaten sandwich, no chips, and a bottle of water. When I glanced back up, Jared was putting his garbage in the can, one item at a time. He placed his cleared tray on top of the can and headed out of the cafeteria.

The anxiety left me no longer hungry. I wrapped the other half of my sandwich, stuck it in my bag and tossed the rest of my items in the trash. Without knowing why, or maybe it was the extra energy I needed to release, I followed Jared. He walked toward the left which led to building four. I sat on one of the couches outside of the cafeteria and took out my phone. While I pretended to surf the internet, I took furtive glances toward him. He was waiting at the entrance to the passageway between the two buildings. He glanced at his phone, looked up and smiled at the woman who approached him. She was wearing a red scarf that covered most of her brown hair and wide rimmed sunglasses that hid most of her face. Though I couldn't make out who she was, I knew it wasn't his wife. Sherry Able was shorter and thicker than this woman and was perfectly blonde. To be perfectly honest, I wasn't surprised, disgusted, or enraged when they fell into a familiar embrace and kiss.

Both brothers? Really?

While I didn't want to see this, following Jared here made me see that the images portrayed to the office might have just been smoke and mirrors. I wondered if that meant, Jared knew what was going on and knew where Justin was. I took one last look at Jared and the woman who now seemed so familiar to me and headed back to work, through building three to the staircase that took me to the second floor.

Mrs. Munch and Hector were leaving a note at my desk. Prior to this, I had never been called to management's office so many times or had to deal with such a situation and in that moment, I felt as though I might lose my half-eaten lunch. Patti Anne, Wilma, and Sheila were pretending to do their work as they listened intently.

"Hi." I tried to sound relaxed and normal. Mrs. Munch smiled. It didn't feel warm and friendly.

"Hi Nikki. We just wanted to have you find us when you were back from lunch. And now you're here." She stood up from my chair and motioned me to join her. I glanced at Hector. He couldn't make eye contact with me. His jaw tightened and the cords on his neck stood out. I followed both of them to Mrs. Munch's office.

I entered her office, a sterile space devoid of pictures and personal items. It surprised me; although she mostly worked out of the St. Louis office and was only here a few days a month, she was married with one son, and she had a grandchild. I would have thought she'd have a picture of them when she was away.

She motioned for me to sit. I did and waited for her to speak. She sat forward eagerly, folder her arms on her desk, and smiled. "The FBI asked us to let them bug your work phone." She said this so matter of factly that even though I knew it was coming I still felt violated. I nodded.

"Who is Emma Cabot?" she asked.

"She's the client in the file that I received. The one that started this ... problem."

Mrs. Munch took out the packet I had left on her desk, the same packet I gave to Hector. She pulled out the Cabot file. "I see you did a thorough background check including a credit report." She folded her hands over the file. "I had more credit history than these clients when I was twenty-one. And they were billed $30,000. It doesn't make sense."

"She called me today. Threatened me. Told me I was to stop looking into her life."

Mrs. Munch and Hector glanced uncomfortably at each other before looking at me. "When was this?"

"Just before I called the FBI. Agent Myles Stanton."

Mrs. Munch tapped her fingers against the files. "I noticed the company Asset Investments. Any thought on that?"

"Money laundering. Embezzling. It seems pretty straightforward." I was non-committal. I was starting wonder who I could trust in management, and I didn't want to let on that how much I thought I knew.

"The FBI will bug your work phone. It seems like a prudent plan. We think we might be able to use you to get to Justin."

I glanced at her and had to stop my jaw from dropping open in surprise. "You'd like to use me as bait?" Hector looked as though he was going to wretch. I'm guessed he wasn't okay with this plan.

"Yes," Mrs. Munch said. She slipped me a sheet of paper. "I had the accounting department set up an account and throw this money into it. The account can be tracked and traced. Give them to Justin since this is what he wanted in the first place. See if you could find out what else he knows or needs. We'll feed you bits of the information and see if we can smoke him out." She smiled pleasantly. I felt sick.

"Does the FBI know this is happening?"

"Yes. As does the Lake County Sheriff's department. We need to find him, regardless of what he did or knows. You can help us bring him in." I looked at the account numbers and shoved the paper into my pocket.

"Did you notice the account numbers I put together?"

Mrs. Munch pulled out the spreadsheet. "Yes. We'll start the process of pulling the bank records and see where the money is coming from. I see you have nothing here about the money leaving though."

"I thought I'd contact the bank. Since they have me on record as opening the account, I can pull the bank records on those. That should tell me where the money is going."

Mrs. Munch nodded. I stood.

"Nikki. I'm very sorry that you've gotten caught up in this. I do hope it won't affect you too much. You do very good work for us. So much so we were speaking about offering you a promotion."

This time I couldn't hide the surprise. "I'd be honored." I paused. "The timing's odd. But I appreciate your confidence in me." *Or worried that this is a bribe*, I thought. "I'll contact Justin tonight and let him know I managed to get into the files and get the data he requested." I turned and left, not sure what to make of this turn of events.

It got even weirder as I arrived at my desk to my phone ringing. "Nicole Page," I said as I glanced at the caller ID and grimaced.

"Hi Nikki. Can you come down to my office?"

"Sure Jared. I'm on my way."

****

To reach Jared's office, I would have to pass Hector's and Mrs. Munch's. I wasn't sure why that left me unnerved. Instead, I bypassed prying eyes by leaving the office and coming back in through the second set of side doors that led me to Jared's office. I wasn't sure why I was hiding this little misadventure from Mrs. Munch and Hector, but there you go, I was.

My first impression of the relationship was simply that they were purposely keeping Jared out of the loop because they either thought he was helping Justin or working with him.

Jared's door was open, so I knocked on the jamb and he motioned me inside. "Close the door, please." His way of asking was more an order, and it was odd for him. He was usually more congenial and warm. I took a seat.

He finished reading a document, scratched off the summation paragraph, made a note, and placed it back inside the folder. When he finished, he slid it off to the side, folded his arms on the desk and offered me a weak smile.

"I think they're hiding something from me."

My lips pursed as I bit my tongue. I wanted to laugh at the ridiculousness of it. Jared had always been a nice man, rumpled but fair, and even after seeing him with someone not his wife, I thought—just for a moment—that maybe he was feeling left out. Or a bit accused.

"I'm not sure what to say, Jared. I just work here. I do what they ask." I held my hands out wide.

"What are they asking about? What's going on?" This surprised me; he was a partner in the firm, and he seemed to know nothing. I got a tingling feeling at the base of my neck, like the hairs were standing straight out.

Is he trying to figure out how much I know?

"All I know is that something is wonky with several client files and my name is attached to them. They're trying to ascertain whether or not I was involved."

As much as he tried to keep his expression neutral, he seemed worried. I knew I couldn't trust any of them. After a moment to reflect, he said, "Well, that just can't be. You are such a good paralegal. You'd never do something like that. Why would they think you'd be disloyal? That's an outrage!" As much as I appreciated his righteous indignation, it felt wrong, off, overwrought.

"I think they just want clarification over some client files." Again, worry deepened the lines around his mouth.

"What's wrong with the files?"

He was fishing. Not only was Mrs. Munch and Hector withholding information, the FBI and the Sheriff's Department hadn't been apprising him of the situation either. Either Hector and Mrs. Munch knew something prior to Justin's disappearance, or they believed that Jared was part of whatever was going on. It was now more imperative that I keep my mouth shut.

"I only saw the one file. There seemed to be a breach of procedure. It coincided with Justin's disappearance."

Jared unclenched his jaw as if knowing it was still all about Justin was a good thing for him. "Anything else new come up?"

Beads of sweat gathered along his hair line and above his chin. He knew now that certain files were in the hands of the FBI. He didn't know which ones or why. I could feel his anxiety.

He glanced out the vertical window beside his door. "If you can, you know, just keep me apprised of the situation. What's going on. I'd appreciate it."

I nodded quickly. "Sure. I'll keep you posted." I stood and left, nearly running for the safety of my cubicle.

****

I've never had a longer day of work in my life. Before five o'clock hit, I was signed out and made a bee line for the door. Hector had the same thought and matched my stride as I headed down the two flights of stairs.

"Jared called you in today." We turned down the landing for the second flight of stairs.

"You're watching me."

"Yes."

I sighed as we hit the first floor. I moved to the side of the staircase, away from other people. "Listen. He wants to know what's going on. I kept my comments as vague as possible."

"What exactly did you tell him?"

I explained the brief conversation. He nodded. "Nikki. I'm so sorry. We're in a pickle here. Just give Justin the account numbers so we can see what he does with it."

"I suggest you tell Jared something. He's paranoid and will probably do something stupid," I whispered loudly, and it was a good thing. Jared was coming down the first flight of stairs and turning on the landing. He saw me with Hector. His face was red from exertion, and he didn't smile.

"Nikki. Hector." Jared nodded once and headed toward the door for building two.

"Give him something," I said again.

"If he asks, give him the account numbers. We can track both of them."

"This better work itself out soon. I haven't eaten or slept well in a week." I turned and walked away.

****

I swung by the middle school on my way home from work. Julia was there for a detention and then the basketball game. I pulled up and Julia and her friend climbed inside the car. Julia had been friends with Minnie since they were about a year old. They were nothing alike; Julia was outgoing and a bit of a troublemaker, Minnie was quiet, sweet, and unfortunately a follower. I had told Julia on several occasions not to drag her into anything, but sometimes it happened anyway.

Once they slammed the car door shut, they jabbered on as if I wasn't there. I smiled to myself and drove to Minnie's neighborhood.

When we got to her house, the girls were still in the throes of a deep conversation.

"We're here," I said. They both glanced up and looked around.

"Thanks Mrs. Page."

"No problem." I watched Minnie take careful, cautious steps up the stairs to the front door. "Is she okay?" I asked Julia.

"Yeah. She doesn't like to fall. And she does that a lot because she walks too fast." Okay. I waited until Minnie arrived at the door. She turned and waved. Once she was inside, I backed out of the driveway and headed home.

I saw him just as I left Minnie's neighborhood, less than a mile from our house, turning on Cuba Road. Justin was in a junker; a small Camry from the 1980's. It was rusted, the paint faded. I don't know if he thought that would be a good enough disguise, but I made him quickly. When I turned left into my neighborhood, he followed.

I pulled into my garage. "Julia, my boss was following us. Get in the house, now!"

She turned around, shaking slightly, and climbed out of the backseat. She ran for the house and slammed the door.

Justin got out of the car. I watched him carefully and cautiously. In the week he'd been gone, he had lost weight. His hair was unkempt; his beard was thick. I doubted he showered regularly, but at least he was wearing a different outfit from the last time I saw him. It was his eyes, though. They were red, watering, frantic.

"You need to turn yourself in," I said.

"I can't. I need to prove I didn't do it."

I glanced at the door to the house before walking across the slightly icy driveway. There was no way I was going to let him back in the house. I pulled out the sheet of paper from Hector and Mrs. Munch with the fake accounts and passed it to him.

"Go slither back to your hiding spot."

He blinked several times and smiled. Not relief, it was more like he had the answer, and it would save everything. I'm not sure how it would have helped even if they were legitimate account numbers, except I thought he'd be trying to move the money if they were real. I didn't even feel guilty that they were fake.

"Thanks Nikki. I owe you. I'll… I'll call you when I get something." He folded the paper and placed it in the pocket inside his jacket.

"Don't. I'm done. I'm not sure if I can get anything else out of the files. I'm blocked out." I turned and headed into the garage, closing it before he had a chance to come after me.

I'm not a criminal mastermind. I never do anything intentionally wrong or skirt the line, but in this, I didn't care that it was fake, and I was lying to him. I had a feeling he was going to try and pull the money out. Even though I've been vacillating between his innocence and his guilt, I had a strong suspicion that he and Jared were in it together. Possibly even Mrs. Munch and Hector. Now more than ever, I worried that their actions would affect me, my kids, my life and the lives of everyone else who depended on that firm for their livelihoods.

CHAPTER 19

I tossed and turned all night and dragged myself out of bed to do a half-assed workout on the treadmill. I never got above three miles per hour. I took my time with my tea and my breakfast, watched a little news before taking my shower.

After finding an dressing and doing hair and makeup, I still had thirty minutes before I would normally leave for the office.

I checked on my kids. Julia was bouncing through the house from too much sugar or caffeine. Jacob was still asleep. I helped Julia with her lunch, packed her backpack, and watched her walk through our backyard to the school on the other side of the fence. When she was safely on school grounds, I headed to work.

My plan was to work my normal workload and forget about everything else.

Traffic seemed light today as I found my spot at the end of the row. Just like any other day, I walked up the winding staircase to the second floor. I turned right to the side door, opened the lock with my key card and headed down the aisle to my cubicle.

Hector was hanging from the ceiling, dangling above my desk.

My knees buckled. My hands shook. I might have screamed. I don't remember. The office was empty this early in the morning; usually only Justin was here before eight. I fell to my knees, taking rapid breaths. When my hands stopped shaking, I dialed Andy Butcher.

"Hello." It was a female voice.

"Mm... my name is Nikki Page. I... I need to talk to Andy Butcher. It's an emergency." My voice rose, high with panic. I heard a whine escape my throat.

"Do you need 911, Ms. Page?"

My mind went blank for a moment as I looked up at Hector. He was already bloated, his face pale, his eyes open and clouded. "Yes. But I need Andy Butcher to come. I just found a dead body."

I don't remember telling the dispatcher where I was. I don't remember getting up from the floor, I don't remember leaving the office or the EMTs entering with the police. But there I was, in the chair outside of the office door, staring at the vending machine. My knees were knocking together while my hands trembled. Andy handed me a bottle of water. It sloshed out of the opening as I tried to take a sip.

"Feeling any better?" Andy asked as he sat beside me in the second chair. The office was closed, and employees were milling outside the main door; this corridor and the one opposite of this, had been cordoned off. I could hear the whispers. Adrienne Mox glared at me as if this too were my fault because I got involved. I focused on Andy.

"Marginally better." I leaned back in the chair. "Was there a note?"

"Yeah. He claimed he did it. He moved the money and set up the offshore accounts. He's taking responsibility for it all."

I shook my head. "It wasn't Hector."

Andy looked at the half open door to the law office. The crime scene unit was sweeping the area for clues, Hector's body was being removed from his noose. I shuddered.

"Why don't you think he did this?"

"Besides knowing him for three years, knowing he loved his wife, his job? He asked me to dig into the files. If he was responsible, I don't think he would have. I think whatever I found in those files, he figured it out. I'm betting he knew something."

I rubbed my temples; they were already throbbing.

"And Justin?"

I opened one eye. "The FBI will need to know this. Mrs. Munch and Hector gave me some account numbers to give Justin. They're tracing what he's doing. I gave the numbers to Justin last night when he stopped at my house, again." I closed both eyes and breathed slowly and evenly, as if that could truly calm me.

Agitated voices grew louder, footsteps slapped against the marble floor. "What's going on? Who's in charge?" Mrs. Munch pushed and shoved her way through the tightly packed crowd. Andy touched my hand and left for Mrs. Munch, speaking to her softly. "No!" she shouted and rushed for the open door with Andy following closely. She ran inside as Hector was zipped into the body bag. We could hear her shouting, demanding to know what happened, demanding to see Hector for herself. "Oh dear," she said as she was led from the office to the seat beside me.

She bent over with her head between her legs. I figured she saw Hector and felt faint and nauseated. I had when I saw him.

"You found him," she said.

I nodded. "I found him." Tears rolled down my cheeks, I couldn't hold in the loss of a friend or what's been happening at work. It had just been too much.

"I'm going to send everyone home. I'll …" she leaned back. "He figured something out from your notes, didn't he?"

I looked at her. Mrs. Munch always looked pulled together and sharp. She was smart, she was confident, and I trusted she could run the law firm. But right now, she seemed small and scared. "I think so."

"What did I miss?" Mrs. Munch rubbed her hands across her face and looked defeated. I could only guess the entire law firm would be transferred to St. Louis. I could feel the layoff coming.

"I don't know. I only gave you the first five. If he saw something and recognized it, it might have been in one or more of the other fifteen I hadn't printed yet."

Mrs. Munch was crying softly. She pulled a handkerchief from her jacket pocket and wiped her eyes. "So why would Hector claim he was responsible?"

"I bet it wasn't his handwriting. If it was…" I looked at Andy. "I think Hector figured something out and contacted someone. And then…"

"You think Hector called the killer and asked him or told him what he knew?" Andy asked.

I shrugged. I yawned. My lack of sleep the night before mixed with my fear of being next was exhausting. I needed a nap; I needed a new job. I needed to figure out who killed my friend.

They wheeled the stretch with Hector's body to the maintenance elevator so no one would see. It rumbled to stop on the second floor, the doors squeaked open and the stretcher disappeared. I wiped a tear and turned back to Andy.

"I gave Hector and Mrs. Munch the client files that seemed odd. He must have found something that concerned him. I think he saw it when I first gave him the files. I don't know what he found. He didn't tell me. I haven't made a connection yet."

I looked at Mrs. Munch. She nodded, pulled a small notebook out of her very large bag, and ripped a page from it. "You keep at it, Nikki. Go home and figure out what he found." She dropped the notebook back inside her bag and pursed her lips. "So, this will be a crime scene. I suppose I need to close down the office."

We heard the heavy footsteps of Jared Able as he ran through the crowd and made his way to us. "I just heard. What the hell happened?" He glanced at the door, still half open. We could see the police and crime scene workers as they moved back and forth, still collecting evidence.

"Mr. Able. We're not sure. But it appears that Hector Garcia committed suicide sometime last night. The ME will confirm time of death, but he was left hanging, coincidentally over Mrs. Page's desk," Andy said.

Jared pursed his lips, glanced at the door, and then to me. "Why? Was there a note?"

"He confessed to the file tampering," Andy offered.

Jared looked at him and then Mrs. Munch. "But that was Justin." His eyes widened; his mouth formed an O. "You don't think Justin killed him to take the pressure off of himself? That seems so like him. Never taking responsibility for his actions." Jared huffed out a breath and held his arms across his chest in righteous indignation. If I wasn't so horrified, I would have laughed.

"We don't know for certain if it was suicide or not. We're investigating." Andy tuned to Mrs. Munch. "Yes. This will be a crime scene for at least the rest of the week, possibly next. You'll have to work out of your homes until we release the scene."

I thought back to when I first saw Hector hanging above my desk. I closed my eyes, blocked out his face as my mind traveled down his body to his shoes. But what I couldn't place was that there was nothing below him. No ladder or step stool, no chair or boxes on which to stand on when he looped the ropes around the steel beams that crossed the office ceiling. "How did he get up there?" I murmured mostly to myself.

"What?" Jared asked.

I opened my eyes. Andy, Jared, and Mrs. Munch all looked at me.

"How did he get up there? There was nothing below him to climb."

Andy made notes in his little notebook and placed it back in his jacket pocket when he was finished.

"I'm sorry, but for now, the office is closed. Mrs. Munch, Mr. Able, Ms. Page." He nodded and stepped away, heading for the side door. When he slipped through, he closed the door. I looked at Mrs. Munch.

She stood, smoothed out her skirt and hooked her purse in the crook of her arm. She looked at Jared. "Inform the staff that everyone has today off. We'll be working from home for the foreseeable future." She strode away and the crowd parted as she marched down the stairs. I shoved the note she gave me into my purse and stood. I waited for Jared to clear the floor.

People were shocked when he told them what happened. Some cried, others didn't seem to care. They all seemed grateful to be going home. When the crowd thinned, I took the stairs back down and exited the building. The ambulance was still in the parking lot, surrounded by several police cars, one of which was blocking me in.

I opened the door. The officer who came with the car walked to me. "Needing to get out?"

I nodded and watched as he got into his car and backed it up, giving me room to get out. The lights were still blaring as I pulled away. The sadness in my heart grew deeper, echoed by the massive headache pounding in my head.

****

I called Myles when I returned home.

"Mrs. Page." It sounded like I had called a robocomputer.

"Hector Garcia, the office manager for Able, Able, and Munch was found hanging in the office this morning. He's the one who requested I search for additional client accounts that were… odd."

Myles was typing on his computer. He wasn't very fast; I suspected he was hunting and pecking with two fingers.

"Andy Butcher just called me. He said you thought Hector discovered something. Any idea what?"

"Something important enough to kill for." I rolled my eyes. How the hell would I know what he found? I pulled out the note from Mrs. Munch and turned on my computer as I waited for Myles to ask another stupid question.

"I'm sorry, Mrs. Page. Was there anything you think he might have found that would lead to his murder?"

"I'm sorry. I'm just very… I don't know. I haven't found anything to implicate anyone but Justin. I suppose you'll find out when the security tapes are reviewed. Whose card was used. And has Justin been in the accounts I gave him last night?"

"In the murder of Hector Garcia, the Lake Zurich police are handling that and will procure the digital readout for the key cards and the video of the front and side doors. And yes, Justin went into those accounts. I'm sure he's not happy that there wasn't anything in them."

"So now what?" I pulled up the website I needed to track the money and typed in the information Mrs. Munch had given me.

"I suppose the best place to check would be Hector's files at work. If you haven't seen something that connected all of this, he must have had the key in his files," Myles suggested.

"I wouldn't have that information. I suppose you'll have to talk to the LZPD."

He stopped typing. "I'm sorry you lost your co-worker. His murder, for now, will be handled by them and we'll work the embezzlement and laundering aspect."

I sighed. "I'll see if I can get into his files through the computer. Otherwise, Andy will have to figure it out. Thanks." I clicked off my phone, though I'm not sure Myles Stanton knew I had hung up.

I typed in the first account number from the Cabot file, pulled it up on the bank website and found the wire transfer number from Asset Investments. On a hunch, I entered the number Mrs. Munch gave me into the system and gaped. I followed the money.

There invoices were paid by Emma and London Cabot.

Were they real?

I kept following the trail and found the same amount had been withdrawn from the Able, Able, and Munch bank account and put into another.

I curled up on the sofa with my laptop and looked at a company, MW Enterprises, that received the money. I pulled up the account information. It was owned by Justin Able and Marcie Winkler.

Did Hector call Justin?

In the Cabot client file, I found a bank statement I hadn't seen before. It was for Asset Investments, the account in the Caymans. And there was the payment to Emma and London Cabot that had been sent to Able, Able, and Munch.

It seemed to me that the money flowed from Asset Investments into a client bank account which was then used to pay the Able, Able, and Munch invoices, but then rather than heading to the firm's bank account, it was transferred back out to MW Enterprises.

My only question was, where did the money come from before it went into Asset Investments?

****

It felt like a lifetime since I went to work that morning, and I couldn't believe it was only 2:15 when I looked at the clock in the family room. I had found the money trail: in and out of Asset Investments to MW Enterprises.

I wrote up what I found and emailed it as an attachment to Myles Stanton, Mrs. Munch, and almost sent one to Hector. The thought made me tear up. I had been so preoccupied with the work that my mind traveled away from him and his murder for a few hours. I typed a quick note to Mrs. Munch, advising her what I had found. I could have told her that I wasn't sure this is what got Hector killed, but I didn't mention his murder.

I worried I might be next.

Before Julia walked through the door, I put my computer away, took all of my copies and auxiliary notes and slipped them under my bed. Julia would be walking through the door at 3:15, after her detention. I didn't want her to know about this. I sat and channel surfed until it was almost time for her to come home.

I pulled out some frozen cookie dough that was already sliced into pieces, filled a tray and popped it into the oven. While it backed, I watched from the window over the sink as Julia walked through the path at the end of the fence that separated our yard from the school property. All the middle schoolers in my neighborhood used that path to get to and from school. She had her backpack hanging from one shoulder, and she seemed happy as she texted on her phone.

She walked in through the garage door as I placed the baked cookies placed them on the stone countertop to cool.

"Mom?" her eyes widened. "Why are you home?"

"Why'd you ask? Planning on causing trouble?"

She smiled and eyed the cookies; she was nearly salivating. "Are these for me?"

I nodded. "I'm home because there was an accident at work and now it's a crime scene. I'll be home for the next few days," my heart ached as I simplified what had happened with an explanation so filled with holes. It didn't do Hector's death any justice.

She looked at me with confusion.

I sighed. I couldn't put it off. "Mr. Garcia, you know, Hector. He was found dead in the office this morning. We don't know why."

Julia's lip trembled. "I liked him. I'm sorry mom." She wrapped her arms around me and gave me a hug.

"Thanks, kid. It's been a weird few weeks there," I said. I held on a little longer than necessary. It seemed we both needed the comfort.

When I pulled away, I scooped the cookies up with a small spatula and placed them on a paper towel. She looked at me with sad eyes. "I feel the same way." I offered a smile. "Go on. Eat up. I have some work to do in my room."

When I was sure she was settled in front of the television, her book bag open and her homework in her lap, I went to my room, closed the door, and locked it. I pulled all the work out from under the bed and took another look at the data I found.

What did you find, Hector? Marcie was on the account that received the final payment, as was Justin. *Did you confront Marcie? Or Justin? Or someone else?*

Justin had denied any knowledge of the accounts and yet someone opened those accounts using my ID. Could they really be using him as the fall guy? And if so, what am I?

I pulled up my computer and looked again at the accounts and the money that filed into Asset Investments. I kept my search to the five clients I gave to Mrs. Munch and Hector. I worked my way through the Cabots, the Hinkles, Watermans, Brights, and the Cantors.

It was there, the last client I searched, the one payment. While I had been over all of the notes multiple times, I had missed it. It was there, buried deep, one payment from one company: JA Associates. When I pulled that company up, I expected Justin, maybe even Jared. I wasn't expecting Jared and a man named Sherman Munch.

He was Mrs. Munch's son and had nothing to do with the law firm. All I knew was that he was in entertainment or something, but not law. Was this what Hector discovered? I called Andy Butcher, because for now, Hector's murder was still being handled by the Lake Zurich police.

"Nikki? Is everything okay?"

"I want the truth. Who did Hector call last night?"

He let out a long sigh. "What did you find?"

"You first."

"We're looking at Jared Able. But I suspect you know this?"

"Yes. Who did Hector call?" I was feeling impatient as I paced my bedroom. It was 4:45 and a thought hit me that I was missing something important. Something not concerning work.

"He called a man named Sherman Munch."

I closed my eyes and grimaced. It was the closest to smiling I could get under the circumstances. "He's Mrs. Munch's son. He and Jared own a company called JA Associates. Money comes from there to Asset Investments and then to Able, Able and Munch. And then it goes out to MW Enterprises."

I held my breath when he stopped typing.

"Money laundering."

"Yes."

"And Jared owns this other company?"

"Yes. I sent an early report to Mrs. Munch and to Myles Stanton. I can send it to you."

Oh crap! I remembered what I had forgotten.

I quickly forwarded my first email to Andy. "I need to go. I forgot my son's basketball game."

"I'll look into all of this and call if I have any other questions."

After hanging up, I threw on my gym shoes and flew down the stairs. "I'm heading to the basketball game. You want to come?"

Julia switched off the television and we headed to the high school.

"You forgot, didn't you?" Julia asked as we pulled out of the driveway.

"Yeah. Lots on my mind."

In the darkness, I could only see the headlights, not the cars they belonged to. It didn't seem strange to see lights following us as I turned right out of the subdivision and hung a left at Rand Road. It didn't seem odd that the lights followed me down Old Rand Road or down Main Street or even that it followed me down Church Street to the high school. It was, after all, a varsity basketball game.

Julia and I got out of the car and walked across the parking lot with the cold wind whipping against us. Footsteps belonging to students and parents followed behind us as we all came late to the game. A rather common occurrence.

We ran up the sidewalk and entered the first open door we came to. I pulled off my jacket as we walked into the gym and found empty seats at the very top of the bleachers.

I scanned the bench and found Jacob at the scorekeeper's table waiting for the next time-out so he could enter the game. As timeout was called, Jacob ran in, replacing Micah on the court. Within seconds, the ball was thrown back into play and cheers reverberated across the room.

When Jacob scored a two-pointer I jumped up and cheered. As the ball bounced, as they set up defenses, a momentary lull in the action hung over the room. I looked around for familiar faces in the crowd, other parents I knew from the PTO, basketball games and camps, or from the fourteen other sports Jacob has played. I waved to several and I continued to scan during the next timeout.

I saw a familiar face but couldn't place it. It wasn't from basketball, or other sports, and it wasn't from school or PTO. He was wearing a knitted cap and a pea coat. I stared again. Justin had shaved and showered and changed clothes. He was scanning the crowd. Our gazes found each other.

He followed me.

I shuddered. He must have parked somewhere around my house and waited for me to get home. He watched me intently, his eyes slanted in anger, his jaw so tightly clenched, I could see it from the last row of the bleachers. I knew he looked at the fake accounts. I also knew he was pissed.

He left the gym. I figured he would be waiting for me when I left. I only hoped having Julia with me would protect both of us.

****

Justin was in his car, parked beside mine, engine running when I arrived at my car. Even in the darkness I could see him glare at me as I loaded Julia in the car and slid into the driver's side. I backed out, and when I drove around the parking lot, he followed me. I made a decision as I drove through the heavy traffic through downtown Lake Zurich, out past the lake, past the grocery store, and down Cuba Road. I finally turned down my street and pulled into the driveway.

"You okay, Mom?" Julia asked as I shut off the car. Justin's Jaguar idled in the driveway, lights still on.

"Yeah. My former boss wants to talk to me. Do me a favor. Grab a snack, go to your room and lock the door."

Julia looked at me, confused and scared; her bottom lip quivered. "But Mom."

"Now, Julia. I can handle him." I had never in a million years thought I'd have to protect my kids and myself quite like this. My hands shook and my stomach burned with anger as Julia raced from the car and slammed the door shut when she entered the house.

I got out and strolled to Justin's car. He rolled down his window.

"Those were fake accounts!" he screamed. I glanced at the house, stared at the window that was Julia's room. She had her light on and was peering outside. I turned back to Justin. I hoped he wasn't armed, that he hadn't plans to take me out now, especially with my child watching. I worried for her safety, for mine. I could only hope if he tried to come after me, I could get inside and the lock the door before he could hurt me or her. I hid my trembling hands behind my back and stared him in the eyes.

"I was supposed to feed you the information they gave me. I don't have any more. I need the truth. Did you launder money?"

Justin glared at me. "No. I'm being set up." He rubbed his hand against his now-smooth chin.

"You're on an account that received all the laundered money."

He looked at me, sad and tired. His whole life had been turned upside down. "Marcie had access to everything. She could have opened the accounts. Yours too."

"Come inside," I said, before I thought it through. I waited as he turned off his car and followed me inside. I switched on the sunroom lights. It was cold and I turned on the floorboard heater. "Stay here," I told him. I grabbed leftovers, warmed them up, and carried them to the sunroom. He paced in front of the French doors and glanced at me when I offered food. The sunroom was large, awkward space that felt stuffed with furniture. No matter what I did, I could never seem to find a comfortable seating arrangement. I led him to the small table and chairs.

He ate like he was starving. He shoveled spaghetti into his mouth, and he stabbed at the meatballs. Julia sent me a text.

I'm okay. I texted back.

"I found twenty accounts that were wonky. I've been working with five. And there's definitely money coming and in and out. So, what happened?"

"Marcie. She had been acting weird in the few days before you got the file. Like she was getting ready to split anyway. She had been asking me for months to divorce my wife, run off with her. I … I couldn't. I treated my wife poorly, but I still love her."

He pushed the rest of the plate away. I waited for him to talk again.

"I told her no. And then she pulled away. Okay. I wasn't going to push her. But she began to run hot and cold. She'd hand me documents to sign and I trusted her and signed them. Suddenly, she was very nice again. All things forgiven, she wanted to pick up our relationship again. I was such an idiot." He looked at me. "For everything."

"So, then?"

He wiped his hand across his mouth. "We had sex in the office. You caught us and she convinced me to run. She must have given you the file. The Cabot file. She knew you'd mark your time in the database and would think something was up. It had to be her."

"I saw Jared with a woman, not his wife." A brunette like Marcie. Had Marcie brazenly returned to the office building to see Jared? "I think it might have been Marcie."

Justin opened his mouth to speak but closed it again.

"I didn't recognize her when I saw them, but now… Maybe it was her." I sat back in the small chair and crossed my arms against my chest.

"I thought maybe they were, you know. But more discreet than me."

"She's been leading you around. Telling you what's been going on, what you should be doing."

He nodded.

"The evidence against you is overwhelming." His eyes widened in fear.

"I didn't launder the money."

"I'm sure you'll be proven innocent of the murders. That might help with the other." Tears trailed down his cheek. I wasn't sure exactly what part of this he was crying over. His failed marriage, Marcie's deception, his own bad decisions. The fact he was crying, could have been the fear of his future or simply that he lacked sleep. Whichever it was, I didn't care anymore. His choices brought me to this bad place and I squarely blamed him. "Hector was found hanging above my desk this morning."

He didn't respond immediately as he processed the information that Marcie hadn't told him yet. "He hung himself?" He asked with some shock in his voice.

"I think it was staged. I think the note was written by someone else." I explained the lack of a stool or chair beneath him.

"He found something and approached the person responsible?"

I nodded. "I think he found the company owned by Jared and Simon Munch." He glanced at me. His eyes got so wide I thought they would bug out of his head.

"Mrs. Munch's son?"

"Yeah. I think they've got some business together and needed to launder the money from that. I'm not sure if the clients are real, but it appears to be a way to get the money to Able, Able, and Munch."

"Who did Hector talk to?"

I shook my head. "I've said more than enough. You need to go to the police."

"No. Not yet. I can pull these accounts, do a little digging. Find out why they chose to implicate me."

"My guess, Jared feels underappreciated and underpaid. Simon Munch, maybe his mother pissed him off and they came up with this plan. Maybe Marcie was pissed off enough at you for what you did to her, and she wanted to get back at you." I felt (fill in the emotion, I'm not sure) and stopped my righteous indignation.

Justin looked at me. There was anguish in his eyes. "My wife kicked me out. Ironically, this family lawyer will need to hire a divorce attorney." When he chuckled, it was devoid of real emotion. He seemed to have lost some of his will. "Does Jared know he's a suspect?"

"No. And if you tell him, I'm screwed. I've already said way too much."

"Contrary to what people believe, Jared and I don't get along. Knowing he put me in this position makes me want to kill him. He's always been outwardly sweet, but evil behind closed doors. I can see him doing this. Did you run a query on the lawyers in the firm?"

"Why would I do that?"

"To find out who and why they'd set up this whole scam," he said.

Justin ran his hands through his hair and wrung them in his lap. "I can help. Run searches. Look for new purchases, lifestyles above their means."

It was my turn to give him a pointed look. "Why? It appears to be coming from a partner."

"This enterprise was too much for two people who I would say aren't the brightest lights on the strand. You said there were twenty client accounts that were weird; plus, all of the companies. We need to run a check on who else in the firm is part of this. " I could hear the bitterness in his voice.

"Hold on a minute." I left the quiet of the sunroom and climbed the steps, finding my computer on my bed where I left it. I checked on Julia. "It's me. Open up." Her lock clicked open. She was standing there, still sad, maybe scared.

"Are you okay?"

I closed the door and pulled her in a hug and kissed the top of her head. I knew I shouldn't have brought Justin into the house, but helping him seemed to be helping me, and keeping my children safe. If I could keep him talking, I might be able to find out what was truly going on. I just hope it didn't get me killed.

I pulled from Julia and found her gaze. "Yeah. I'm okay. I... I think if I can get Justin to talk, I might reach the answers." I glanced at her bed, her books were strewn across her bed, unopened. I knew she was worried. I tried to smile. "Finish your homework. He should be out of here soon." I glanced in Jacob's room. He was working on his computer, ear buds in his ears, head bopping up and down. "Lock the door." When I heard the lock click, I went downstairs.

Justin was in the sunroom staring into the dark hole that was my backyard. "Jared told me about JA Associates in 2013. He wanted to know if I wanted in on the ground floor. The specs for the company seemed a little dubious. There was no real plan. He insisted it was a sure thing. I passed on it."

"What was the company supposed to do?"

He slumped in the chair beside the fireplace. "All encompassing law firm, just..." He looked at me. "A little too close to the legal limits. We opened Able and Able and then Mrs. Munch asked us to merge with her."

He took my computer. "They've locked me out of everything. I'd show you the proof if I could get in." He grimaced.

I thought of the access Mrs. Munch had given me and I flipped open the lid. I logged into the employee website.

"What do you want me to find?" I asked.

"Payroll."

I had never been into the payroll files and I searched, clicked on the link and pulled up the payroll search field.

"Who?"

"Jared."

I typed in Jared's name and waited for it to pull his payroll records. "What am I looking for?"

My jaw dropped. "He doesn't bill very much, does he?"

"No. His paralegals do all of the work. He goes to meetings, he reviews it all, but no. They do everything. They have substantial hours and are paid for that. Jared also received a smaller salary than I do. Much less than Mrs. Munch. She brought me in first. We worked well together. Jared, he was good with people, not such a good lawyer. Pull up my information."

I typed Justin into the search and again, found myself surprised. He earned three times what Jared made. But then, he bill that much more than Jared.

Was this truly a case of a brother jealous of another and wanting to stick it to him. I glanced at Justin, he seemed almost giddy after showing me his 'proof.'

"Why would he do all this to set you up. He could have billed more hours, made more money, stepped up as a leader in the company. Why?" I asked Justin. It seemed like a lot of work to get caught so easily.

"He wasn't a good student. Barely got his law degree. He begged to be brought into the firm. Mrs. Munch set him up like this. He knows enough to do the job, but he's not extraordinary. He's just eh."

"Still, it doesn't make sense. He could bill more, make more money."

Justin shook his head and chuckled. "He couldn't he didn't know that much. We kept him at the end of a leash. Gave him just enough to make it look good." This time Justin sat back in the chair with his hands behind his head, relaxed. It unnerved me.

"That still…"

"I think he was jealous. He stole my girl. He wants me out of the company. Think of it. It makes sense!" he seemed excited as if it was all figured out.

"So, a jealous brother set you up with the help of your lover to get back at you?" I asked incredulously.

"So, it seems." He flashed me a smile. I felt nauseated. "Don't tell anyone about this. But I think he did it. All of it. He lives beyond his means. Maybe I'm wrong, but I don't think I am."

I shut down the computer and made a mental note to call Will. I couldn't help but worry, that I had been manipulated into Justin's side.

He opened the sliding door and stepped onto the deck. "Thank you, Nikki. You just gave me hope that we can end this thing." He began to turn away. Turned back to me placed his finger on his lips as if to silence me. "Keep quiet about this. I don't want you to be next." He touched my cheek and I pulled away. I felt creeped out by his behavior, and I locked the sliding door, returned to the garage to lock both door and tried the front door. Still, I felt unsafe, used.

I hid my computer and the rest of the report under my bed. Just in case I was truly marked for next.

I dialed Will.

"Hey Nikki, what's up?"

"Justin was here."

There was silence on the other end of the line. He wasn't typing, there was no television rambling in the background. I wondered if I had interrupted a date. "I'm sorry if this is a bad time?" I said.

"It's not. I thought you weren't going to speak to him again." Paper rustled. "What did he want?"

"The FBI wanted me to feed him bad data." I repeated my conversation with agent Stanton and waited for Will to say something. When he didn't, I continued. "Justin's coming here crying that he's been set up. Because I seemed to have been, it's plausible."

"But…"

"Everything is pointing toward him being framed and he seems to be leading me to Jared."

"How is he doing that?"

I told him about the payroll records. "It seems Jared wasn't billing as much as Justin. His paralegals do all the work. He just reviews. Justin claims he wasn't that good with the law, just with the people."

"You obviously don't believe Justin."

"I get a bad vibe. Like I'm being set up. If he can get me on his side, I can fight for him."

"Nikki. You need to stop helping him."

I could hear the worry in Will's voice and I knew he was right. "But if he thinks he has me on his side, he might not be inclined to take me out."

"Nikki. You don't know if it was him who killed Hector. It could have been Jared!" I could hear him staring to pace. "Damn it!"

I knew I had screwed up if he was that worried.

"I know. I put myself and the kids in danger. I was trying to calm him. Trying to stay friendly so he wouldn't come after me." Tears welled in my eyes.

"I'm sorry I was so terse. I'm worried about you. I know you. You think you'll be able to handle this. Figure this out. But you need to leave it to the FBI and the police. It's their job."

"Okay. I'll be careful. And I don't think he killed Hector. Hector went to Jared's partner, Sherman Munch with whatever he found. Though I'm not sure which of them killed Hector." Again, at the mention of Hector, my heart hurt. My anxiety grew with the silence between us. Was someone with Will? Was he calling someone else on the house phone? I held my breath.

"Why did he call Sherman Munch?"

I told him about the connection.

"Don't tell Jared or Mrs. Munch. You don't have access to certain files to know what he was billing or what he made. They, the law firm, or the police might be tracking who gets into the system. You might need to explain that to someone."

"Mrs. Munch gave me access to the system, so I could follow the money. I used what I was given. That includes payroll. But it doesn't matter. I'm starting to get scared. It's getting heavy."

"You think? Nikki. Promise me you'll be careful. Don't tell anyone else what you know and stop talking to Justin. I think you're right. He's using you for his own gain."

My heart pounded. "I'm sorry. I'll be more careful." I could barely speak.

"I'm sorry I scared you. It's getting complicated. The police are verifying yours and Justin's signatures. You'll be clear and then I'm worried you'll be dangerous to whoever is in charge."

"I can call Andy in the morning."

"No. I'll do it. I don't want you talking to anyone without me."

"Okay. I'll keep it quiet. I'm sorry to bother you. I'm just so uneasy about all of this."

"You can call me any time. I just want you and the kids to be safe."

After we hung up I paced the bedroom, worried and wondering. At 9 p.m. I received a text from Mrs. Munch. *Please see me at 8 a.m. I'll open the office for you.* My heart pounded. She had never sent a text to me, never at night for a morning meeting. I had a feeling I knew what it would be about.

I went against Will's suggestion and called Andy Butcher and told him everything I knew.

CHAPTER 20

I had stayed awake most of the night, nervous about my early morning meeting with Mrs. Munch. Sometime during the night, I had a thought; did Mrs. Munch give me the computer access in order to spy on me. It had been stupid to be lulled into believing I was helping stop a criminal without knowing who it was. I knew I had been putting myself in danger.

Then why meet her at the empty law firm?

I had tossed and turned all night, my thoughts jumbled and scarry. I reached my phone once with the idea that I'd lie, claim I had a sick kid and cancel. But then, maybe it wasn't what I thought it would be. Maybe she got all she needed from me and I'd just be fired.

I chuckled at the thought, covered myself up but I still couldn't still myself to sleep.

Eventually five o'clock in the morning rolled around. Still dark outside, I got up. My anxiety was ratcheted up, and I skipped my workout. I showered, dressed, and packed a lunch for Julia.

It was only 6:05 and my stomach roiled as I sipped my tea. I stared at my phone, Andy Butcher's phone number filled the screen. All I had to do was hit call, and yet I didn't. I had been waffling for an hour at the merits of calling him and letting him know Mrs. Munch called me in to work. Why should I be afraid?

Because Hector died after discovering something.

I texted Will instead. *Mrs. Munch texted me. I'm probably going to get fired.*

I grimaced and headed to work, filled with a sense of dread. Outside the main office door, I glanced at my phone. Will simply said, *Call me when you get home.*

At least someone knew where I had gone.

I stared at the gleaming door, Able, Able, and Munch and the fancy logo on the glass door. I pulled out my phone again, turned on the recorder and slipped the phone into the pocket on my shirt.

The crime scene tape had been taken down at the left corner of the door frame and was laying on the floor like a dead snake. I slid in my key card, surprised it worked as normal and stepped over the tape into a mostly darkened space. Before turning the corner to Mrs. Munch's office, I patted my pocket where my phone had been recording sound.

I was amazed by the quiet and the stillness of the once busy office. Rows and rows of cubicles at empty, computers were off, lights dark all except the sliver of light came from Mrs. Munch's almost closed office. I was alone with her and took a deep breath as I knocked on her door.

"Come in."

She sat at her desk in a sweater and jeans, not her typical work attire. The casualness unsettled me. I had never seen her dressed like that.

"Have a seat," she said curtly. I watched her sign a sheet of paper and shove it in a thick envelope. She handed it to me.

"There's three month's pay in here and information about your insurance. The law firm will pay on your insurance for a year. I've also included reference letters from myself and one from Jared." She folded her arms on her desk and stared at me. "I'm moving all the business to St. Louis."

I sat stunned for a moment, but then I had just joked about this with Will an hour before. I couldn't hide the smile that cracked my lips.

"I'm sorry, Nikki. Do you find this funny?"

I bit my cheek to stop from laughing. "No ma'am. Lack of sleep and stress." I resisted the urge look inside the packet. "What about everyone else?"

She smiled, but it no longer felt warm. "I'll be laying everyone off this week. Some, might come to St. Louis." She tried to smile again but it looked more like she ate a lemon. "You unfortunately got laid off first because you figured out what happened. I can't have this getting out to the public or to the clients. I'll be ruined. Justin ruined everything." She seemed rattled, and unsure. It was so unlike her.

"I was just doing what I was asked to do." I held up the folder. "Thanks for this." I stood, ready to bolt for the safety of home.

"I am sorry, Nikki. You're a great paralegal. I could always count on you. Is there anything on your desk you need? If there is, please retrieve it and leave your badge when you go."

Mrs. Munch, in not so many words, dismissed me when she returned her attention to the pile on her desk. There was a large stack of envelopes and she signed another letter, slipping it inside. I wasn't the only one getting laid off.

Crime scene tape still roped off my cubicle and Shelia's across from mine. I looked up at the crushed ceiling tile and see Hector dangling above my desk as if he was still there. I shuddered and felt anger boil up inside of me. Angry that I was brought into this on purpose, angry that I was being used for information, angry that I was a potential fall guy. I was most angry that someone else made a plan to destroy several lives for their personal gain and I had a sudden, desperate need to leave. I yanked opened desk drawers, showing notebooks, pens and post it notes in my bag. In the bottom drawer I grabbed my mug, water bottle and a shawl I wore when it was cold.

I pulled pictures of my kids from the cubicle walls and the clock I had sitting by the desk lamp. My inbox was still full, I resisted the urge to see which clients weren't getting my help today.

With one more look around the cubicle, I knew I had everything I wanted. I tossed my badge on the desk, hiked the bag up on my shoulder and turned away, leaving behind what had been a good job. I opened the door to the hallway and let the door slam shut behind me without a final look. It was done, over. I had lost a job, a friend.

I held off the tears until I was safely tucked away in my car. As I pulled away, I saw Adrienne Mox enter the building. I was sure she was next on the chopping block unless they really wanted to transfer her to St. Louis. I had a feeling she knew something they would find useful.

****

It was only 9:15 when I got home. The kids were off at school, and I had the whole day without work. I called Andy Butcher first. He picked up on the first ring.

"Hi. It's Nikki Page."

"Hi Nikki, how can I help you."

He seemed chipper so early in the morning and all I wanted was to throw up. "They're starting layoffs at the firm. I was the first they let go."

"I'm sorry to hear that." He was typing; he sounded quite proficient.

"Has Justin been found?" I asked him. Last night I gave in and told him about Justin coming to my house. I didn't quite tell him what I did for Justin though.

"No, he hasn't. You know Mrs. Page, you keep telling us that you're asking him to come in, but he doesn't seem to be willing to do that. If I was a suspicious man, I'd think you're only tell me this to make it seem like you're doing the right thing. Are you actually helping him?"

I stopped pacing, could feel my face burn with anger. He got me there. "I'm helping myself since no one seems willing to find Justin and stop him!" I said.

"Helping you helps him too, don't you think."

I pounded on the counter. "Listen. I've been honest with you about what I know. I've been trying to help. I called you about this to let you know what's going on. I didn't have to do this. Everything I do where my job is concerned or where this case is going has to do with protecting myself and my children!"

My heart raced. I pursed my lips because I thought I might vomit.

"Are you sure you're telling me everything. If I find you're not, I can charge you aiding and abetting when you don't call me when he's there," he said calmly.

"Then do it. He won't listen when I tell him to turn himself in. And no, I have no idea where he's staying. I'm giving the FBI the information I have about the supposed money laundering. There's nothing more I can do to help."

Andy sighed loudly. "I don't want to arrest you. I don't think you've done anything wrong, except talk to your former boss. I worry that you're hindering the case. I just want you to be sure you've told me everything. Have you told me everything?"

Everything you need to know.

I should tell him I pulled up the payroll data, and that I've been helping Justin. But the guilt I was carrying for not telling him this, was eased when I admitted to myself that I was holding some information back so that maybe whoever killed Hector would think I didn't know as much as I did. It wasn't great logic, I knew, but it was the best I had.

"I've told you everything I know."

He was silent for a moment. I wondered if he took a deep breath or planted his palm on his forehead. That thought made me chuckled.

"I'm not going to press any further. But what I do want to impress upon you is that you need to tell me everything so that we can resolve this. And keep you safe."

I shuddered.

"I promise I will."

"As long as we're clear. I do have one thing. Have you given any thought to what Hector discovered?"

I thought of JA Associates and Jared's involvement with Sherman Munch. I told Andy what I had discovered.

The typing stopped. Andy's end of the line grew eerily quiet. "I told you Hector called Sherman Munch. Discovering JA Associates is a link to both Jared Able and Sherman Munch means he knew too much. That's motive for murder and a link to the other brother. And if Mrs. Munch realizes you know this too…" He was thinking at that made me nervous. I knew what he was going to say.

"Be careful Mrs. Page. I'm hoping by firing you they'll think you're done with this. But I'm not sure that would be the case."

"Mrs. Munch knows what I know. I gave her and Hector everything I have." That feeling in the pit of my stomach grew.

"Where does Justin fall in this?" Andy asked but I think it was to himself.

"The fall guy," I said anyway.

"He's not the one in charge?" That piqued his interest.

"No. Maybe. I really don't know. I think Jared is involved with both Marcie Winkler and Sherman Munch. If this was a detective novel, I'd say Marcie was pissed as Justin for their affair and set up the whole thing to get back at him. But I'm not sure how that fits into the whole thing." After stating it, even to my ears, it sounded not right.

"Without proof there's not much I can do with that except dig for a connection. Just remember to tell me EVERYTHING you know. I'll let you go."

I tapped my fingers on the counter and counted to ten. I didn't say anything. "Mrs. Page?"

"Jared wasn't making as much as Justin. He wasn't billing as much, because according to Justin, his paralegals do all the work. He knows enough to review and sign off on documents." It came out in one stream. I needed a deep breath when I finished.

"And that means," he said.

"He wasn't billing as much or making as much. Mrs. Munch, Justin, Hector, they didn't keep him in the loop. Not over this, not about much. He was jealous, at least that's how Justin made it seem. Jared wanted information from me. Saying they weren't…" Damn it!

"Mrs. Page?"

"They've been playing me. All of them. Jared knew what was going on. He just wanted to know what I knew. Mrs. Munch and Hector…"

Who else was part of this? Who wanted to know what I knew, who wanted to learn what was going on?

"Mrs. Page… Nikki. I implore you to be careful. Don't talk to anyone else about this. Something is going on at the firm and you know too much." He pulled the phone from his mouth and spoke to someone. Papers rustled.

"I'm glad you called. Please be careful. And good news. The FBI handwriting analysis just confirmed the signature on the bank cards was definitely not yours. We used some documents Justin signed to verify his signature. His signature appears to have been forged as well."

For the first time in a week, I felt like I could breathe. "So, are you or the FBI still looking at me as an accomplice?"

Andy was silent for a moment and my heart skipped a beat. "No. We're not. But we still have questions for Justin. I suspect that if you have an epiphany as to where he is, you'll let me know."

"I wish I knew where he was hiding. And I'm sorry I didn't text you when he was at my house. Justin shouldn't have run; I should have turned him in. Hector might still be alive and I might still have a job."

What was I thinking? Did I really think what I did for Justin was going to save me? I wish I had turned him in and vowed I'd call Andy as soon as I saw Justin again.

"I'm sorry you had to go through all of this. It will get better. I wish you the best. Mrs. Munch and Hector Garcia thought very highly of you."

That might have made me happy, once upon a time. Now I just felt numb. "Thanks, Andy, that's kind of you to tell me."

"No problem. I promise I'll keep you posted on my end as long as you promise the same." I promised I'd call and we said goodbye, and though he said he would call the FBI, I called Myles Stanton.

"Mrs. Page. How can I help you?"

I told him about my morning, being laid off, about Jared's potential activities, and the information I got from the payroll system.

"That's quite a bit of information, you've been allowed to find."

"You think they've been playing me too, don't you."

"I might not state it quite like that, but after reviewing the files you had for us, I do think someone wanted the world to know what was going on and you were that conduit for the information. I implore you to be careful. I don't think the person in charge quite expect you." I wasn't sure if I should be happy with that assessment or insulted.

He typed slowly and said, "We've found more on JA Associates, MK and Asset Investments. We're still going through all of the files we confiscated, but you're help has been so help in pinpointing exactly where we need to go."

He was kind and accommodating.

When I finished with Myles, I dialed Will.

"Nikki. How did it go?" I could almost hear him smiling over the phone.

"I was laid off today." I sounded as gloomy as I felt and shivered at the thought.

"Oh. While I'm not surprised they're laying off the firm, I am sorry you got caught in all of this."

"Thanks. I thought I ought to let you know about the new developments." I regaled him with my long morning. Everything I told Andy and Myles. It left me feeling overwhelmed. The tears welled up and the story left me nauseated and warm.

"I'm on my way to a client meeting. If they call you in for anything else, just call me. In the meantime, can I bring you dinner tonight?"

The offer made me laugh. "You don't have to do that. I'm sure you have a life." I wiped tears from my cheeks.

"I have time to comfort an old friend. Let me bring dinner. Enough for four. I can be there at six."

"Thanks. That would be great."

After hanging up, I stared at the bulging envelope on my counter. I wanted to look away but couldn't; if I didn't look at the contents then the layoff didn't really happen.

It was still morning, but I rationalized that it was five o'clock somewhere in the world and poured myself a glass of wine. I stared at it before taking a sip. This was not how I normally handled stress. I sat myself on the sofa, turned on the television and prepared for a day of home decorating.

****

I managed to stay mostly sober through the morning and early afternoon when I had enough tv and felt a little more settled. I stared at the nearly empty bottle of wine and pulled out my records that I had been collecting. I copied some for the FBI and included the spreadsheet, all the check and wire information— all of it. I slipped it all into a nice thick manila envelope and addressed it to Myles Stanton at the FBI. I covered it in stamps and stuck it in the mailbox. I waved to the mailman as he carried it away. Okay, maybe I was a little drunk.

Julia came home at 2:40 like she always did when she wasn't in detention. She was pulling off her backpack when she saw me. "Mom?"

"Hi sweetie. Why are you home early? Detention done?"

"Yeah. Why are you home so early?"

"Lost my job and my friend Will is bringing dinner. Eat a snack. Not sure what he's bringing." I was revved up, nearly chipper.

"You lost your job?" Julia's lip quivered. I thought she might cry.

I think that was the moment I sobered up. I patted her shoulder. "I discovered something at work, and it's put the firm in a bad place. They're laying off all of the employees and moving to a new office in St. Louis." I put my arm around her.

"Are we gonna have to move?" Tears filled her eyes and her lower lip trembled. I put my hands on her shoulders and sat on the stool at the island, nearly falling. I might have felt sober in the moment, but soon knew I wasn't.

"I know it's been scaring here the last two weeks and it sounds bad, but we don't have to move." I kept my gaze on her. "The firm is giving me a severance package; I have my insurance. And I'll get new job." My phone rang. I grimaced when I checked the screen. "Okay." I patted her hair.

The ring grew louder. Julia didn't seem to calm after my explanation. I wrapped my arms around her and kissed her head. "We'll be fine. I promise." The phone stopped ringing. I sighed with relief.

"Is your boss going to come back here?"

"If he does, I promise, I won't talk to him again. He'll after to figure it out on his own."

Julia held me tight as my phone beeped. My mom must have left a message. It could wait.

My daughter held me tighter, and I fought the tears from falling. It had been too much. All the time Justin came to the house and followed me out and put us in danger. I didn't do enough to keep the safe. I vowed I'd do better. My daughter shouldn't be trembling in my arms.

"Will you be okay?" She pulled away and nodded.

"I'm so sorry."

Julia slunk to the den and slowly emptied her backpack as I dialed my mom.

"Hey, Mom. What's up?"

I felt way too cheery. Julia looked at me with confusion before turning on the television.

"You sound happy. Where are you?" Mom asked.

"At home." It all started to spill out. "My friend Hector, from work, died yesterday. I found him hanging over my desk." I started to chuckle. Damn wine. "They closed the office now that it's a crime scene. Oh shit." My empty wine glass toppled over rolled off the counter and fell to the floor, smashing into hundreds of shards.

"Are you drunk?" my mother asked incredulously.

That made me laugh, deeply. "Just a little. Listen. My boss, you know, Justin. He's innocent. He didn't do any… thing. But he's still in hiding. Hector was a good man. Who was killed because he realized what had happened and someone made it look like a suicide. And the best part… the best part is today; they had the nerve to lay me off!" I was winded after relaying my day. I was happy. No. Not happy. Lightheaded. No. No. I was just drunk.

"So, you drank. It's the afternoon," Mom said.

"Yep. So, it is. I think had my first glass at 9. I'm good." Julia turned to face me a quizzical look on her face. I gave her a thumbs up. Her mouth opened wide in disbelief and when she realized I was drunk, she smiled as if she learned a great secret. I tried to not drink in excess, I hated hangovers and I didn't like being drunk in front of my kids. Sometimes my rigidity waned. While I thought I should have felt guilty, in that moment, I felt justified and wondered if my mom was rolling her eyes. That image made me giggle.

"Do I need to come over?" she asked.

"Nope, I'm aaall good."

Julia rested her arms on the back of the sofa and watched me with fascination. I might have to pay for this with cookies, or worse.

"I'm sorry about your friend and your job Nics, but you have kids and shouldn't be handling all of this with drink. Go take a shower, drink some coffee and take an aspirin," Mom chided me.

"Will do. Gotta go. Gotta thing tonight."

I think I said goodbye before hanging up. I looked back at Julia, still watching.

"You're drunk."

"Yeah. I guess I am." I began to pick up the small shards of glass lying on the floor feeling a bit stupid for drinking in the middle of the day.

"Why?"

I thought of my mom's reaction to my news, and how my drunkenness was what she took from it. Julia came over.

"Be careful. There's small pieces everywhere." Julia emulated me picking up the larger pieces and dumping them in the trash.

When we finished with that I rolled the vacuum cleaner over and picked up the rest.

I observed Julia as she pulled the full garbage bag out of the trash and tied it closed. She dropped it by the island, reached under the sink and put a new one in.

"I'm drunk because the last two weeks have been horrible and I just…" I sat on the island stool. Julia seemed to be hanging on my every word. "I got drunk because I didn't want to have to deal with everything. I wanted the world to stop for just an hour so I could take a breath. And grandma…" I looked at my phone when it beeped.

Nics. Sorry I was so harsh. I can come and help. Give you a hug.

No. I'll be fine. I just need to sleep.

I knew part of what my mom had said was correct. This was not me.

I turned on the coffee machine, made myself a strong coffee and sat in the den with Julia as I tried to ease the coming hangover and forgive my lapse in judgement.

****

Wilma, Shelia, and Patti Anne had called me in a conference call just as my hangover was starting to recede. "I got mine at 10:00," Wilma said about her severance package. "When did you get yours?" she asked me.

"8:00," I mumbled. I glanced at the clock. Will would be at my house in two hours. I sighed.

"We're just so busted up about it," Shelia said.

"I can't believe they fired you first. Girl, you discovered the laundering they should be happy about it," Patti Anne said.

"And that's why they fired me first." I wanted to tell them the rest of it, Justin calling me, his visits, Jared's role. I kept my mouth shut. The less they knew, the better.

"Oh, I'll miss you all so much," Shelia cried. I could tell she was emotional. If I wasn't so angry about all that had happened, I might have been too.

"Can't you tell us what you know, hon?" Patti Anne asked.

"I wish I could. I think it would be best if you let the investigators put it all together." I couldn't think of anything else to say. I glanced at the clock again. "Actually, I have a meeting tonight. I need to prepare." I thought that would be enough.

"A date maybe," Wilma joked.

It wasn't a date and yet I was nervous, or maybe it was the alcohol still in my system. "No. A lawyer friend is helping me navigate all of this stuff with the law firm. I just need to get ready. I'm going to miss you all."

We said teary goodbyes.

I jumped in the shower, put on clean clothes, brushed my teeth, and drank loads of water. I didn't want Will to know I had been drunk by the afternoon and I wished Julia hadn't seen it, but she had. And when she looked at me she gave me a smirk, like she knew a secret and was willing to spread it all over.

"So, what's it gonna take to not spread rumors about me and my drunk afternoon," I asked her.

"Well, since you're not working tomorrow, I think cookies would be awesome."

I figured.

"Chocolate chip would be awesome too, I suppose."

I turned when Jacob entered. He had just gotten home from basketball practice. He was sweaty and his gangly body moved through the kitchen. He looked at me with concern when he saw me rubbing at my temple.

"You okay mom?" he cocked an eyebrow.

"She's drunk off her ass," Julia called out. She was at the island with a shit-eating grin on her face.

"Shhh. That was our little secret." I held my fingers to my lips.

He smiled. "Uh, what happened?"

"Lost my job today and got a wee bit carried away." I lifted the empty bottle and put it back down.

Jacob laughed a little. "You've had a few crappy weeks."

I shrugged. "I suppose they have been. Thanks for being so helpful and kind and not telling all of your friends."

He shook his head. "What's for dinner?"

"My friend Will is bringing it. I'll call you when he gets here."

Jacob carried his bag upstairs, headed toward a shower. Julia watched me intently. I blinked rapidly. "Don't you have homework?"

She smiled again.

"I've never seen you drunk. It's kinda funny."

I stuck my tongue out at her. She laughed and turned back to continue her homework. I took a bottle of water, sat in the sunroom, and stared out my windows. My neighbor's lights were on, and the school behind the house lit up the night sky. But my backyard, you could get lost in the darkness. For just a moment, I wanted to hide in it. Quiet, silent, alone. I wanted to forget that I ever got the Cabot file, that I ever discovered the money laundering. And mostly I wished that I hadn't learned the truth about Jared, about Justin, and about Sherman Munch.

I chugged down more water when the doorbell rang. Before I could answer, Julia was already opening the door.

Will smiled when he saw me. Julia held her hand on the door handle and smirked at him. Will smiled.

"You must be Julia. I'm Will."

"Julia, let him in." I reached for the food and kissed his cheek. He held my arms and looked down at me.

"You look a little…"

"Drunk would be the word you're looking for. Come in. We'll eat. I'm starving."

I laid out the plates and silverware, Julia pulled down the glasses and found the napkins. Jacob lumbered downstairs. "Will, Jacob. Jacob, Will." Jacob nodded, took a seat, and began emptying the bags of food. There was a bucket of broasted chicken, rolls, roasted potatoes, and coleslaw.

"Thanks for all of this. It's been a day," I said as I scooped a little of each on my own plate.

"No problem." He glanced around the house. It had been so long since we had seen each other socially. "Nice house."

He took his food. I watched the kids eat, shoveling chicken and potatoes into their faces. Julia looked up at Will and studied his face. "Are you marrying my mom?" she asked. It was almost innocent, though I knew Julia well.

Will smiled. "I've been friends with your mom for a long time. Nearly twenty-five years, I think. I'm just here for moral support. She's had a very rough two weeks." He smiled again and looked at me with raised eyebrows.

"I've never seen you," Julia said.

"It's been a very long time since your mom, and I have seen each other. You were probably a baby last time I saw you. I'm helping your mom with a problem right now."

That seemed to satisfy her, but her curiosity was strong and she periodically looked at him when he was eating. We talked about the cooling weather, about the Cubs blowing it in the playoffs. He asked Jacob about his basketball season. Jacob even answered without a mouthful of food.

When the plates were cleared off and placed in the dishwasher, I turned it on and brought Will to the sunroom.

"Very nice house. Very sweet kids," he said as he sipped his coffee on the sofa. I sat across from him in the large chair and tucked my legs underneath myself. I held my tea but didn't drink.

"Thanks." I kept talking before I could stop myself. "I told Justin what I know."

Will looked at me over the top of the mug. "Did you let the FBI know that?"

I shook my pounding head. I wished I hadn't told him. "Will I be in trouble?"

"Don't tell them, and I'll pretend I didn't hear that. He's still wanted for questioning." He took another sip. "Who did it?"

I shrugged. "I'm thinking Jared. I looked at some payroll information. He doesn't make much and doesn't bill as much as the other two partners. It's always about money. And sex. But mostly money." I blushed slightly and took a long sip of tea.

Will chuckled. "If he calls again, tell him to go to the police." He put his mug down on the table. "You look tired."

"Drunk, remember?"

"You were serious about that?"

I nodded. "I guess I haven't really been handling the stress."

"Have you ever thought you should give yourself a break?"

I took a sip of tea. He watched me thoughtfully.

"What?" I asked.

"It will be okay. I'm thinking they laid off everyone to reduce their liability. Make a quick change to save face."

"Do you think I'm safe?"

He sipped his coffee. "I will advise you to keep your eyes open. Be careful. Whoever killed Hector is still out there." He reached over and held my hand.

"What are you going to do now?"

I moved to the edge of the chair. "Update my resume. I'm sure I can find a job somewhere." I closed my eyes. I was still dizzy. "Hopefully."

"My administrative assistant is going on maternity leave next week. I'm not a large firm. I'm not big enough for a second paralegal, but I could use the help. It would be a combination of admin and paralegal if you're interested."

I glanced at him and grimaced. "Are you making that up?"

He laughed and shook his head. "No. I'm not. It's serious. I thought about it on the way over. It would be nice to have an admin who can do the legal stuff too. At least it'll keep you working."

"Can I think about it when I'm not drunk or hungover? My head is about to explode." I made a motion with my hands, expanding them from my temples and blowing them out. I laid my head against the high armrest and smiled at Will.

"I'll call you in the morning. If there's anything you need from me until then, call me."

He pulled me up from the chair and I walked him to the front door. He brushed his lips against mine. It had been a while since I was kissed. I wanted to wrap my arms around him, but we've never had that kind of relationship and I was still feeling the effects of the wine. I stepped back.

"I'll talk to you in the morning. Drive safe." Behind him, rain fell against the sidewalk. He walked to his car and backed it down the curvy driveway. I stood at the door even after I could no longer see his brake lights. I raised my head to the sky, my arms outward letting the rain cool me, and in a funny way, lift my spirits. When I started to tremble in the cold, I stepped back inside and locked the door for the night.

CHAPTER 21

I always kept my cell phone on, on the off chance that Emily needed to reach me in the middle of the night. When the doorbell rang at 2:11 a.m., it took me a moment to wake and realize it wasn't the phone. Someone was leaning on the doorbell. I jolted awake with a hammering heart. I worried Emily was in a car accident, dead at the side of the road, drunk and in jail, or dead in the hospital. I grabbed my robe, turned on the outside light and without looking through the viewer, I flung open the door. My heart stopped when I looked at the strange man at my door.

"Nikki Page?"

"Y...yes. Who are you?" I felt like my legs were going to buckle under me.

"I'm Detective Angelo Martino from the Chicago Police Department." He held up his identification. I blinked away the tears.

"How can I help you at two in the morning?" My mouth went dry, I rubbed my lips with my trembling hand.

"Do you know Justin Able?"

Justin? I felt my heart calm, my legs stand straighter. Not Emily. And then I thought of Justin and the police here at two in the morning. Only answer the questions, nothing more.

"Yes. He was my former boss." It was nothing but the truth.

"I'm sorry to inform you, he was found dead at midnight."

I leaned against the wall as I took that in. "I... have you called his wife?"

I couldn't fathom why they'd be contacting me.

"We have. The reason I'm here, he was found with an empty messenger bag, with a note stuck inside. It had your name and phone number." He held up the plastic bag with the sticky note inside, my name and number clearly visible. "Do you know why he had this?"

He was dripping wet from the steady rain, and I invited him inside the foyer to drip on my rung inside. I felt lightheaded and sat on the stairs looking up at detective Martino.

"I'm sorry. It's just a shock."

"I'm sure seeing me here so early is. If you could just tell me why he had your name and number."

I nodded. "Justin's been calling me for a week, wanting help with several cases he was working on." Not exactly the truth.

"He had been wanted for questioning. Did you know this?"

"Yes." Only answer the question, I reminded myself.

"You could be charged with obstruction of justice for not advising the police that he was contacting you."

My stomach sunk and roiled and my hands trembled. I didn't bother hiding it. I felt the anger boil over. "I did call the police! I called the FBI! Neither was interested enough to follow through on tracing my phone. I don't know what they were doing to find him! They wanted me to pass on fake information. I did. It's not my fault he wouldn't turn himself in!" My heart raced and I tried to catch my breath.

Detective Martino grimaced and marked something in his little notebook. "You say the FBI gave you information to pass to him but didn't prepare to pick him up should he come to your house?"

I gave him the name of my two FBI contacts. "Call them for the details." I stifled a nervous yawn. "I'm sorry, but how did he die?"

He continued to make notes in his book. "He was shot between the eyes. It looked like a pro hit."

I was startled by that news. I would have expected Jared or his partner Sherman to pull the trigger, not a pro. Maybe they hired someone.

"Do you have any idea who might want him dead?" Detective Martin asked.

Only answer the question. "It looked like he was laundering money through the law firm. While I don't think he did it, I think whoever did do it, is responsible for his death and for the murder of Hector Garcia. Though I have no proof, just educated guesses."

I was silent for a moment. He asked, "So, who do you guess?"

I rolled my eyes, frustrated, and tired. "I'd start with his brother Jared Able or Jared's business partner Sherman Munch. Yes, the son of Mrs. Munch, the other partner in the firm."

I did a mental palm plant to my forehead. It was too much. Too much information.

"Did you want him dead?"

My eyes widened. "No. I didn't. I had no beef with him. I just wanted to know who was implicating me in the money laundering and most of all, I want to know who killed my friend Hector." I sighed as the tears welled in my eyes.

"Thank you, Mrs. Page. I'll contact you again if I have any other questions."

He pulled his collar up against his neck and walked out in the rain. I didn't watch him back out or drive down the street. I sat on the bottom step, hung my head, and cried.

****

"Hey Nikki. I was going to call you in about an hour. What's up?" Will sounded awfully cheery this morning. I couldn't say the same. I finally pulled myself out of bed at six, having not slept at all since Detective Martino appeared at my door at 2 a.m. I was on my second cup of coffee, and it was only 8 a.m.

"Justin was killed with one bullet to the head. I got a visit from a Detective Angelo Martino with the CPD early this morning."

Will stopped typing. "Oh. Jeez. Nikki. I'm sorry. But why did he come to you?"

I began to speak but my voice was raw. I took a sip of coffee and swallowed. "Justin had a sticky note in an empty messenger bag with my name and number on it."

"What did you tell this Detective Martino?"

"I told him Justin's been calling me. Martino threatened me with obstruction of justice and I explained to him that the police and the FBI both know he's been contacting me. He seemed confused by that. He also asked if I wanted Justin dead."

Will held the phone away from his face and spoke to someone in his office. When he returned, he said, "Okay. Next time any police organization calls you, ask for a lawyer and then call me. This is getting ridiculous. It seems to me like someone is still trying to implicate you in this."

"The handwriting expert determined my handwriting isn't a match to the bank account signature cards."

"Well, that's something."

"I didn't do anything." My voice rose an octave. I dropped my head in my hands. "I'm sorry. This is just too much."

"Get me all the files you have. I think I need to take a deep dive into what you've found."

The files were sitting on my counter; I stared at them. "I'll be at your office in an hour." After we hung up, I put them all in my bag, locked up and headed out.

****

Traffic flowed around me as I made my way to Will's office, but one car caught my eye. It was three cars behind mine and seemed to follow me as I turned on Quentin Road. It hadn't left my tail as I made the twenty-minute drive south. I suppose it could have just been heading to Schaumburg like me, but when it turned on Algonquin Rd left like me, my heart sped up. I wondered if it might be police protection or a stake out and tried to see if it was Andy Butcher, the FBI, or Detective Martino.

While I couldn't see who was inside, my hands trembled as I turned into Will's business complex. When the car slowed but continued down the street, I let out a breath and found a parking spot outside the office.

I had worked at Able, Able, and Munch for three years. It was a beehive of activity with three partners and five lawyers, a whole department of paralegals, administrative assistants, and human resource staff. Will's office was quiet and clean, with marble floors and a reception desk near the front door. I approached the administrative assistant with an outstretched hand. "Hi I'm Nikki Page. I'm here to see Will Mann." The admin smiled at me, and I noticed her round belly.

"Hi. I'm Angie. I heard you might be taking over for me while I'm on maternity leave. I hope you take the job; poor Will doesn't know what he'll do."

She called Will to let him know I was there, and I didn't wait long. Will opened the two glass doors and smiled at me. He offered me a hug, a kiss on the cheek. "I'm glad you're here. Follow me."

The hallway led in both directions. At each end of the hallway were doors with a third in the middle of the hall. "That way is the library, my paralegal works in there. Here's the storage room, the bathroom is outside the main doors." I followed him to the left; he opened the door to an office. It felt just right, just like Will. Bookshelves lined the wall opposite his desk. It was filled with books and mementos. His desk held a few small piles of files, an open law book. The window across from the door let in light and had a great view of the highway.

The floors were marble, and the paint was light and bright. I sat across from him in one of two visitor's chairs that were more like something I might have in a living room at home, cushioned well with a sage green fabric. I sat back with my briefcase in my lap, my hands holding the strap tightly, as if I were fighting to not give away the information inside. I held my breath as I watched Will take a seat behind his desk. He smiled, folded his hands together.

"You look nervous," he said.

"I am. I just keep thinking it's getting worse and there's no end in sight." I opened the briefcase and pulled out all the information I accumulated.

"I basically know what you've told me." He opened the first folder with my notes and took a moment to take in the information. He perused several other papers, stopping on the spreadsheet. "That's quite an enterprise." He squinted and took a closer look. "I can see how Justin was implicated." He turned the page.

I was fidgety and tapped my fingers against my leg. Sweat began to bead on my lower back. I watched Will take a second look.

"It looks thorough. I'm sure that firm will have nothing left. I wonder what Jared will do," Will said.

I hadn't thought about where he would be going. If evidence truly pointed to Justin, Jared would be out free. "Someone wanted the enterprise to be exposed. I'm sure of that considering the document came to me. They knew I'd question it. I'm guessing it wasn't Jared and I'm guessing Mrs. Munch won't bring him with her." I ran my hand through my hair and leaned against the arm of the chair.

"You look tired. Didn't sleep?"

"I hit my breaking point." My voice squeaked and I grimaced.

"You exposed this. I worry about you."

That sent shivers up my spine. I had the same worry and thought of the car that followed me here.

"Do you have copies of this?" he asked.

"Yes."

He took the files, neatly stacked them, and put them inside the drawer. He locked it, pocketed the key, and looked at me. "So, can I convince you to come work here? At least while Angie's on maternity leave?"

I could use the money. It would help not having to use my severance pay. "Yeah. I could do that. Typing, filing, some paralegal stuff?"

"Yeah. I'm not sure how much training you'd need. It's probably pretty much what you do now."

"So, no training today?"

"No. I think you need to get some sleep. Like I said, it's pretty much what you did at Able, Able, and Munch."

I nodded. I was feeling the lack of sleep and thought a mug of coffee, a bucket actually, might be good right now.

"No problem. You want me in at eight on Monday? Seven-thirty maybe?"

He raised an eyebrow. "Eight is perfect. I'm busy, but I'm much smaller than what you're used to." He wrote something on a piece of paper and passed it to me. I opened it.

It was less than what I was making at Able, Able, and Munch, but not by much. I glanced at him. "Really?"

"You're a paralegal. It's more than Angie makes but, you'd be doing more specialized work. My paralegal's name is Stacey. She's good but doesn't have your experience. I have a feeling you'll be able to do more for me than she does. If it works out that way, I'll readjust. But yeah. I'll pay you that." He pointed to the piece of paper. I stood and held out my hand.

"Well then, I'll see you Monday morning."

He walked around the desk, offered a friendly hug. "Thanks. We'll keep things loose and open when her maternity leave is over. Okay?"

I was overwhelmed by my luck and could only nod.

"In the meantime, be careful. If you see something odd, call the police." He kissed my forehead. As of now, he was still a friend, not my boss. It might be different Monday.

"Thanks, Will. This will help. It definitely helps."

I stopped at Angie's desk. "I'll be here Monday. Good luck with the baby."

Angie smiled. "Thanks. I'm glad he found you. I was worried about him. I think the divorce has him a little absent minded about some things."

I stared back through the glass doors and nodded. I said goodbye and headed home.

****

As a cautious driver, I checked my mirrors often, drove carefully, in the middle lane or the lane I'd be turning in even if it wasn't for miles. I had three kids, and whatever I did, I put them first. But the ride home from Will's office had me on edge as I paid extra careful attention to the cars that passed me, or followed me, or turned with me.

I noticed the same car I saw when I drove to Will's. It was a beige Buick, I'm sure hand-picked for being innocuous, but right now it stood out. It turned left with me, it stayed back about two cars, and when I turned right onto Quentin, it followed me.

I worried, I was tired, and this was crazy, and I was imagining it. But I changed lanes and so did the Buick's driver. I changed lanes again, driving around a car. It was a last-minute decision and the car that was following me was now four cars behind mine. I sped up as the light turned yellow; the car that was tailing me hadn't made the light and was stopped. I figured whoever was following me must know where I live so I took a different way home. Maybe, I thought for a minute, maybe they'd give up and leave me alone.

But whoever was driving that innocuous car found me on Rand Rd. I switched lanes again and it followed me. I swung back around down Long Grove Road and ran through the red light. I wouldn't have minded a cop finding me, but of course when I wanted one, there wasn't one around.

I pulled into my neighborhood and sped a little faster than I should have through the residential streets. In the mirror, the beige car was close to my back end. And rather than turning on my street. I drove to the stop sign and stopped. He didn't.

I felt the force of the other car as it hit my trunk and crunched. I flew forward against the steering wheel and slammed back. The driver's seat flew forward and then backwards until it was lying flat, and I was staring at the ceiling of my Camry. I momentarily worried that the driver would stop, pull me from the wreckage, and take me away. I wondered if I should call my ex, have him take the kids, keep them safe. Instead, I heard the crunching of the car behind me as it pulled away from the wreck and tires squealed away. It was a warning. I knew they wanted me to back off. And as of now, I would.

I was still in shock, unable to move, my body trembling. Someone yanked my car door open, and I stared up at my neighbor.

"Are you okay, Nikki?"

It was Tony. He had lived next to me for fourteen years. His wife died last year, and his kids were grown, off and away with their own families. He helped me sit. When I tried to release my seat belt, it was stuck.

"I can't get out." I felt the rising panic, my heart raced as I realized that someone purposely ran into me.

Tony pushed on the seat belt button as a police car pulled up next to me, blocking the entrance to the neighborhood.

"Hi. We got a call of a hit-and-run. How are you feeling?" According to his name tag, he was Officer Roberts. I glanced up at him as he looked inside. His gaze landed on my seat belt where it had broken and trapped me inside.

"I'm okay. My seatbelt's stuck."

He returned to his car, came back with a bolt cutter, and cut the belt from my waist. I swung my legs out of the car as Officer Robert checked on the back end of my Camry. It had been crunched like an accordion.

When I stood, I felt lightheaded and sat back down.

"Take it easy ma'am. I have an ambulance coming to check on you. Are you up for telling me what happened?" Officer Roberts asked when he returned.

The last two weeks ran through my head, bits and pieces of scenes, Hector, the Cabot file, Justin's unshaven face, my friends, the beige car. My head was swimming, and when I took a breath in, I could feel the bruises forming.

"I had a job interview this morning. I thought I saw a beige Buick following me. When I turned into the office complex, it continued ahead. I…" I took a deep breath and shuddered. "When I left the interview, it followed me home."

Officer Roberts looked at me and back at the trunk of my car. "I'm guessing there's part of the story I'm missing, like why would you be followed?"

I felt chilled. Officer Roberts held up his hand, walked to his car and returned with a blanket, slipping it over my shoulders. "Can you continue?"

I shook my head, wishing I hadn't. The dizziness was increasing.

"Detective Andy Butcher can give you background. Why…" Tears welled in my eyes and slowly rolled down my cheeks. Officer Roberts dialed Andy.

I heard uh huhs, and ohs. And he'd glance at me and return to Andy. I rested on the steering wheel. When Officer Roberts returned, the ambulance sirens were close, he squatted beside me.

"Detective Butcher's on his way. He thinks it might be a warning to you, to back off. Do you have any idea who wants you to back off?"

I shook my head, something I shouldn't have done, again. I was pretty sure I had a concussion.

The ambulance pulled in front of my car, just as an innocuous black sedan pulled into the neighborhood.

I looked at Officer Roberts. "All I can say is, someone with Able, Able, and Munch. Beyond that, I don't know."

Officer Roberts walked to the EMT explained the situation and two young men walked to me, one carrying a large case.

"Mrs. Page. How are you feeling?" I explained the forming headache, the bruising, the nausea. They did a cursory exam. I could hear Officer Roberts and Detective Butcher, speaking in low tones. My neighbor, Tony stood behind my car watching intently, a worried look on his face. When our gaze met, he offered a smile.

After my short exam, the EMT named Brian asked, "It appears to be a mild concussion. Would you like to go to the hospital?" The EMT named Philip was taking my pulse.

"No. I'm fine. Just dizzy." I swung my legs out of the car. Brian took my hand and helped me stand.

"Ma'am. Mrs. Page. I would rest for today and tomorrow. Follow up with your regular doctor," Philip said.

"I will, thanks."

They packed up their bag and reloaded the ambulance. I turned and took a first look at the back of my car.

It had been crushed in, like an accordion. My knees buckled. Tony reached for my arm and held me up.

"It looks pretty bad. Are you okay?" he asked.

"I will be. I just don't know what I'm going to do?" It came out rather whiny. I think this was the last straw.

"I'm a little dizzy and nauseated. But it could just be the shock. Or hunger." I tried to smile. "I think I'm okay."

He put an arm around me and pulled me into him and that made me feel steadier. "Thanks, Tony. I'll probably have to get checked out."

"Yeah." He paused for a moment. "I heard the cop. Why would someone do this, warn you off?"

"It's a long story and it just got more complicated. I was laid off because of it."

When Officer Roberts finished talking to Andy Butcher, he walked over to us. "I talked to Andy. I'm going to write this up and send it to him, and the FBI. I'll send you the report for insurance. We're towing your car; as it's evidence now." He let that sink in for a moment.

"Thanks for your help." He nodded once and returned to his cruiser. Andy joined me."

"How are you feeling?"

"Nauseated, headachy, achy…" I wiped tears from my cheeks. "Scared," I managed to say.

"I'll have the police send a cruiser more often until we figure out who did this to you. I spoke with Myles Stanton. They are looking into several people. In the meantime, I'll be working on the car that followed you. Can I ask where you had gone this morning?"

I told him about my job interview and gave him Will's address. I leaned against Tony. The accident had worn me out.

"Can I give you a ride home?" Andy asked.

I smiled through the tears. "No. I live down there." I pointed without enthusiasm.

"I'll take her home. I'm her neighbor."

A tow truck arrived, and I watched as the operator lined up with my car, got out and hooked the car up.

Officer Roberts went to speak with the driver, pointed to me and returned. "Why don't you grab what you need and then you can go."

I grabbed my purse, my phone, a jacket. There was nothing else I could think I'd need. I returned to Tony, and we watched as the tow truck pulled my car onto the truck bed.

"I'll send you my report tonight. When I have information for you, I'll pass that on. You sure you don't need a ride?"

"I'm good, thanks." I said, still in shock. After a few minutes, Officer Roberts climbed into his cruiser and followed the tow truck. When we were alone, Tony led me back down the road to home.

CHAPTER 22

I'm fine, Mom," I said for what felt like the tenth time. After Tony left me securely in my house, I called my mom and told her about the fender bender. She'd eventually find out if I didn't. The new car I was going to have to buy would have been a sure giveaway.

"A car accident! I'll be right over."

"Mom." But she had already hung up. I still felt shocked and now pain in my neck and back.

When the phone rang, I hoped it was Mom telling me she wasn't coming. It was my daughter, Emily, calling from college. I rubbed my temples and answered.

"Hi sweetie. What's up?"

"I think I'm failing math." I stifled a chuckle. I had always been failing math growing up. I spent most of high school in the tutor's office and barely got a C.

"Go to the student center and find a math tutor." I said. I know I've given this advice before, but for Emily, it seemed as though she needed something more. I wasn't sure what I could give her from home.

"But Mom."

I bit my tongue to keep from speaking. She had anxiety, and ADHD. She was sensitive and I've spent so much time accommodating her. It was hard to find that line between let her go and being there for support. And with my head starting to pound, I really didn't have much to say.

"Emily, honey, math was my worst subject growing up, there's not much I can do to help. So just tell me what you need. Do you need to just vent, do you need advice, or do you need me to do something for you? I can't do much from here."

"School's hard," she said in a small voice. She was crying.

"It's college."

"Mom!"

"Sweetie." I closed my eyes, took a breath. "You are so smart. So, determined. You know you could do this. I know you can do this. I need you to remember." I couldn't keep the emotion from my voice.

"I'm trying but it's so hard."

"What would you do when it was hard in high school." I leaned back on the sofa. I had spent so much time accommodating my children, and I feared that I had done more harm than good. Was she ready for college or had I hindered her? I felt as lost as she did.

"Go to my teacher. Ask for help."

"Aren't there tutors there?"

"Yeah, I guess." She sniffled. I could imagine her sitting on her bed, cross legs, wiping her tears. I shuddered.

"Then what should you do?"

"Go to the tutors and talk to my teacher."

I couldn't help but smile, but my heart ached.

"I'm sorry sweetie. I wish I could help. But I can't."

"I know," she said.

"If you promise to get help, and you're okay now, I need to get off the phone. I'm not feeling well."

"What's wrong mom? You sound tired."

"I just lost my job and now the car is smashed up because I was in a fender bender." My mom watched in horror as I started to cry.

"What do you mean you lost your job? Am I going to have to come home? I…" She was scared. So was I.

"School is fine. Dad and I have a college fund for you."

I sighed again.

"You're okay though. The car… Do you need a new car?"

I pictured my bumper. "I'll wait and see what my insurance says. I'm okay. A concussion. I'll be fine. You will be too. I know you."

"I just, it's so hard here."

"I remember thinking the same thing when I started college. I was so good in English through high school and then college... Got my first C on an essay. I was crushed. Scared maybe."

"How did you do it?"

"I wanted a career. I wanted to take care of myself. Be independent. I just studied harder. Met your dad, eventually grew up." Was this enough to convince my daughter to want to adult. I learned the hard way that you couldn't force them to grow up or make changes if they didn't want to. I supposed all I could do was be there for her. I hoped it would be enough.

After a few more supportive words, we finally hung up. I was almost secure in the knowledge she was a lot less stressed than when she called.

The phone beeped again. It was Susie. "Hey Suz, what's up?" Her husband Gary was a Lake Zurich police officer. I knew why she was calling.

"I just heard you had a hit and run. The driver really just left?" I could hear the tinge of worry in her voice.

"Yeah. It's weird. Officer Roberts, the police officer on the scene, followed my car to the station. It's evidence now. Hopefully the damage is enough for a newer car."

"John Roberts. He's a good guy. And single." I rolled my eyes and it made me dizzy. "So how do you feel, though?" I could hear her youngest babbling and the television in the background.

"Actually, I'm already feeling achy. But I'm fine."

"First your job, now this. You're having a horrendous month."

This time I laughed out loud. I really was having a bad stretch. "Yeah. I guess I am."

"Next thing you know that bitch will have her baby and your kids will have a new sibling." She was rushing through her house after the toddler, shouting. "Come back here with that glass!"

"Thanks for reminding me," I said.

"I shouldn't have said anything. This can't be easy for you. Sometimes I wish you weren't alone. Had someone to help you." She's been saying that for the last year. I really didn't think that would have stopped me from losing my job or getting into that accident. Though it would be nice to have someone make me tea.

And as if on cue, Mom walked through the garage door into the kitchen. She only lived ten minutes away. I waved from the sofa in the den, and she went ahead and turned on the Keurig without me needing to ask.

"Listen, my mom's here. I need to go. Tell Gary I'm fine and Officer Roberts was kind. I'll talk to you later."

Before she could say goodbye, I could hear her running after her youngest, I wondered if she was still after the glass.

"How are you feeling?" Mom asked as she sat beside me, waiting for the tea to drizzle from the maker.

"I'm fine, Mom. I feel silly that you dragged yourself here. I think I just need sleep and time.

"How hard did that car hit you?"

I shuddered thinking of the back end of my car. "Hard. I guess." I curled into the corner and let Mom cover me with a blanket.

She touched my cheek and went to make me the tea.

When the tea was made, Mom prepared it how I liked, and came back, handing me the hot mug. I watched the billowing steam.

"You need help," she said. I glanced at her.

"I'm fine. I'll be fine."

"I'm not telling you to get married. I'm worried because after the divorce you through yourself into your kids and you completely ignored you."

I looked at her, unsure if I was angry that she was interfering or frightened that she was correct. *Why couldn't I just accept the help? Why did I feel so guilty?*

I didn't know what to say and searched my mom's face as if that would give me an answer.

"You're speechless."

She touched my hand. My first thought was to pull away, I let her rest hers on mine. "No. You're right and I have no answer for that. I just needed to focus on them. I still do."

"No. Emily's an adult..."

I held up my hand. "She's struggling in school. She calls all the time. I still have to be there."

"So be there but less. They're older. They can do for themselves. It's time you do for them. That ass of an ex moved on. It's time for you too, as well."

"I don't want to date."

Mom rolled her eyes. "Go out with friends. Take up a hobby. Do for you." She sat back and fumbled with the remote as she turned on the tv and search for a show.

"So how are they going to find the car that hit you?" she asked as she settled on a documentary.

"They probably won't." I blew on the tea and took a sip.

"So, now what, Nics?" Mom, never one to just sit, got up to fold the two blankets that on the edge of the sofa. She piled up the coasters that were scattered across the coffee table and placed them in the basket. She wiped away some crumbs on the tabletop.

"Nothing. I'm going to sit here and watch tv until Julia comes home, and then figure out what to make for dinner." I offered a wan smile. The longer I sat, the stiffer my muscles got.

"I'll make dinner." Before I could protest, she was up and searching in the kitchen freezer, for what, I had no idea. She went into the garage and looked in the tall freezer and came back with two boxes of frozen lasagna that she placed in the sink. When she was done, she sat back down on the couch and stared at me.

"What?" I asked as I took a sip of tea.

"This will hinder your job search."

I wrapped the blanket tighter around me. "Remember my friend Will, from college?"

She thought for a moment and then smiled. "Yes. He was a good-looking boy. You should have married him."

I shook my head and felt the world spin. That couldn't be good. Not wanting to think about it, I ignored the dizziness and ignored her comment. "You know the issues I had at work before losing my job. He's helping me with those, and as it turns out, he needs someone to take over for his admin assistant while she's on maternity leave. I start Monday."

"It's not a paralegal position." Mom focused her attention on the television screen, changed the channel and watched about a house in the Bahamas. I laid my head on the back of the sofa.

"I'll be doing paralegal things for him as well as secretarial. It will keep me working until I find something."

"Is he married?" Mom tucked her legs beneath her and grabbed the second blanket, laying it on her lap.

"No. Divorcing right now. And please don't start. He's a good friend and helping me out." I stared at my phone and placed my tea on the table. "I'm getting the mail."

Mom put her hand on my lap. "I'll go. You rest."

I sighed as she left, and I continued to channel surf. There wasn't much daytime television I liked to watch, and I wasn't in the mood to stream something new. Mom returned and placed the pile of mail on my lap. She retrieved the remote and turned it to the cooking channel.

I shuffled through the envelopes: bills in one pile, junk mail on the floor, a handwritten envelope to me with no return address on it. It was flat and felt almost empty. I opened the flap and looked inside. It was a nice, thick card stock, the inside just as neatly written as my address.

You know too much. Meet me in the brewery parking lot at midnight, October 22.

My hand shook as I put the note back into the envelope and shoved it between the cushions. I texted Will about the note as mom oohed and ahhed over a recipe.

Will texted back. *Call the police!*

"I need to make a call." I slipped inside the sunroom and closed the French doors behind me. I sat in the armchair and dialed Andy Butcher. He answered on the first ring.

"Mrs. Page. How are you feeling?"

"I'm okay. A little tired and achy."

"Well, go to the doctor if you feel worse. How can I help you?"

I explained the note that I had just received in the mail.

He was typing quickly and stopped.

"That could be a break in this case. Hmmm…" He was thoughtful for a moment. "This is what we'll do. I'll swing by and pick up the note and drop off the accident report for you. Once I have the note, I'll advise the FBI. We know the murders here and the illegal activity both fall under FBI purview but we're assisting. This meeting could be exactly what we need to put this away." He almost sounded gleeful.

After hanging up, I remained in the sunroom with the door closed. The world was spinning out of control and I wondered if maybe it didn't have to do with the concussion.

****

My mother waited impatiently for Julia to arrive home before we headed to the urgent care to get my head checked out. Mom told Julia about the accident as soon as she walked through the door. I grimaced as Julia ran for me.

"Mom?" Julia asked as she looked at me with a bruise on my temple and my eyes half shut.

"I was just napping a bit. I'm fine, baby. Probably just a concussion." I looked at my daughter, her worry kicked me in the gut.

"Your boss was after you. He came here and scared us. Did he do this?"

I held my breath, let it out slowly. "No, he didn't. It was a fender bender kind of thing." I debated with myself whether to tell her, but she had been here for all of Justin's frantic visits and she felt my fear. I didn't want to worry her. Would I regret that?

"We're going to the doctor."

"I can come too." She pleaded at me with big brown eyes.

I pointed to my colorful and bloated face. "See Grandma packing her purse? She'll take me. I'm not sure how long it's gonna take. I'd rather you stay here and finish homework or eat and watch tv." I squeezed her shoulder and worried for my children as Julia slunk away to her waiting backpack and homework. Why couldn't I tell my children what was really going on, the danger I might be in. Was this my way of protecting them or was I only going to hurt them?

I shuddered, wanted to speak up but she had settled down and watched me as we left.

It was a difficult walk to the car, but I made it and buckled myself in. The urgent care was two miles away in a newly built hospital building, with an urgent care on one side and doctors' offices on the other.

We stepped into the waiting room. I went to the reception desk, gave the woman my name and found a seat along the wall. Mom was already seated and searching for something in her purse.

"This has just been a crazy two weeks for you, Nics." Mom was still digging through her large purse. I think she was organizing it for something to do. And with the headache, it was loud, and I wanted her stop. I bit my lip.

Thankfully, at three in the afternoon, the waiting room was relatively empty, and I was called to register. I gave the receptionist my insurance card, grateful the law firm would be paying for my insurance for the next twelve months. I signed form after form. She put my id bracelet around my left wrist, and I followed the nurse through the doors to the patient rooms, followed by Mom, her purse hitched over her shoulder, her lips now covered in lipstick, her hair fluffed.

I sat on the bed; mom took the chair. I was hooked up to the pulse oxygen monitor and the blood pressure cuff. I held my breath as the cuff tightened and breathed out as the nurse took my temperature. I explained the car accident and the headache and general achiness.

I lay back as the nurse walked out.

"We should have stayed home." I glanced at my phone. We had been here twenty minutes and Jacob had left a text message asking if I was ok. I texted him back, letting him know I was feeling better, as the doctor entered my room.

The doctor walked in. "So, you had a car accident?" After re-explaining the symptoms, he looked at my eyes, felt around my neck, and had me stand and bend at the waist, watching my back.

When he finished, the doctor looked at me. "It's a minor concussion," he said and typed into the computer on the wall by the bed. "I'll give you something for the pain." He typed something else and then hit print. "I'll be right back."

"I know you didn't want to come but I'm glad you did."

"The EMTs said the same. I could have called my doctor in a few days." I was crabby now and ready to go home.

"Nics. It's time you care for yourself. The kids are old enough."

"Habit." I waited not-so-patiently, and I drummed my fingers against my leg. Mom gave me a look I stopped.

"Change your habits," she started to say when the doctor entered. After receiving my discharge papers and instructions for my care tonight, Mom led me out to the car and drove me home.

"Mom." Jacob jumped up from the table where he was doing his homework. "You okay?"

I waved him away, Mom shot me a dirty look. "I'm fine. I…" I reached around and pulled Jacob into an embrace. As much as I loved my children, I think I had been pushing them away in my attempt to protect them from their father and what he had been doing to them. Guilt for past indiscretions.

"I'm fine. I'm…" I pulled Jacob to the sofa where Julia was waiting patiently. While they sat across from me, I sat on the coffee table. "I'm not fine. I mean, I have a concussion and I'll be fine. But the last two weeks… I discovered illegal activities at work and with the job loss, I'm stressed. I'm sorry I've been pushing you away. I just need to take care of this problem and I didn't want you to get hurt."

Jacob and Julia each held a hand. "We're not kids anymore. We can help," Jacob said.

I chuckled in that moment. "I know. I know. Grandma's making dinner and I just want to sit here. Go finish homework and we can sit and watch a movie if you'd like."

I felt lucky and grateful as I lay on the sofa with the television on, watching my kids doing their homework. Periodically they'd glance at me, make sure I was still there and still okay. Absently I stared at my phone until I realized that tonight, at midnight, was October 22.

****

Andy Butcher stopped by my house during dinner. Mom ran for the door and let him in.

"Sorry for disturbing you. I just came by for that letter we spoke about."

The card was where I left it, sandwiched between the sofa cushions. I handed it to him. "Is the FBI going to wait for them? See who shows up?"

"That's the plan. So, I'll say this once. Do not go to the brewery parking lot. We're already concerned they won't be happy you're not there. We just want to grab them when they come." We were talking in the sunroom, away from Mom and the kids, the door closed, the light low. I paced along the patio door.

"Andy, I'm not feeling great, but wouldn't it make sense to put me in a car so they see me? You can nab them before they get to me."

"Can't risk it. We'll have someone watching the house in case they stop here, but we want to grab them without incident."

"My guess is Jared Able." I crossed my arms on my chest and stared at Andy. He nodded.

"Well, if it is, it is. We'll get him and he'll have a lot to explain." He pocketed the card that was now in a plastic bag and closed his jacket. "I'll let you know what happens."

He left, but I didn't feel any better.

CHAPTER 23

I don't think of myself as brave. I'm kind of a fraidy cat when it comes to adventure. When I was a kid, I counted on Susie, my fearless friend, to drag me anywhere and everywhere. So tonight, just before midnight—and I'm not sure why I did what did—I snuck out of the house.

In that moment, as I carefully climbed down the stairs, and grabbed Jacob's car keys, all I could think was, I needed to end this. I needed whoever was in charge to know, no more. I wouldn't let them use me, torment me or put myself in danger anymore.

I started the car and drove to the brewery.

It was weirdly exhilarating as I drove through the empty streets. The nausea and dizziness from earlier in the day had subsided, and as I drove the two miles to the brewery, I glanced into the rearview mirror, looking for a tail, finding none and wondered where the police were who were supposed to be watching my house.

Pushing thoughts aside, I found a sense of freedom the closer I came to my target. I hadn't felt this free in years. I realized—in that moment—how freeing it was to do something you were clearly told not to do. I understood Julia a little better as I pulled into the brewery parking lot.

If the FBI and LZPD were already here, they had hidden themselves well. As I pulled into the parking lot, my eyes darted from the tops of the building to the trees that lined the back side of the parking lot. I completed a three-point turn and faced the only entrance to the lot. I thought this was the best option if I needed to escape.

I shut off the car, watched my lights finally blink out, and pulled my warm winter coat around me. Cold air quickly filled my car.

I wasn't much into beer, but I passed the brewery whenever I was on this side of town. Since I drive this way often, the neighborhood on the other side of the trees was unfamiliar to me. I glanced through the leafless trees and noticed several lumps that I assumed were police officers waiting for the killer or killers. I shuddered as anxiety overcame me. I continued to scan every inch of the brewery lot, trees, and the houses beyond them. It was nearly midnight, and the only lights came from a few scattered houses and two on the corners of the brewery.

Twenty minutes before midnight and I was in place with little time for the Lake Zurich police department and the FBI could kick me out. I wondered how angry they were that I showed up and wondered when they'd be coming to kick me out. I knew they were out there, but they were mostly well hidden—until they weren't. I jumped when Andy tapped on my passenger side window and bumped my head on the roof of Jacob's car.

"You're not supposed to be here," he said when I rolled down my window.

"The killer or whoever wrote that note is expecting me. I need to be here."

His jaw tightened. So did his fists. "You were in a car accident this morning. I can see you still have a concussion." He shone his flashlight in my eyes. *Not fair*, I thought, as I turned away.

There was movement in the trees. I was resolved to stay and turned toward him, giving him my best mom face; the one I gave my kids when I had had enough, and my kids needed to stop what they were doing. I wasn't sure if it would work on a cop. He just sighed.

Several FBI agents in marked jackets and hats, entered the parking lot and Andy joined them. I watched them discuss me and a revised plan; I was determined to stay. When Andy returned to my car ten minutes later, he slipped inside beside me.

"You can stay under certain conditions."

I glanced at him, still wearing my mom face.

He chuckled. "I'll be in here, ducked below the dash, and the FBI agent brought in who resembles you, will sit in the back seat."

I supposed that was fair considering they didn't want me here at all, for safety reasons. A woman my size and with my coloring opened the back door and slid inside. It didn't make me feel any safer and I gripped the steering wheel; I couldn't seem to remove my hands.

"Mrs. Page. You're making this difficult. I really wish you'd go home." She admonished. I felt like one of my kids and turned toward her without the mom face.

"You look a lot like me, I'll give you that. But there's two things. What if he gets a good look and takes off? They might still come after me. They know who I am. Second, I want this over. I'm tired. I'm crabby and my life's been spun around. Besides, there's tons of FBI and the LZ police are here."

I looked back into the parking lot. Empty. I held the steering wheel for support as I turned and was white knuckled as I observed the last of the officers return to their hiding spots.

There was movement above us on the roof of the brewery. I caught the shadows against the streetlights as what I assumed was a SWAT team settled into their places. It felt like overkill, but then, maybe not. I took a deep breath in hopes my heart would stop pounding wildly and my hands would stop trembling.

It was 11:51.

Andy grew tense as did the agent behind me. Both reached for their guns, resting their hands around the handles, ready to pull them out should they need to. My mouth went dry and sweat beaded down my neck and back.

Minutes slowly ticked away, and with each passing minute, I thought I could finally see the light at the end of this nightmarish tunnel. But first, I had to get through this. Just before midnight, Andy ducked below the dash and the FBI agent ducked below the seat. I swallowed, mouth dry, as my leg began to shake.

At midnight a car rolled into the parking lot, its tires crunching on loose blacktop and gravel. It stopped within feet of my car. The headlights blinded me. I held tightly to my steering wheel as the passenger door opened. I concentrated on the silhouette, a man, medium height, a rounded belly.

"What's happening?" Andy asked.

I glanced at the driver, but he was covered in darkness. "At least two people in the car. It appears to be a man exiting the passenger side."

"Can you make out who it is?" Andy asked, anxious to sit up and see for himself.

I turned on my car lights and the man stared at me, at first shocked and then dismayed as he made his way to my car. I stared at the face. He looked just like his mother.

"It's Sherman Munch," I murmured.

He took one step, two steps.

A shot rang out, echoing through the parking lot. A bullet pierced the side of the man's head. Teams ran from the trees as the car backed up and out of the parking lot with the passenger door swinging in and out. Out of the lot, the car shot away from the brewery; a SWAT member took a shot and I heard broken glass. Before anyone could reach the other car, it was gone.

I shook in my seat. My knees knocked together, my hands trembled, I could barely breathe as my stomach churned. I tried to not look back at Sherman Munch crumpled on the black top, but I couldn't look away.

"Stay here." I nodded as Andy and the FBI agent ran from the car. They stood over Sherman who face up. Blood had poured from his temple and seeped across the ground. And from where I sat, I could see his eyes wide open, frozen in surprise.

Nausea rushed through my belly. I pushed my door open and ran for the trees. I held on to the tree until there was nothing left in my stomach. I took shaky steps back to my car, slid down the side and sat on the cold pavement.

Andy found me. I was sweaty and shocked and couldn't stop shaking.

"Can you make a positive ID?" Andy asked.

I glanced at him, nodded, and pulled myself up. My legs shook as I walked over and stared down at a man that was so familiar to me.

"His ID says Sherman Munch. Mrs. Munch's son?"

I nodded. "Yeah. That's definitely him."

"He's owner of JA Associates?" Myles was reading from his notes.

I nodded again. "Yeah." I could still feel the concussion, the waves of dizziness and nausea setting in. "I'm sorry. I should have stayed home. He wouldn't have…" My voice trailed off as I glanced into the trees. They had been packed with the FBI and the LZ police. So where had the killer been hiding and where were they now?

"What do you see?" Andy asked.

"The killer. Where did he hide?"

Andy followed my gaze, his eyes darted across the trees and the neighborhood that lay on the other side. He motioned for one of the cops to join him.

"Watch her," he said to another, and he entered the trees.

"You okay, ma'am?" the officer asked.

I nodded but continued to watch for Andy's form as he exited the trees to the parking lot. It couldn't have been more than five minutes, but it felt like much longer when he finally returned. He came over to me. I was leaning against my car.

"There's a house just on the other side of the trees. It looks empty, and the window beside the front door had been broken. I'm guessing whoever killed him knew this meeting was going down. Most likely either Sherman Munch or his killer was in the car that hit you." Andy leaned against the car. "When they say it's okay, I'll drive you home." He touched my shoulder and joined the group still lingering by the dead body.

The parking lot was filling quickly with the medical examiner, an ambulance, a fire truck, and more people. The medical examiner took his time reviewing the body and making his notes. When he finished, he gave the okay to remove the body from the scene. I watched Sherman Munch being loaded into a body bag and loaded into the ambulance. The doors closed and the ambulance left, the ME following.

Andy finally helped me into the passenger seat and drove me home.

****

I'm a stomach sleeper, but it leaves my back aching when I wake in the morning. Last night, it didn't matter which position I tried, the pain stayed in my head and in my shoulders. I didn't sleep.

By six a.m., I couldn't stare at the ceiling or the dark, deep shadows that crept across my room anymore. I showered and dressed in record time and made myself some tea. The sunroom was cool, almost cold, even with sun light penetrating the many windows and the sliding door. It burned my eyes to look at it, so I turned a quarter of an inch in the large chair, squinted as I read my phone, and took another sip of tea.

Minutes ticked away, and as soon as I could, I called Will. He answered right away.

"What's up?" he was almost cheery for so early.

"The murderer wanted to meet me last night at midnight. I went."

There was silence on the other end, he stopped typing, maybe even stopped breathing. I figured he was holding back anger or worry.

"Why?... Are you okay?"

I took a sip of tea and closed my eyes.

"It was Sherman Munch. Look at the notes I gave you. He's part owner with Jared in JA Associates. He was the passenger in the car. No clue who was driving. He was killed by an unknown assassin." I hadn't expected to tear up. Maybe it was the lack of sleep, or watching someone die, or just losing my job and the rest of it was just too much. I lay back against the tall pillows and stared at the wood ceiling; it needed to be re-stained.

"And you're, okay?"

"Define okay?"

"Nikki, you could have been killed." His voice was strained.

"I wanted it to end. But the killer had other plans." I sipped the tea. The heat felt good as I swallowed.

"You're still in danger."

"Probably. I wish I could have seen the other driver," I mostly murmured that to myself as I heard that familiar whirling of a printer coming awake. Will typed and stopped.

"Stay home today. Please take care of yourself."

"I promise." I meant it. I wasn't feeling great today and based on how I looked in the mirror when I woke up, I didn't want anyone seeing me anyway.

"I have a client coming in. Keep me posted and stay safe."

After hanging up, I spent the next couple hours on my morning routine, rinsing my tea mug, making Julia's lunch, waving both kids off to school and promising my mom if she left this morning, I would spend the day caring for myself. When I was finally alone, I pulled the client files for another review.

****

JA Associates, Asset Investment, MW Enterprises, Investments Unlimited. I pulled a list of the twenty client files. All of them had dubious businesses, with little to no information about them online. There was no social media, very little personal information. I scrutinized every available website and search site we had used at the office.

My pile of printed sheets was growing; I added more paper to the printer.

The doorbell rang.

When I opened the door, the delivery man was already sliding into his van and the package was on the stoop. I picked up the thick envelope, glanced up and down my street and closed and locked the front door.

I recognized the handwriting. It had come from Hector, sent before he died. I slipped a letter opener up and through the seal and looked at the files inside. There was a handwritten note on the top of them.

Nikki,

It was all there in your notes. Sherman Munch. I knew when I saw it, when I saw the notes in the payroll file. You wouldn't have seen it. You haven't worked for Mrs. Munch as long as I have. It was her odd notes. When I deciphered them, I completed my own spreadsheet. All of the money entered into Asset Investment and out through all of the other

*companies. It was all in her notes, in the payroll
system.*

*I copied you and sent it to you and now I'll talk
to her. If it goes wrong, you'll know, you'll get it to
the right people.*

I should have seen it sooner.

Best always.

Hector

I pulled out his spreadsheet and there it was, all twenty clients, all the money into Asset Management, all the money out to MW Enterprises and one last cleansing to JA Associates. It was simple and clean and deadly. But it didn't tell me exactly who killed Justin, Hector and it didn't tell me where Marcie was, or who gave me the file that exposed it all. Or who killed Sherman and who was driving the car.

I ran the files up to my room and hid them in my closet, under several boxes of shoes. My heart hammered in my chest; my eyes grew bleary.

Or did it explain everything? Did she fire me to keep me quiet? Did she think I'd drop it, forget it, no longer be involved? Was everyone else gone?

I called Patti Anne. She answered on the second ring.

"Nikki. Girl. Did something else happen?" She said in her Southern drawl.

"Is everyone gone now?" I asked. I could never read her emotions; she was always even.

"Yes. Mrs. Munch let the rest of us go yesterday. They still haven't told us what happened. Justin's dead, Hector's dead, and Marcie's missing. I heard Sherman Munch was killed last night. That's the last news I heard." She stopped talking and took a breath.

"Yeah. I heard the same thing. I thought she might not have fired everyone. I thought some people might go with her."

"No. Everyone was let go. They still won't tell us what happened. Why is Justin dead? And Hector?" Her voice rose with her anxiety. I had never heard that happen before.

"Client accounts used to launder money. Someone gave me a file that brought my attention to it. It got out of hand."

"What kind of cooked books?"

"It's an FBI case. All I can say is money laundering. I can't get you caught up in it." Patti Anne was quiet, either wanting to ask me more or afraid to. Either way, it was odd for her to be quiet. My other line was ringing but I wasn't sure I wanted to answer.

"Okay. I need to go." Patti Anne said.

"Take care and keep in touch," I replied.

The phone rang again as I sat in the corner of the sunroom couch.

I answered the phone without knowing who was calling. It belonged to the number that flashed across the screen. Maybe I shouldn't answer. "Hello?"

"Is this Nikki?"

I recognized the voice, though he didn't sound jovial. "Jared?"

"I need to talk to you."

My hands shook.

"What do you need, Jared?" I asked as I moved from the sunroom to the front living room; I stared out onto my street. It was quiet. No one was outside.

"The files."

I swallowed and closed my eyes.

"Everything should be in the archives. It's all there."

"All of them?"

"Yes."

He was quiet for a moment. I wondered what went on in his mind, what thoughts were churning.

"I've been removed from the system. I need in." *Someone's been cleaning up the mess*, I thought.

"You're no longer with the firm?"

Something crashed around him, and while it was muffled, I still jumped. "There is no firm anymore. If that asshole brother of mine hadn't laundered money through the business, we'd all still have jobs."

He was lying. He wanted to know what I knew. I walked to the back of the house, there was no one in my yard. I glanced at the clock on the wall. It was two and Julia would be home soon. I ran for my bedroom and locked the door. I found my laptop and logged on.

"So, you don't know how it worked?"

"No! Why would I know?"

I pulled up my email and sent an important one, hoping against hope it would be received.

"Where are you?" I asked him. He was clearly somewhere loud, with lots of activities.

"I'm at home. Where are you?"

"I'm at my temp job." I wished I was there with Will, where he could protect me from this maniac. The owner of JA Associates.

"No, I don't think that's where you are." My mind blanked as I glanced out the window, still the street was empty. What did I want to ask him?

"Did Hector confront you?" I sent a second email, also hoping it would be received in time. Jared groaned lightly.

"No! He went to Mrs. Munch. Mrs. Munch. Damn, Justin and Mrs. Munch, they cut me out of this."

Justin was in it! That liar!

My email refreshed. I breathed a sigh of relief when I saw Andy's response. "Did you drive the car that rammed into me?"

"No. That wasn't me."

"It was Mrs. Munch?"

Jared laughed a hearty laugh. "No."

Wherever Jared was, he was pacing. I could hear his hard soles against the floor. He picked up his pace.

My bedroom was over the garage. It was still too early for Julia to come home, and yet the garage door to outside had opened and someone was walking into my garage. I wasn't much for guns, and here I was, alone, without a weapon, locked in my bedroom. I had two thoughts, first that these were my last few minutes on earth, and second, I hoped whoever was here would leave before my kids would get hurt.

My legs trembled and I held the footboard of my bed to steady myself when the door from the garage to the laundry room was slammed shut and the intruder was inside.

"What do you want, Jared?"

"It's over, you know." He was eerily calm as he spoke to me. Footsteps crossed the wood floors to my staircase.

"Who's in my house?"

"Mrs. Munch is angry with you." Jared hung up and I looked out the window, hoping Andy was here. There was no one on the street.

The intruder walked up the stairs and stepped on the squeaky tread. Mrs. Munch was three stairs away.

I stared at my bedroom door. The handle jiggled but was locked. Mrs. Munch kicked at the door. It shook in the jamb. A gunshot echoed through the house. My bedroom door splintered. Mrs. Munch pushed open what was left of it and stared at me.

"Will Mann, the FBI, the Lake Zurich Police." She waved the gun around. "You had to tell them all, didn't you? You couldn't have just shown up at the brewery. I could have ended this." I stared at the gun and swallowed. I thought of my children, my friends. My heart pounded.

"Who gave me the file?"

Mrs. Munch smiled, licked her dark red lips. "Marcie. He wouldn't leave his wife, so she came up with the plan. She's very smart, that girl. It was a shame that I had to kill her." Mrs. Munch smiled at the memory; my stomach churned.

"Nikki, did you really think catching them was a complete coincidence? You caught her because Marcie planned it that way. Knew you were trying to reach him to sign that document, knew you'd be in early. She studied you. Always punctual, to a fault, always efficient. She finally got tired of being used. Came up with the plan to frame him for the money laundering. I could get out of Chicago and go home."

She pointed the gun at me.

I swallowed when I saw Andy's cruiser speed down my street. I held the footboard tighter.

"Why did you kill her?" My voice was high and frightened. I just needed to keep her talking, just long enough.

"It was a good plan. I was hoping the police would blame Justin. They just couldn't get there."

I knew Jared was lying to me about being in the car that hit me. He had to be driving last night when Sherman was shot. Then she had to have killed him. My mouth flew open.

"You were always a smart girl. What did you realize?" she cooed.

"You killed your son."

She smiled. But it wasn't warm, it wasn't motherly. It was nuts. Crazy. "Loose ends, my dear. He was only supposed to follow you and scare you. Then he hit you. Thirty-nine years old and he couldn't get anything right. I should have known Marcie's vengeance would be the downfall." She cocked the gun, ready to pull the trigger.

"How long have you been doing this?"

She smiled again, this time it felt genuine, happy. "I got my law degree when there weren't many women who did. I could get a job, but I couldn't advance. Couldn't break that glass ceiling. Worked for crappy bosses doing little more than paralegal work. I worked my ass off to get to where I was. And then, I fell in with clients that offered me… an opportunity for more power, more money. I took it." She snapped her fingers, she was proud of what she had done. I pursed my lips. I thought I might throw up.

"I brought Jared and Justin in thinking they were narcissistic enough to do what it took to keep the enterprise going. They are my godsons, after all. But Jared's too stupid and went after his brother's mistress. He bragged to that girl. And Justin." She shook her head and smiled. "Justin was too arrogant and let his vices run his life. Pissed off the wrong woman. I was wrong about them."

While she bragged, the garage door opened, and footsteps crossed the floor. I hoped Andy could stop her before it was too late. When the stair squeak, Mrs. Munch frowned and turned. Andy stepped inside my bedroom, his gun drawn, facing Mrs. Munch.

"Drop your gun," he said.

"You're not taking me alive," Mrs. Munch hissed. I dropped to the floor as Andy rushed her. Her gun fell to the hardwood floor and slid under the bed. I grabbed it. Andy wrestled with Mrs. Munch before he could slap the handcuffs on her. When I stood, she was on the floor face-down, hands behind her back, and Andy was on his knees beside her.

"She did it all. Killed Marcie, Justin, and her son. Jared called me; he knew she was coming." I said through raspy breaths. I could barely breathe. I handed Andy her gun.

"You, okay?"

I nodded. "I was next." Tears welled in my eyes. I let them fall as I shook and shuddered. Officer Roberts, the cop from the crash, raced up the stairs with his partner behind him. They quickly assessed the room, dragged Mrs. Munch up, and marched her downstairs. She glared at me as she stumbled in their grasps. My lips trembled and Andy pulled me into him and I cried, finally letting it all go.

****

My kitchen table was covered in folders and notes from the package from Hector. They were scattered in makeshift piles as I explained the spreadsheets, Mrs. Munch's notes on the payments in and the payoffs out, and the clients that were overcharged on purpose.

Myles returned to the table. "You did well. What you started got us on the right path. We did another pass at the client list. There's about fifty more we think follow the same pattern. We're not familiar with notes and the system like you but we have a sizable number of accounts to review. There are several more companies we found, too. Jared and Justin had their own companies they funneled money to." He gave me a heartfelt look. "You did a lot of the work for us. I thank you, and I'm sorry we couldn't help you more. We weren't sure how much you knew and if you were in on the scheme."

Myles offered a smile. I shrugged. He pulled the piles together and shoved them in one of several boxes on the kitchen table. Silvia came in and grabbed one of the full boxes.

"Justin was staying in a house in Lake Barrington. It had been owned by his parents about fifteen years ago. The current owners live in Florida part time. They happened to be there now and were very surprised when we told them."

I sighed. "Did he leave anything behind?"

Silvia raised her eyebrows. "Yeah. All the books for this enterprise. Additional companies we hadn't found yet. Other client accounts. Good news. The LZ police did find Jared. He's locked away, waiting for us." She smiled softly when she caught my gaze.

I glanced into the sunroom. Julia was playing on her phone. Every once and a while she'd look out and wonder what was happening. I didn't know how I'd explain the splintered bedroom door. I just hoped she'd believe we were finally safe.

"Mrs. Munch said she killed Marcie. Any signs of her?" I asked. Myles and Silvia glanced at each other.

"We found blood and hair in the house where Justin was hiding. It's too long to be Justin's. I expect it's hers. It's all bagged as evidence. When you gave Hector the evidence, he called Sherman, and Sherman called his mother. She decided to kill Hector, hoping Justin would be implicated. They were hoping Justin would be found and arrested. Everything implicated him. Justin had no idea. I think when you received the Cabot file, he realized what they had planned. I'm surprised he didn't go after Mrs. Munch or Jared for what they had done to him. However, you look at it, it's all such a waste." Silvia shook her head slowly and took another evidence box from Myles. She nodded once and walked away.

"I'll be going as well. Call me if you think of anything else." He patted my hand and followed Silvia out.

"Thanks. Myles. Hopefully this is it." I hadn't realized how much I collected, how much work I had put into this. I wondered if I should change careers.

Andy chuckled. "You did a good job. You're smart and figured it out before they could put it all together. You pushed the investigation ahead by a lot. And Mrs. Munch will pay for what she did."

Andy touched my hand. I glanced at him, and for the first time, realized he had lovely green eyes.

****

Will brought me a glass of wine and a plate of chicken parmesan into the sunroom. "You did good," he said when he sat.

I took a bite. The chicken was crispy and tender and the sauce was sweet and spicy. I wiped excess cheese from my chin.

My kids had taken their dinners into the basement to watch movies. Jacob had rolled his eyes when Will arrived but chuckled as he went down the stairs. Julia watched Will intently as he unpacked the rest of dinner. When he smiled at her, she scampered away with her fried shrimp and French fries.

"You haven't dated since the divorce?" he asked as he sipped his wine.

"Yes and no. Just one-off dates. Nothing special. I don't think I'm ready. Why?"

"They think something's up." He cocked his head toward the basement.

I raised my eyebrows. "You're my boss. It's not appropriate."

"Temporary boss." He took a bite of his lemon chicken.

"Temporary's good."

"I let Jack know everything's been resolved. I'm sure he would have found out in the news." Will sipped his wine and watched me.

I shrugged. "I know he was worried, but it's not his business. And I'm fine. The kids are fine. He's fine." I looked at him and smiled. "Thanks for taking care of that though."

"That's what I'm here for."

I hadn't meant to walk down a new road or turn to a new page in my life. I thought I had been happy with the old page. But it happened. I inadvertently ran into this mess. But it was a tale as old as time: money makes people crazy, jealous, mean, and deadly. But I was still alive. And over the course of the next few weeks, I'd have to come completely clean with my children and let them know how close I came to not being here.

I watched Will eat for a moment. I thought about how much had changed over the course of our friendship with our kids, our spouses, our lives. He caught me watching him.

"What?" he asked.

I shook my head. "Nothing. It's just been a very long time since I've felt this free."

The End

Milton Keynes UK
Ingram Content Group UK Ltd.
UKHW012307160324
439511UK00012B/273